"There are so many reasons this would be a mistake," Gavin said, his voice lower, rougher.

"And only one reason it wouldn't?"

"I can think of several, but they're all just different words for the same thing."

He turned to go, clearly determined not to make that mistake, as he called it. Katie stiffened her spine, reeled in her uncooperative senses. *Fine. I'm certainly not going to beg the man to kiss me. Even if that's what I feel like doing.*

And yet Gavin turned back suddenly. Crossed the three feet between them in one stride. Katie felt his hands cup her face in the moment before he lowered his mouth to hers. The unexpectedness of it didn't lessen the jolt, or slow the fire that leaped to life in her anew, as if it had only been banked, not extinguished. The feel of Gavin's mouth on hers rekindled it thoroughly, sending heat and sensation racing along every nerve...

* * *

Be sure to check out the rest of the books in this miniseries.

Cutter's Code: A clever and mysterious canine helps a group of secret operatives crack the case.

* * *

If you're on Twitter, tell us what you think of Harlequin Romantic Suspense! #harlequinromsuspense

Dear Reader,

Like many writers, I'm sure, in the process of writing a continuing series like Cutter's Code, I often find myself mentioning in passing the names of characters I never really expect to write an entire book about. They serve their purpose and then vanish, perhaps to be mentioned from time to time. But sometimes they reappear, full grown and knocking on my consciousness, saying, "Hey, remember me?"

Gavin de Marco is one of those. I had worn a uniform and a badge for many years, so attorneys in general were not always at the top of my guest list, except for ones I knew were good guys. But I think it does us good to take out old perceptions and rattle them around a bit, and see what happens. And Gavin turned out to be quite a good guy in the end. I'm glad he came knocking. I hope you will be, too.

Happy reading!

Justine

OPERATION NOTORIOUS

Justine Davis

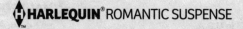

HARLEQUIN® ROMANTIC SUSPENSE

Recycling programs
for this product may
not exist in your area.

ISBN-13: 978-0-373-40239-7

Operation Notorious

Copyright © 2017 by Janice Davis Smith

All rights reserved. Except for use in any review, the reproduction or utilization of this work in whole or in part in any form by any electronic, mechanical or other means, now known or hereinafter invented, including xerography, photocopying and recording, or in any information storage or retrieval system, is forbidden without the written permission of the publisher, Harlequin Enterprises Limited, 225 Duncan Mill Road, Don Mills, Ontario M3B 3K9, Canada.

This is a work of fiction. Names, characters, places and incidents are either the product of the author's imagination or are used fictitiously, and any resemblance to actual persons, living or dead, business establishments, events or locales is entirely coincidental.

This edition published by arrangement with Harlequin Books S.A.

For questions and comments about the quality of this book, please contact us at CustomerService@Harlequin.com.

® and TM are trademarks of Harlequin Enterprises Limited or its corporate affiliates. Trademarks indicated with ® are registered in the United States Patent and Trademark Office, the Canadian Intellectual Property Office and in other countries.

Printed in U.S.A.

Justine Davis lives on Puget Sound in Washington State, watching big ships and the occasional submarine go by and sharing the neighborhood with assorted wildlife, including a pair of bald eagles, deer, a bear or two and a tailless raccoon. In the few hours when she's not planning, plotting or writing her next book, her favorite things are photography, knitting her way through a huge yarn stash and driving her restored 1967 Corvette roadster—top down, of course.

Connect with Justine at her website, justinedavis.com, at Twitter.com/justine_d_davis, or on Facebook at Facebook.com/justinedaredavis.

Books by Justine Davis

Visit the Author Profile page at Harlequin.com, or justinedavis.com, for more titles.

SAM

Sometimes the best things just end up on your doorstep...

One day a little puppy, lost and alone, somehow managed to pick the right house to show up at. He was a two-color pup, black-and-white fur, with one blue eye and one black eye. Irresistible, because when it became clear no one knew where he came from, the people at that house took him in.

They dubbed him Sam, sometimes called Perky because he was, and he became a member of the family. He took to life on a farm, with cattle, horses and chickens, grew to a nice medium size and functioned as buddy, playmate and, if necessary, protector. He loved them as only a dog can, and they loved him very much in return, for all the many years they were blessed with. And, as all dogs should be, he is remembered with love to this day.

To all who loved him, from Granny Thrasher.

This is the latest in a series of dedications from readers who have shared the pain of the loss of a beloved dog. For more information visit my website at www.justinedavis.com.

Chapter 1

"I'm sending him to you. Make up something you need him for."

Quinn Foxworth blinked, and frowned at his phone. "What?"

"Fight info's en route. You've got six hours to come up with something. Good luck."

"What am I supposed—"

He stopped when he realized he was talking to dead air. He lowered the phone, staring at the screen that told him the call had lasted eighteen seconds.

Funny, it seemed shorter.

He turned to his wife, Hayley, who had come out onto the deck with two mugs of coffee and was now looking at him curiously.

"Charlie."

"Ruh-roh," she said with exaggeratedly widened eyes as she handed him his coffee.

"Yeah."

He wrapped his hand around the mug. It was due to rain by this evening, and he'd come out to scan the clouds. The warmth of the coffee was welcome against the chill of the shifting season.

"Dare I ask?" Hayley said after taking a sip from her own morning brew.

"Gavin's on his way here."

"Our Gavin? De Marco?" Her brow furrowed. "Do we need him?"

"No."

"Then why—"

He offered her his phone. "Call Charlie and ask."

She laughed. "No, thank you. So she didn't say why?"

He shook his head. "Only that it was life-and-death that he get out of there."

Her eyebrows rose. "Whose?"

"No clue. Maybe he's just driving Charlie crazy."

"Now that," Hayley said with a grin, "is a frightening thought."

Quinn laughed. "For you? I don't believe it."

And he didn't. The first time she'd met his fearsome sibling, and gotten that up and down, assessing, calculating look that intimidated less hardy souls, Hayley had never wavered.

So you're the one who thinks she can tame my brother?

I don't want him tamed. I love him as he is. And he loves me. So if you hurt me, you hurt him. Don't.

Charlie had blinked, stared, then burst into laughter. *She'll do, little brother. She'll do.*

Indeed she would. Forever.

"Well," Hayley went on after a moment, "if something's really eating at him, one of us should be able to get him to talk."

A quiet woof turned both their heads. And simultaneously, they laughed at their dog, Cutter.

"You can, is that what you're saying?" Hayley asked the clever animal.

Cutter's plumed tail wagged, and his amber-flecked dark eyes gleamed with amusement. Given the dog's history, Quinn wouldn't put it past him to have even the man who had once been the most famous attorney in the country spilling his guts to him.

And then the dog's expression changed, and his head swiveled around, looking north. Never one to waste time, he trotted off to investigate whatever had caught his attention.

"Good thing all the neighbors know him," Quinn said.

"And we don't live in a city of leash laws," Hayley added.

Once they'd realized what they had on their hands, they had introduced Cutter to all of those neighbors. Most were receptive to a trained watchdog who would look out for all of them as part of his home duties. The dog was respectful of the older neighbors, gentle with the young children, playful with the pets in the zone he'd mapped out for himself, and somehow realized that the rather reclusive residents on the corner didn't care for dogs and kept his distance.

"Maybe he can help Gavin," Hayley said.

Quinn grimaced. "Sure. Because Gav is so good about accepting help."

"Because he doesn't trust anyone. Except Foxworth. Cutter is part of Foxworth. Besides there's one thing he can be surer of with Cutter than anyone."

Quinn lifted a brow at her. "Which is?"

"Cutter," she said seriously, "will never, ever lie to him."

And that, Quinn thought, was the key to Gavin de Marco. He would tolerate much, never blinked at the grimness and unfairness he sometimes encountered in his work for them but, with very good reason, he refused to put up with liars.

And now he was going to get therapy from a dog. A dog Gavin didn't quite understand yet. But he would. He'd have no choice.

Quinn nearly grinned at the prospect.

Katie Moore drew her knees up tighter to her chest, wrapping her arms around herself as if that could keep her from flying into pieces. The nightmare hadn't been this bad for a while, and she'd dared to hope it might eventually go away entirely. But last night it had returned with a vengeance and now, three hours after waking up screaming, she was still shaken.

She sat on the floor of the small garden gazebo, amid a patch of roses stubbornly refusing to admit it was almost November. She stared at one of the blooms, studying each curving petal as if it held the answer. When she had moved here, away from the city where life had turned so ugly, she'd planted the roses around the gazebo with some vague idea in her mind that someday when the worst was over, she would sit here and breathe in the sweet scented air and remember the good times. She'd never had a sister by birth, but she'd found her sister of the heart, and since they'd met in elementary school they'd rarely gone a day without communicating in some way.

And still sometimes she had her hand on her phone to call before she remembered she would never speak to Laurel again.

Images from last night's horrific dream seethed just below the surface, and her barricades seemed particularly weak this morning. She wished it was a workday; losing herself amid the books she loved would help get her mind off this ugly track. Maybe she should go in anyway. Surely, there were things she could do.

Being the librarian in a town this small wasn't a difficult job, but she loved it. The new library was a beautiful, light, airy space that was a delight to the community that had worked so hard to make it happen.

Laurel would never see it.

That quickly, she was back in the morass. She felt so lost without the steady, loving friend who had always been there for her. If she hadn't been the one to find her body, maybe it wouldn't be so bad. The loss would be just as great, but she wouldn't have those horrifying images seared into her brain. Maybe—

"Woof?"

Katie snapped out of her grim thoughts, startled by the quiet sound. She smiled when she saw the dog sitting politely at the bottom of the gazebo steps. Cutter, Hayley's dog, from down the street. He was unmistakable with his black fur over face, head and shoulders, shifting to a rich reddish brown over his back down to his fluffy tail. She'd seen him often since her neighbor had come by to introduce him, and had been amusedly grateful he had apparently taken it upon himself to protect this entire block. More than ever now she needed reassurance of safety.

"Hello, boy. On your rounds?"

For an instant she could have sworn the dog shook his dark head. She laughed at herself. She'd never had the tendency to anthropomorphize animals, but it was hard to avoid with this one. Especially when he came up the steps, turned and sat down beside her, and leaned in. As if to comfort her, as if he knew how roiled her inner self was this morning.

As, perhaps, he did. Dogs did wonders as therapy animals, she knew. One of the most popular nonfiction books in the library last month had been the story of one such dog. But she wasn't sure anything could alleviate this kind of pain. What could possibly make this any easier to bear? She shuddered, her throat going tight, nearly strangling her airway. Cutter leaned in harder, and when instinctively her hand came up to stroke his soft fur, she found, to her surprise, that the horror receded slightly. Only slightly, but enough to allow her to breathe again.

She hugged the dog. And by the time he trotted off toward home, his rounds completed for the morning, she realized she was going to have to read that book.

Gavin de Marco shifted the backpack slung over one shoulder, and adjusted his grip on the duffel in his left hand as he walked through the airport parking structure to the rental car area. The crisp Seattle air was like a gulp of pure, clean ice water after the humidity he'd left in St. Louis, which was having trouble surrendering its grip on a muggy summer even two months into fall.

Two children in Halloween gear raced past him, shrieking. He'd almost forgotten the day of costumes and candy was nearly upon them. A man he'd noticed on his flight let go of the suitcase he'd been wheeling and bent to greet the two mini-superheroes, a wide, loving smile on his face. The woman with the children joined them, and the look the man gave her made Gavin turn away. It was personal, intimate, even here among the throngs of a busy afternoon at SeaTac Airport. That "you're mine and I'm yours" kind of look that meant a deep, irrevocable bond that might change over the years, but would never fade or break.

The kind of look Hayley gave Quinn, and more surprisingly, Quinn gave Hayley.

The kind of look no woman had ever given him.

Not, he thought wryly, that he'd ever earned it.

He let out a disgusted breath. The disgust was aimed, as it usually was lately, inwardly, not at Quinn Foxworth, one of the last few people on earth he trusted without reservation.

Unfortunately that few did not include himself any longer.

He made himself focus on the task of picking up the car. He'd refused Quinn's offer that they would pick him up—by car, plane or helicopter, whichever he preferred—and insisted on the rental car. He wanted to be independently mobile, because recently there were times when he just couldn't stay put.

He said he just felt restless.

Charlie said he was crazy-making.

So here he was, sent off to make the other Foxworth sibling crazy. Maybe that's all it was, Charlie getting him off nerves he'd trod on too often.

He hoped Quinn had something going on he could seriously gnaw on. Not that it hadn't been a challenging go-round last time. Taking down a governor was not simple, even when they mostly did the job for you. Gavin didn't want to admit he'd been exhilarated by walking through that minefield; it made him wonder if he'd become some kind of adrenaline junky.

He knew some had assumed he always had been, what with the kind of headline grabbing cases he'd been involved in during his career in criminal defense, but that hadn't been it at all. He'd been coolly analytical, helped by his knack for anticipating the moves of others. He'd been able to think on the fly and draw up almost any precedent-setting case he'd ever read about. He'd been—

Wrong. Don't forget that one.

He interrupted his own thoughts with the sharp, bitter reminder. For he had been wrong. Very wrong, and it had pulled the rug out from under not just his career but his entire life.

By the time Gavin's phone warned him he'd reached his destination even he had to admit his brain had eased up a bit, as if responding to the more peaceful surroundings. Just as Quinn said it did for him. Here on the other side of Puget Sound seemed a world away from the bustling city in feeling if not distance. He never would have thought he'd say it, but maybe Quinn was on to something here.

A light rain had begun just as he stepped under cover of the porch, and his hosts congratulated him on his timing. He was welcomed, his bags stowed in the guest room, and a drink poured and waiting for him by the fire crackling in the hearth before he recognized the luscious smell wafting from the kitchen was Quinn's famous spicy chicken.

"I'm honored." He tilted the glass of wine in a salute. "You cooked for me?"

"Don't get used to it," Quinn said.

Gavin managed a creditable grin before asking, "Where's that rascal dog of yours?"

"On his nightly rounds," Quinn said.

Gavin found himself laughing, to his own surprise. "Patrolling the neighborhood?"

"Morning and evening, every day we're not on a case," Hayley said.

"Strong sense of duty, that one," Gavin said, not really kidding.

Quinn nodded. "Like most good operatives."

Gavin had heard enough stories of the uncannily clever canine to know Quinn was dead serious. "Even Charlie has finally accepted that he's an integral part of your team."

"Speaking of Charlie," Hayley began, then stopped.

Gavin studied her for a moment, then let out a long breath as he lowered his gaze. Quietly, he voiced what he'd been suspecting since his plane had cleared the Rockies. "You don't have a case, do you?"

Hayley exchanged a glance with her husband. Quinn grimaced.

Quinn had never lied to him—one reason he trusted him—and Gavin knew he wouldn't now. But before he could answer there was a sound at the rear door that drew their attention. Gavin turned just as a hinged section at the bottom of the door swung open. A second later Cutter was there, looking a bit damp from the rain, which had picked up now. He had something in his mouth, some toy Gavin guessed.

"He has his own door now?" he asked as Hayley grabbed a towel clearly kept by the door for that reason and turned to the dog.

"It's easier," Quinn said. "He's got a mind of his own and—"

He stopped as the animal walked past Hayley and the towel, toward Gavin. He guessed that figured, given he hadn't been here when the dog had left the house. Cutter sat at his feet, looking up at him intently. Did he even remember him? Gavin wondered. He hadn't spent much time here last time, and—

His speculation broke off when he saw what the dog had in his mouth. It was not a toy. A cell phone? What was the dog doing with a phone? Whose phone? Where had he found it? And why the hell was he bringing it to him?

By the time he got through the string of mental questions Quinn and Hayley were at his side. Cutter allowed Hayley to take the phone from him, but the dog's steady gaze never left Gavin. He found it strangely unsettling.

"It doesn't look like it's been lying around and he just found it," Quinn said.

"No," she agreed. "It's not damaged at all. And it's on, so it's working."

"Is he given to stealing things?" Gavin asked neutrally.

Quinn gave him a sideways glance. "In the interest of a good cause, it's not unheard of."

Gavin didn't know what to say to that, so he said nothing as Hayley pressed a button on the side of the phone.

"Locked," she said. "Charge is at 65 per cent."

"Good. The owner will probably call it once they realize it's gone," Quinn said.

"Assuming they have another phone, and don't already know because Cutter snatched it right out of their hand," Hayley said, sounding a bit glum.

"Well, there's that," Quinn said, glancing at the dog. Hayley handed him the phone and went to work on the dog with the towel.

She had just finished when the doorbell rang. She put down the towel and looked at Quinn. "And maybe," she said, "whoever it was—"

"—followed him here," Quinn finished for her.

"I'll get it, shall I?" Gavin said lightly, telling himself a buffer between a possibly irate phone owner and the owners of the dog who'd grabbed it might be a good idea. Quinn didn't immediately answer him, but moved across the living room to where he could get a glimpse out the window to the porch, where a motion-sensor light had come on. Only then did he nod.

"Sometimes I forget," Gavin muttered under his breath as he reached for the door handle. Coming in as he did, usually after everything had happened and there was nothing left but cleanup, he did sometimes forget that Foxworth occasionally irritated people with minimal impulse control. People who could be dangerous.

He pulled the door open, revealing a woman who looked

a bit damper than the dog had. Rain glistened on hair pulled back in a wavy ponytail, and a couple of drops clung to long, soft-looking eyelashes. Lashes that surrounded eyes that seemed vividly blue even in the artificial glow of the porch light. Her face, with a slightly upturned nose and a nicely shaped mouth, was turned up to him since she was probably about five-four to his five-eleven. Her cheeks looked even wetter than her hair, and if it hadn't been raining he might have thought she'd been crying. Which would explain the distress he saw in both her eyes and her body language; she was hunched into herself against more than the chill.

"Is Hayley here?" she asked. "Or at least Cutter?"

Chill, he thought again, only this time in the nature of a self-command. Belatedly he realized she wore no jacket over her jeans and light sweater, as if she had come hastily. In pursuit of her phone? He shook off the strange sluggishness that had overtaken him.

"Sorry," he said, stepping back to let her in. Obviously she knew Hayley and she hardly looked like a threat, even if he'd been studying her as if she were one.

"Katie, isn't it?" Hayley said, coming forward. "Katie Moore? The blue house?"

"Yes," she said, sounding grateful.

Quinn had disappeared from his position by the window, but now reappeared with a fresh, dry towel, which he handed to the newcomer.

"Here, dry off. I'm Quinn, Hayley's husband."

"Thank you," the woman said, then applied the towel. "I'm sorry to intrude, but—"

"It's no intrusion. Neighbors are always welcome. Come in by the fire and get warmed up," Hayley said.

"Thank you," she repeated, folding the used towel. Gavin noticed, because it was what he did, that her hands trembled slightly. And again he was certain there was more to it than simply being cold. "I don't quite know what happened. I—"

She stopped then. Because Cutter the phone thief had stepped between them and stood at Katie's feet. And then he turned and sat, staring up at Quinn and Hayley.

"Ah," Quinn said, as if the dog's action explained everything.

Gavin had heard about this, although he'd never seen it in person. But even if he hadn't known, he could have seen that this was a signal.

Fix it.

That's what Quinn called it, the dog's "fix it" look. And eyeing the clever animal now, he believed it. What he found harder to believe was the thought that popped into his head then.

In the interest of a good cause...

That was a bridge too far, thinking the dog had stolen the phone specifically to get this woman here because she had a problem that Foxworth could fix.

Wasn't it?

Quinn and Hayley exchanged a glance. And then Quinn looked at Gavin.

"That question you asked, about a case? The answer just changed."

Chapter 2

"Sorry, I'm a bit scattered," Katie said, hands wrapped around the steaming mug of hot cocoa Hayley had fixed for her.

She was starting to feel warm again, thanks to it and the fire. And Cutter's presence. The dog had taken up residence at her feet, lying on them in fact, and his body heat was doing nearly as much as the fire and cocoa to warm her up. She felt miles away from the new pit of shock and despair she'd been cast into just a short time ago, and for the moment she let herself revel in the warmth.

"This rascal is good at distractions, when needed," Quinn said. His voice was quiet, steady, but it took nothing away from his formidable appearance. In fact it added to it. This was a man, she thought, who had nothing to prove to anyone.

"He's been visiting me a lot lately," she said. "He's really been quite sweet. I don't know why he did this."

Quinn and Hayley exchanged a look that was both know-ing and wary, but also seemed slightly amused. They didn't seem the type to take their pet's misbehavior as funny, not after Hayley had gone to the trouble of introducing Cutter to the neighbors, but maybe she was wrong. She hoped not.

As for their guest, introduced as Gavin visiting from St. Louis, he was something else altogether. When a complete stranger had answered the door, all sorts of crazy thoughts had run through her mind. She'd known she had the right house; she'd done her due diligence on the neighborhood before she'd moved in five months ago. But when the man who now sat slightly apart from them, as if he were in the room but not the group, had opened the door, her heart had slammed into her throat.

Hayley's husband was tall, looked strong, and his mili-tary background showed in his demeanor. This Gavin might be a little less imposing physically but there was some-thing about the way he looked, something in eyes so dark they almost appeared black, that she found even more im-posing—a bright, quick intelligence that to her crackled as tangibly as the fire she was sitting beside. And the way he'd stared at her, making her overly conscious of how wet and bedraggled she must look, left her feeling she had been thoroughly assessed and cataloged.

Could you tell I'm a basket case? About to fly into a million pieces?

"Katie runs our new library," Hayley was saying to their friend. "And it's become quite the success thanks to some of her ideas."

Katie found herself watching the man who'd opened the door, awaiting his reaction, half expecting some kind of joke or comment she'd heard too many times before. Somehow being a librarian came with certain judgments or stereotypes, many of them wrong, some of them very,

very wrong. But nothing showed in his expression, and he said nothing. She wasn't sure why she had reacted to him so strongly, with that startled leap of her heart.

"So, Cutter's been visiting you a lot?"

Hayley's quiet question snapped her out of her ruminations. "Yes. I haven't minded," she put in quickly. "He's been…quite comforting, actually."

"He has the knack," Quinn said.

"He does," Hayley agreed. "He can always sense when someone is in turmoil. Or pain. Or has a problem."

Well, all three of those fit her just now, Katie thought.

"And," Hayley said, her voice even softer now, "he'll do whatever it takes to get that person the help they need."

"Including making off with their cell phone," Quinn added.

Katie blinked. She stared at them both, then at the dog at her feet. Then she looked back to Quinn. "Wait. You're saying he took my phone on purpose? To…what? What are you saying?"

Hayley leaned forward, focusing on Katie. Her voice was gentle, encouraging, like a hug from a friend. "He can always sense when someone needs the kind of help the Foxworth Foundation can provide."

Katie frowned, puzzled. She remembered the name from when Hayley had come by, but she'd been too entranced by the charming Cutter to really focus on the brief mention of the foundation she and her husband—and the dog—were part of, other than to register she'd heard of it before. But while she appreciated the concern—and heaven knows she needed any support she could get—she doubted this foundation of theirs could help, even though she had only a vague idea of what kind of work they did.

"I'm afraid your foundation can't solve my problem," she said. "Because what I need is a really, really good attorney."

Neither Foxworth answered her. There was no sound but a loud pop from the fire. But Hayley, Quinn and even Cutter had all shifted their gaze. And they were staring at the man sitting in the chair opposite her. The man who had gone suddenly very still.

"Told you," Quinn said, breaking the silence.

Katie had no idea what Quinn was referencing, but Gavin muttered something she guessed she was glad not to have heard.

"Katie," Hayley said in a more formal tone that was no less gentle, "let me more fully introduce someone to you. This—" she gestured at Gavin "—is the Foxworth Foundation's attorney, Gavin de Marco."

She was so startled at the coincidence of their guest being an attorney, on top of their dog seemingly leading her here, that it was a moment before the name registered. When it did she gaped at him, she was sure gracelessly.

"De Marco? *The* Gavin de Marco?"

She'd known the name since before the scandalous downfall of the governor last spring, but once it was discovered that the formerly famous but now rarely heard from attorney was involved in sorting out the aftermath, his name had been included in every news story. And suddenly she remembered that was where she'd heard about the Foxworth Foundation before, in those stories. She just hadn't realized that Quinn and Hayley were *those* Foxworths.

But she doubted there was any adult in the entire country, except perhaps those who lived purposely in ignorance, who hadn't heard the name Gavin de Marco. Any criminal case that had hit the national news in the last decade, there was a 50 per cent chance de Marco's name was attached. After blasting into the public awareness at a young age when a senior attorney had died midcase and he'd had to take over—he often referred to himself as the understudy who made good—his record was so amazing that it had become, in the public mind, an indicator of guilt or innocence in itself. Not because of lawyerly tricks or clever dodges, but because he always seemed to turn up the evidence or get testimony or make an argument that exonerated his client so thoroughly juries could vote no other way.

And then there were the other cases. She'd read about them, back when she'd been living and working down in Tacoma, because they were hard to avoid as she shelved the newspapers patrons had still wanted in those days. The Reed fraud case, the Redmond murder case, and the others where he had withdrawn from the defense. By then his reputation was such that it was practically a conviction in itself, no matter what reason was given.

All these thoughts raced through her mind in the embarrassingly long moment when she simply stared at him. Along with a rapid recalculation. She'd thought he must be about her age, but he had to be older. College, three years of law school, however long it had taken to hit the national stage, all those famous cases, and then the three or four years since he'd dropped out of sight for reasons still a matter of wide speculation.

He didn't look like the pictures and video images she remembered. Gone was the exquisitely tailored suit and the haircuts that had likely cost more than her monthly food budget. Now he was wearing a pair of black, low-slung jeans and a knit, long-sleeved shirt that stretched over broad shoulders and clung to a narrow waist and hips. His hair was longer, with a couple of dark strands kicking forward over his brow. Outward signs of inward changes? she wondered. It all made him less intimidating…until you looked at his eyes. No one with those eyes could be anything less than intimidating.

She had no idea how long she'd been sitting there gaping at him when he said, in a level tone that told her he was familiar with her reaction, "And you need an attorney because…?"

No preamble, no "Nice to meet you" exchange. He'd cut right to the chase. But then, wasn't that what an attorney was supposed to do? Be objective, get to the heart of things, and not be distracted by such messy things as emotions?

Easy, when you're not the one whose life is being blown up.

The spark of emotion she felt at his cool detachment enabled her to pull herself together. And instead of saying the multitude of things piling up in her mind, she made herself answer his question simply.

"I need an attorney because my father is suspected of murdering my best friend."

Chapter 3

Well. He hadn't expected that, Gavin thought.

He'd wanted to cut through her obvious reaction to his name, even as he wondered yet again when it would at last fade from the public consciousness. He looked forward to that day with more longing than he ever had getting into a courtroom, even in the fresh, young days of idealistic fervor.

That it was likely going to take until an entire generation grew up having never heard of him was a thought he tried not to dwell on. For a guy who, unlike many of his fellow attorneys, had never wanted that kind of fame, he surely had acquired enough of it to last a lifetime. And he was likely going to be a crotchety old man before it faded.

And who says you're not a crotchety old man already, de Marco?

"No wonder you're scattered," Hayley was saying. She'd moved to sit next to the woman on the sofa, putting an arm around her. Cutter sat up and shifted so that he could rest his chin on her knee. The woman lifted a hand to stroke the dark head. He could almost feel some of the tension ease from her, even from over here.

That dog was…something. Then again, Gavin couldn't blame the dog for wanting to be stroked by this woman.

He blinked. *Where the hell had* that *come from?*

"Can you tell us the story?" Hayley asked gently.

"I wouldn't know where to start."

Gavin heard the husky tremor in her voice, saw the sudden gleam in her eyes, recognized the welling of moisture. She was on the edge of breaking. He knew there were usually two ways to go with someone who was teetering like this. Let them go, let it gush out uncontrollably and try to make sense of it after, or take the lead and control it for them. Both approaches had their benefits. An emotional flood sometimes netted information the person would not necessarily have revealed had they been in control. But it could also lead to confusion, because emotionally distraught people often saw connections where there were none, assumed cause and effect where it wasn't warranted, or at worst made no sense at all.

He decided on the latter approach, and told himself it was not because he simply did not want to see this woman break down in front of him. And it had nothing to do with that errant thought that had blasted into his mind as he'd watched her stroke Cutter's soft fur.

"Or," he said, intentionally rather briskly, "would you rather just answer some questions, in a logical order?"

Gavin saw her take a deep breath, as if to steady herself. Her mouth tightened slightly, and he found himself disliking the tension of it in a very peculiar way.

"There's no point." She glanced at Gavin. "I need an attorney for my father, but we can't afford Gavin de Marco."

Quinn stepped in then. "If we determine Foxworth can help—and that is a big *if*—you won't have to. Gavin works for us."

"In that case, I probably can't afford you, either."

"Not an issue," Gavin said. "Whether your case meets Foxworth criteria is."

"And if it does," Quinn said, "there's no cost for Foxworth's help."

"No cost?" She glanced at Gavin. "What's your billable rate? A thousand an hour?"

His mouth quirked upward. There had been some bite in the question, a sign she was steadying. Given even what little he knew of her situation from her stark explanation, he found it admirable. He doubted many could manage it.

"It was actually a bit more," he said. "Back in the day."

Her gaze shifted to Quinn. "So you have him on retainer, or what?"

"Actually," Quinn answered mildly, "we don't pay him at all."

She drew back rather sharply. Hayley put a hand on her arm. Cutter nudged her to keep petting. Between the two of them Katie didn't have a chance, Gavin thought, but he hid his amusement.

"Gavin," Hayley said, "works with us because he, like all of us, believes in what we do."

Katie's gaze shifted from Hayley to Quinn to him in rapid succession. "For free?" she said in obvious disbelief.

"I get compensated in…other ways," he said. *Like the easing of my soul.*

She looked genuinely confused. People always were, when first confronted with the idea of an organization like Foxworth. It just didn't seem possible these days that anyone would take up causes like this.

"What exactly is it," Katie said carefully, "that you do?"

Gavin glanced at Quinn, the man who had pulled him out of a quagmire of betrayal and self-doubt and given him a clear and bright path to follow. Were he not here Gavin might have tried to explain himself, but the Foxworth Foundation was Quinn's creation, his and Charlie's. Quinn walked over and sat on the edge of the coffee table in front of Katie, his elbows resting on his knees.

"When I was ten, my parents were killed in a terrorist bombing. I have never felt so helpless or so enraged as when the terrorist was set free and nobody would tell me the truth. Foxworth was founded to help people who are in that same boat, fighting injustice. Honest, good people in the right, who have fought but can't fight anymore, or who haven't been able to get help anywhere else."

Gavin watched with interest as Katie Moore studied Quinn. "And who," she asked after a moment, "decides they're in the right?"

Gavin registered the question that many didn't even think to ask. Ms. Moore was clearly not in the nonthinking category. He could almost hear the click in his mind as he checked off that box in his assessment. She would not be difficult to work with in that way. In other ways…

Again he had to slam on the mental brakes. Maybe Charlie had been right, and he really was going nuts.

"That's the joy of being a private enterprise," Quinn answered with a smile. "We do. We have our values, and our criteria are ours alone."

"We only take cases we can get behind wholeheartedly," Hayley added. "We can't help everyone, but those we do help get it all."

Katie seemed fascinated by the concept, and was now distracted enough that she appeared and sounded calmer than when she had arrived. Gavin knew he was right because Cutter settled back down at her feet, head resting on his front paws.

Her hair had dried now, and he saw it was a sandy sort of blond with strands of a lighter, golden color here and there. And her eyes truly were that blue. Even as he thought it she glanced at him, giving him the full force of that vivid color. Then she turned back to Hayley and Quinn.

"What kind of cases?" Katie asked.

"We've reunited long-lost families—my own included," Hayley said with a smile. "Recovered a kidnap victim. Helped some troubled kids, and adults, find their way. Gave a grieving family a reason they could bear for a suicide. And Quinn found a stolen locket that was the only memento a girl had of her dead mother." She looked at her husband proudly. "That's still his favorite case."

Katie smiled at that. It was a nice smile, Gavin thought, yet it was tinged with a sadness that made him wonder about her own mother. *Not something you need to know. Stop it.*

Katie only asked, "Even more than taking down a corrupt politician?"

"In a way, yes," Quinn said.

"And there you have it," Gavin said, speaking for the first time since this explanation of Foxworth had begun. "The reason Foxworth is what it is. It's in what they value."

Katie's head turned and she studied him for a moment. She clearly took her time, thought through things, processed them. He wondered if she ever did anything on pure impulse. Images flashed into his mind, of things Katie Moore might do on impulse. Heat shot through him, as if the fire they were gathered around had suddenly flared. He quickly shifted his gaze to that fire, wondering what the hell was happening with him, and if she'd seen anything in his eyes.

He looked up again when she spoke, but she was back to looking at Hayley and Quinn, and he could breathe again. He would analyze this later, far away from those eyes.

"I'm sorry," she was saying, "I didn't realize you were the Foxworths mentioned in all the stories last spring."

"We don't advertise it. We work mostly by word of mouth," Hayley said. Then, rather pointedly, she nodded at Cutter. "Although these days, he brings us enough work all by himself."

Katie blinked. Gavin understood. He was more than a bit bemused himself by how easily Quinn and Hayley accepted that their dog had not only sensed this woman needed their help, but apparently had engineered this entire meeting.

Quinn smiled. "I was as skeptical as you are, but he's proven himself time and again. I've learned to just go with it."

"We all have. Even Gavin," Hayley added with a grin and a sideways look at him, "and he's the least fanciful guy you'll ever meet."

"Thanks," Gavin said drily. "I think."

"I would think being fanciful wouldn't be a good trait for an attorney," Katie said.

Gavin found himself oddly curious. "And what traits would be?"

Katie studied him again, perhaps looking for any sign his question had been facetious or snarky. His curiosity was genuine, and apparently she sensed that. Once decided, she seemed to consider the question as thoroughly as she had everything else. After a moment she said, "Sifting. Through all the dross to the essentials, I mean. Empathy that doesn't cloud objectivity. Researching. An affinity for the facts."

Gavin stared at her. "That was very concise."

"I read a lot. Remember most. Was I close?"

"Very." His mouth twisted at one corner. "Except the objectivity and affinity for facts seem to be falling by the wayside these days."

"You asked what traits would be good, not which ones were common."

He blinked. Quinn laughed aloud. "She got you there, Gav."

He laughed himself, something rare enough to be appreciated. "Indeed."

Cutter's head came up, and Gavin found himself the object of the dog's steady gaze. He got the oddest feeling it was a look of approval. Then he almost laughed again, at himself for attributing such things to a look from a dog. And he was glad when Quinn turned things back to Katie's situation.

"It's up to you, of course, but if you tell us the story and Foxworth can't take the case, we can perhaps guide you to someone who can. We have a lot of contacts, people who'd be willing to help."

"That's the payment Foxworth gets," Hayley told her. "The willingness to help someone else down the line."

Katie glanced at Gavin again. He could almost read the question in her glance, if he was one they had helped who was now paying them back.

More than you could imagine, he told her silently.

She continued to look at him. Cutter made a small, low sound, drawing his gaze. The dog was staring at him again, and he felt oddly compelled to tip the troubled woman over that edge, get her to open up. He leaned back in his chair, as if settling in.

"What was your friend's name?" he asked.

"Laurel," she said. "Laurel Brisbane."

The pain that echoed in her voice jabbed at him. The old instincts still kicked in, but the old impartiality was struggling. He tried to ignore it and went for the easiest question that was likely to get her started. They'd get to the rest once she'd gotten used to the idea of talking.

"Tell us about her."

She drew in a deep breath, and he knew the ball was rolling.

Chapter 4

Katie was amazed at what a relief it was to talk about Laurel to people who hadn't heard it all before. People who neither wanted salacious details nor tried to steer her away from the painful subject. She knew her friends and even her family meant well, but the way they shied away from even speaking about Laurel or her death, as if the lively, clever and utterly loyal woman she'd been had never existed, only added to the hurt.

And yet she herself shied away from her death now, choosing to start at the beginning, when two girls had laughed at the same thing in a fourth grade classroom, and a fast, enduring friendship had begun. And they listened, these people she barely knew, even though this wasn't the story they were really waiting for. Even Gavin—she had to think of him by his first name because realizing she was sitting in the same room with the celebrated Gavin de Marco disconcerted her—listened quietly, not interrupting or prompting. That was unexpected to her; she thought he'd be more of a "cut right to the chase" kind of guy. At least, that was the impression he'd always given in news reports and video clips. He'd been renowned for his talent for reducing a case to its simplest aspect in a broadcast-worthy sound bite, succinct and pithy. Of course, the fact that the camera loved him didn't hurt, she'd thought back then when she'd seen him.

Now, however, she knew it wasn't the camera at all. He really was that good-looking, and more compelling in person than any recorded image could be. And that was a path she was not walking, she told herself sternly. But didn't it just figure that the first spark of real response she'd had to a man in a long time would come now, not only amid an impossible situation but with an impossible man?

Ignore it. It will go away. Or he will.

She jumped ahead to where Laurel had, temporarily, moved into Katie's apartment in Tacoma after a final breakup with her boyfriend of a couple of years, Ross Carr. Laurel had seemed both unsurprised and resigned, and Kate's role seemed to mostly be offering commiseration, ice cream and reassurance that she was better off without him.

Until that day a week later, when she had come home from work to find a bloody nightmare of a scene. Her fingers curled into fists as she fought to get it told. The words came out in compressed chunks, in between harsh breaths.

"They told me there was no sign of forced entry. She fought him, they said. Then…he used a kitchen knife. It wasn't mine. He…he slashed her. Blood everywhere. He cut—"

She broke off, nearly choking on what she couldn't, just couldn't give voice to, the horrifying carnage she'd walked in on. She was aware of Hayley putting a comforting arm around her. Cutter jumped up beside her and put his head in her lap. She automatically put a hand on his head, and the feel of the silky fur steadied her again.

"Is that why you moved here?" Hayley asked, and the gentle concern in her voice almost broke Katie. She was holding on to a hair of control when she answered.

"Yes. The opening at the library here came up, I knew the area because my father lives here, and… I wanted new surroundings. Quiet, peace. A place where I could soak in the tranquility, purge the…the ugly."

"Of course," Hayley said.

Katie nodded because she didn't dare speak anymore. This quiet, supportive concern, even from near-strangers, was somehow harder to cope with than the thoughtlessness of people who had no idea. That was another reason she'd moved here, to get away from those who couldn't resist speculating about the shocking murder, never realizing or caring that they were talking to or in front of the collateral damage.

"It's taken me a while, but I reached…tranquility, if not peace." She grimaced. "I wasn't sure of that until I went back to visit a friend and ran into Ross at the coffee shop."

"That must have ripped the scab right off," Quinn said with a grimace.

"Yes. Yes, it did. I couldn't wait to get back here. I could feel the…serenity, I guess, growing the closer I got."

"Sign of a good decision," Hayley said.

"Why isn't he the prime suspect?"

The question, the first time Gavin had spoken since she'd begun her sorry tale, was not quite brusque but close. It had the effect of a blast of cool wind, complete with the rain still falling outside. And it quashed the silly reaction she was having to him.

"He was. In the beginning. Especially since they'd recently broken up. They even grilled me, until they verified

I'd been at work late that night. The ones closest to the… victim always are the first ones they suspect, aren't they?"

"And they're guilty more often than not," Gavin said, in that same tone.

"I know. But Ross had a solid alibi. They verified it. Lots of witnesses."

Odd, she thought. It was somehow easier to deal with that brisk, businesslike tone. Or maybe it was the inexplicable comfort provided by petting Cutter.

"And," she added, "he was as devastated as I was. He genuinely cared for Laurel. He told me the breakup had made him realize how much he loved her. He'd even bought a ring, was about to propose, right before she was killed."

"Then why did they break up in the first place?"

Again, Gavin's clipped tone made it somehow easier to answer. As if they both realized this, Quinn and Hayley stayed silent. Cutter never moved, however, and she was glad of that. Still she hesitated, then said, "I know she's gone, but it still feels like betraying a confidence."

"Weigh it," Gavin said, "against finding out who killed her."

Put like that, there was no question. "*Cheating* was all she said. She hadn't been ready to talk much about it yet."

"And so she turned up on your doorstep, expecting you to take her in?"

Something jabbed through the pain of her recollections. "No," she said, rather sharply herself, "she turned up on my doorstep *knowing* I would take her in. As she would for me."

His expression didn't change, as if he hadn't heard the shift in her tone. She wondered then if he'd done it on purpose, to shake her out of the dreadful memories. Surely he hadn't gotten to where he'd been a household name without having more than a few tricks up his sleeve. And she had to admit this one had worked; she was steadier now. Before she had time to decide how she felt about that, he dragged her back to what she'd been dreading most of all.

"Your father," he said flatly. "He's now a suspect?"

"That's what they're saying. And they're talking like he's now the only suspect. The news, I mean." She gave herself a mental shake; she was sounding very scattered. "A friend heard it and called me."

"Let me guess," Gavin said, his tone sour now. "It was 'according to a source close to the investigation,' or some such."

"Yes, something like that. They didn't say who it was."

"Of course not."

She realized he'd dealt with the media a lot during his career. She saw him exchange a glance with Quinn, and although the other man didn't speak Gavin apparently saw some kind of signal and went back to his questions.

"Has an investigator called you yet?"

"Yes, although I didn't realize it was about this at the time. A detective contacted me about a month ago, said she was following up, and asked several questions they'd already asked. But one of them was if my father had a key to my apartment—he used to, but I got it back to give to Laurel—and if I'd seen him that day."

"That came in the middle of a lot of other questions, I'd guess."

"Yes. Why?"

"Less chance for you to realize that was the whole purpose. Hide that particular tree in a forest of them. So you couldn't tip off your father that they were looking at him."

Her mouth tightened. "Well, it clearly worked on Ms. Oblivious."

He shrugged. "If they're good, it works on most people. What did you say?"

"The truth, of course. I hadn't seen him or talked to him, not that day. Since there's no way he could have done it, it didn't matter. At least I thought it didn't. Until I heard he'd become their prime suspect."

The toxic combination of anger and despair threatened to rise and swamp her, and she barely managed to hold it at bay. She felt a bit like a bug—a helpless one—under a microscope, and wondered if that was what the people Gavin de Marco confronted in court had felt like. She wondered, as she had at the time, why he'd really quit. Cutter gave a low whine and licked at her hand. And again the dog steadied her.

She lifted her gaze from the dog to the man whose attention was so focused on her. "If they were so worried about keeping it secret, then why are the police talking to the media about it now?"

"Likely because they haven't got enough evidence, or it's all circumstantial."

She frowned. "Of course they don't, since he didn't do it. But why would they let it leak that he's a suspect now, after all this time?"

"They may be hoping to prod him into doing something."

Perplexed, she frowned. "Doing something?"

"The knife," he said. "Did they find it?"

"No. The killer took it with him."

"Then they may have wanted him to think he had to get rid of it, if he hadn't already."

Her frown deepened. "My father doesn't own that kind of knife, either." Somehow she was able to say it fairly evenly, and fight off the images that were piling up behind that barricade she'd built in her mind. She suspected it was thanks to his businesslike tone.

Again Gavin glanced at Quinn. This time she saw the

barely perceptible nod. It was odd, she thought, to think of Gavin de Marco having a boss. She would have thought he would call his own shots. And again she wondered why he'd walked away, wondered who left when they were top of the heap?

She remembered the stories after he'd removed himself from the Reed case, his request to the judge stating that there had been a breakdown in the attorney-client relationship that made him unable to provide effective representation. The congressman had later been found guilty of fraud, his political career destroyed by proof of influence peddling and graft. His former attorney had, as required by his professional obligations, never said another word about it, but Gavin de Marco's withdrawal and the resultant verdict had only cemented his reputation. And she couldn't help thinking of the effect having Gavin de Marco publicly on her father's side would have.

When he spoke again his tone was sharper, not accusatory, but not friendly, either. The questions came rapid-fire, as she imagined they would in a courtroom, except he gave her no time to answer. And he was leaning in, into her space.

"What proof is there that he didn't obtain said knife just for this purpose? What makes you sure he would tell you the truth about it? Did he know Laurel? What was his relationship with her? What is his alibi for the time of the murder?"

Her mind was racing as he fired the words at her, trying to decide what he was doing.

"Are you trying to pressure me into saying something I didn't intend to, or just showing me what it would be like dealing with you?"

He leaned back then. Kept his gaze on her. "Yes."

She straightened up, giving Cutter a final stroke between his silky ears. She met that gaze head-on. Her certainty gave her strength.

"I've told you the truth and nothing but. My father is innocent. He would never lie to me. Bring it."

For a brief moment, barely an instant, she thought Gavin de Marco smiled.

And the little jump in her pulse was ridiculous, for just a smile.

Chapter 5

Gavin looked up from the computer he'd been working on as Quinn ended his call. His boss slipped his phone back into his pocket. It was a special piece of equipment modified by Foxworth IT expert Tyler Hewitt back home in St. Louis; he had one just like it, as did everyone at Foxworth.

While Hayley continued to talk with Katie in the living room, they had adjourned to the den that had become an office.

"Brett said he'll make a call. He knows someone down in Tacoma," Quinn said.

"Is there anywhere your sheriff's investigator doesn't know someone?"

Quinn grinned. "If there is, we haven't found it yet. He confirmed that Steven Moore is the main suspect, judging by the bulletins that came out to all local agencies last week."

"That must be when they decided to let it go public,"

Gavin said, leaning back in the office chair. "A knife and that kind of carnage—that screams personal. Rage."

Quinn nodded. "Find anything?" he asked, gesturing toward the computer's wide monitor.

"Nothing that jumped out in a cursory search, no contradictions. Once I eliminated the spate of reports that hit in the last twenty-four hours, he's pretty low profile. Haven't dug into the reporting on the actual murder yet."

"Ty can do that, and send us the report."

Gavin nodded. Ty was an expert at finding things buried deep. Gavin didn't mention that the main reason he hadn't gotten to that search was that he'd also searched on Katie, and found several entries on her taking over the new library and turning it into a welcoming place for all.

Quinn glanced toward the living room. "What's your assessment, Counselor? Is she for real?"

Gavin remembered Katie's response to his string of questions, coming nearly as rapid-fire as his own words had, and, he noted, in the same order and complete. There was nothing slow about Katie Moore, for all her thoughtful consideration of things, but he'd already guessed that.

My only proof is knowing he can barely use a kitchen knife without cutting himself. He has never lied to me in my life, even when it would have been easier, and I have no reason to believe he would start now. Of course he knew Laurel; she'd been my best friend since I was nine. He liked her the most of all my friends, for my sake if nothing else. And obviously he doesn't have a provable alibi or he wouldn't be a suspect, would he?

He'd probed a little further and learned her father's story was that he'd been home, alone, watching an old movie on cable. They'd verified the movie had indeed played when he'd said, but obviously that wasn't proof that he'd watched it. A bit more pushing and he'd learned how close she and her father were, especially since her mother had died when Katie was nine. He got the picture of a loving dad who had focused on his only child during a very difficult time, and that they had gotten through it together.

"I think," he began in answer to Quinn's question, "that she believes every word she said. It's whether it's all really true that's in question."

"Agreed."

Gavin raised a brow at his friend. "Are we taking this on? Not exactly our usual. A straightforward, if ugly, murder case. The police are pursuing it, even months later, so it hasn't been forgotten."

"But they might be pursuing the wrong man."

"True." Gavin looked at Quinn quizzically. "But that alone is still not usually enough to fire your jets. So what is?"

Quinn returned his look. "That she's a beautiful woman with a problem isn't enough for you? And if you say you didn't notice, then I'll know you're lying. I saw your face when you opened the door."

"She was soaking wet. I knew you'd feel guilty if she caught pneumonia."

He wasn't sure why he was deflecting. Katie Moore was beautiful, in that quiet way that had always moved him more than the flash and glitter that had seemed to surround him back in the days when his name could get him entrée into just about anywhere. But that had nothing to do with it. He was moved by her plight, not the woman herself. The kick of his pulse when he looked at her notwithstanding.

"Nice of you to be so concerned about her health," Quinn said drily.

"And you're dodging the question."

Quinn sighed. Then he shrugged. "Cutter."

Gavin drew back slightly. "Seriously?"

"Do you need another rundown of all the cases he's found?"

"No. But hearing about it is different than seeing it."

The image of the dog wiggling through his private door, purloined cell phone in his mouth, played back in Gavin's head. *He knows a Foxworthy case when he sees one*, Liam, a fellow operative, had joked the last time he'd been here.

Gavin had laughed, but he couldn't deny the facts. The cases the dog had brought them, directly or indirectly, had all turned out to be their kind of case. He just didn't see how this one was. But he had meant what he'd told Quinn; he believed that Katie Moore believed every word she'd said. She might have been lied to, but she wasn't lying herself.

Right. And you're sure of this because your judgment is infallible, right?

But in the end, the bottom line was simple. If Quinn—or apparently Cutter—said they were taking the case, they were taking the case.

When they left the office, they could hear that Hayley and Katie were actually laughing. Cutter was at their feet, his tongue lolling happily as Hayley reached out to scratch behind his right ear.

Both women and the dog looked up as they came into the room. Quinn didn't waste any time. "Can you meet us at our headquarters tomorrow, and we'll get started?"

Katie blinked. "You're doing this?" Her gaze flicked to Gavin. "Including you?"

"I'm Foxworth," he said simply. And meant it. In the Foxworth Foundation he had found both something he hadn't been fully aware of missing, and something he hadn't thought existed anymore—good people fighting for good people and good causes. People he was proud to work with, who had given him back a pride in his own work, in what he could do. "I don't do criminal defense any longer, so if it comes to that, we'll find you someone. But I can still prepare a case."

Cutter stood up and gave a woof that Gavin couldn't deny sounded satisfied. Then Katie stood up, her eyes wide and full of hope.

"I don't know how to thank you," she began.

"Don't thank us yet," Quinn warned. "We go after the truth, and there's always a chance you won't like it."

"I know what the truth is," she said confidently. Gavin winced inwardly; he'd heard that before, and seen it explode.

In fact, he'd believed it before and seen it explode, nearly taking him with it.

"We will ask you questions you probably won't like answering," he said, adding to Quinn's warning. "About things you may not see the reason for."

She met his gaze. "They might be new, but they can't be any worse than the ones I've already asked myself."

Self-blame, Gavin guessed. It was common. People always thought there was something they could have or should have done to prevent the tragedy that in fact had nothing to do with them.

"Let's get you a ride home, then, and we'll start fresh tomorrow," Quinn said as he handed her the business card he'd picked up in the office. "Since it's Sunday, maybe a later start? Ten or so?"

"Fine," Katie said, although Gavin had the feeling if Quinn had said 5:00 a.m. she would have been there.

Cutter trotted past them toward the door, as if he'd understood that Katie was leaving and he was a well-trained doorman. Gavin found himself smiling. The smile widened when the dog raised up and grabbed a set of keys from the table just inside the door and trotted back.

"Now he's your parking valet?" he said, half joking and half astonished that the dog had understood.

"I'd say he's more *your* valet at the moment." Quinn laughed as Cutter came to a halt directly in front of Gavin and sat. Only then did he see that the keys the dog had brought were indeed the ones to his rental car. The animal stared at him intently, clearly waiting for him to do the obvious. He reached for the keys rather gingerly, but Cutter released them without protest.

"I guess you're doing the honors, then," Hayley said, and Gavin didn't quite understand the undertone in her voice. Not quite amusement, but he couldn't put a finger on what it was.

"You don't need to," Katie said. "It's only a block and a half, I can walk."

Hayley shook her head. "It's dark, and it's pouring rain. You'll end up twice as wet as you were when you got here." Cutter barked, short and sharp this time, as if to hurry them up. "You might as well give in now, save the energy," Hayley said cheerfully. "He's obviously decided."

As silly as it seemed to acquiesce to their dog, there didn't seem to be anything to do but give in. Hayley handed him an umbrella—with the standard joke about it marking him as a tourist, since practically nobody who lived here used one. But at least it would save Katie from being drenched anew even on the short walk to his rental car parked in the driveway. He would have preferred to give it to her and just take his chances, but when he realized that was because he didn't want to be as close to her, he mentally rolled his eyes at his own childishness and ordered himself to snap out of it.

"That dog," he muttered when they were inside the car and he had the umbrella tossed in the back. "Apparently his word is law around here."

"I didn't come looking for help, just my phone," she said, and he realized she had taken his words as complaint.

"That statement had nothing to do with you," he said as he started the car. "I'm just a bit…bemused at Quinn, who's one of the most grounded, practical guys I know, taking his lead from a dog. An amazing dog, I'll grant you, but a dog."

"I think it's sweet."

Gavin doubted the word *sweet* had ever been applied to the adult Quinn, at least not before he'd met Hayley.

He followed her directions and made a turn into a narrow driveway. In the dark and the deluge he couldn't see much of the yard, other than what appeared to be lots of trees and smaller plants. He grabbed the umbrella and walked around to her side of the car, then sheltered her under it up to her front door. She thanked him rather more than he thought necessary, and ended it with a smile on her upturned face that made his pulse jump oddly. For a moment they just stood there, uncomfortably and deliciously close. The sound of the rain falling on her porch roof seemed to amplify both the chill around them and the body heat between them.

If she hadn't moved first he wasn't sure what would have happened. But she did, hastily, thanking him once more, opening her front door and escaping inside.

Escaping. What a word to come to mind, he thought as the door closed. He shut the umbrella despite the good fifteen feet between him and the car. And when he got back inside it, already good and wet, he turned off the heater. As he drove the short distance back, he had to admit none of it helped, the chill of the rain or the lack of the heater's output. He was still a hell of a lot warmer than he should be, and had been ever since she'd looked up at him with that smile.

And he'd wanted to kiss her.

Chapter 6

Katie closed her door and leaned back against it, all her focus inward, on the odd hammering of her heart and the strange way her house, even at its normal temperature, felt chilly compared to standing outside in the rain.

With Gavin de Marco.

Even thinking the name seemed absurd. As did her reaction to him. She felt foolish; she should have known that that man would have "it," that elusive quality that drew attention even from those who didn't know who he was. Charisma, appeal, magnetism, whatever name you gave it, that man had it in abundance.

And apparently it worked on her just fine. She'd been hyperaware of him from the moment he'd opened the door.

She fought for calm. She began to move, busied herself with mundane things, like locking the back door she'd left unsecured when Cutter had so unexpectedly grabbed her phone and she'd given chase. She put away the bowl she'd gotten out, planning to reheat the leftover chili from last night; she had no appetite for it now, not after reliving her worst and persistent nightmare yet again.

But at least it had been for good reason this time, and intentional. Not like the way it so often snuck up on her and left her paralyzed with grief and horror. She'd reached an equilibrium here, but she knew it didn't take much to upset it. Like pouring out the ugly story to strangers, one of them Gavin de Marco…

Gavin de Marco. How impossible was that?

She went back to the living room and grabbed her phone. And once more she hit the speed dial for her father. She hadn't spoken to him since this morning, when he'd reassured her everything would be all right because he was innocent. He was cooperating with the police, of course, he'd told her. She'd suggested a lawyer then, but he'd said that he didn't need one and that he couldn't afford one anyway.

So how would you like the most famous defense lawyer in the country for nothing, Dad?

When he answered, he sounded different than he had this morning. Not quite so unruffled, but still confident.

"It will be fine, honey. I think they're grasping at straws because they have nothing else." He laughed, and there was only the slightest touch of strain in it. "They even gave me the 'don't leave town' speech. As if I would."

She cut to the chase. "You need a lawyer, Dad."

"We've talked about that, Katie."

She hesitated, but there was no way she would do this behind his back, so she plunged ahead. "I found you one. Or rather he found me. Sort of. Actually it was the dog, I think."

There was a moment's silence before he asked, "Dog? Katie, you're sounding a bit confused."

She laughed then, and it eased the tightness in her chest

a little. Then as concisely as she could she told him the story. She was honest enough to admit that she savored the moment when she dropped the name Gavin de Marco.

"Wow. He was big-league. But I thought he quit?"

"He did, but he's working for them now."

"Doesn't matter. No way on earth I can afford Gavin de Marco."

"That's just it, Dad. You don't have to." She explained about the Foxworth Foundation, and how Quinn and Hayley said it worked. And she pointed out that just having Gavin's name attached to the case could change things, and would certainly assure that the police moved carefully. "It's for your own protection. You have the right."

"I don't need—"

"At least talk to him, Dad. What can that hurt?"

By the time they ended the call, her father had—so reluctantly it surprised her—agreed to at least talk to the man if, after meeting with him tomorrow, Katie still wanted him to.

It was odd. She'd thought he would be pleased. She knew he trusted that the truth would come out, but she couldn't see why he didn't want the insurance that an attorney could provide. Especially one on the level of this one.

She walked to the small den in her house that served as an office of sorts. She opened her laptop and when the familiar screen appeared, she opened a search engine. It was time to do some homework. Research, after all, was a big part of what she did.

She began with the Foxworth Foundation. Their website was clean, simple and gave little clue as to exactly what they did. It was mainly contact numbers for the various regional headquarters. Five, she saw with some surprise, covering every region of the country; she hadn't realized just how big they were. She remembered what Hayley had said about working mainly by word of mouth, and wondered how an organization grew to this size that way. Even if they had the willing help of hundreds of previous clients, it took funding to keep something this size going.

She found a bit more on Quinn's history, including his rather stellar military career. The mentions of the foundation here and there in news articles were always scant, as if they were trying to keep a low profile. As if they didn't want public credit for what they did.

But it was the other entries in various places that told her the most. The almost tearfully thankful blog posts and public letters all made clear that what the Foxworths had said was true, that they really did take on anything that met their own, personal criteria.

This made her feel a new, bubbling kind of hope, to have this kind of organization helping her. She felt something else, a lightening of a burden now that it had been shared. And she wondered if the time of holding herself apart while she tried to rebuild a life with a huge piece missing had passed, if perhaps she should open up, let some people in. New friends, who wouldn't be always aware, who wouldn't assume that any time she grew quiet or thoughtful she was mired in grief. Not that it wasn't true much of the time, but it was easier to get through if everybody around her didn't know it. Social pressure was an effective tool.

She opened a fresh search window. She hesitated for a moment, feeling a tiny bit stalkerish. But she chided herself out of it. If she was going to go through with this she needed to know as much as possible, didn't she? The sensational headlines didn't tell the whole story, they never did. And it wasn't like she was checking out a potential date. Surely he would expect her to gather data. She was sure he did all possible research himself. Settled now, she reached for the keyboard.

And typed in Gavin de Marco.

Gavin traveled enough to be used to waking up in different places. When he slept at all, anyway. This time, realizations tumbled through his mind one after the other. He was in Quinn and Hayley's place. His head was pointing south, the opposite of at home. Weird quirk, but he'd always had it. The rain had stopped.

He wasn't alone.

That was enough of a jolt to bring him fully awake. As if his movement had been the trigger, he heard a soft woof. Cutter. A cool, damp nose nudged his hand. Instinctively he reached out and stroked the dog's head. Odd that he hadn't heard him come in; he slept lightly, and usually the slightest sound woke him. On that thought he sensed more than saw the dog hop up on the bed. Felt the slight give of the mattress as he landed, felt the brush as he went over him and plopped down on the other side. He nearly laughed as he felt the swipe of the dog's tongue over his ear, then smiled into the dark as Cutter curled up and put his head down, his side pressed up against Gavin's back. He'd never been allowed a dog as a kid, so this was a new experience.

It seemed rude to toss and turn as was his wont most nights, not when the dog had just gotten comfortable, so he tried to lie still. It was more difficult than he would have expected.

Maybe he'd been sleeping alone too long, he thought. He rarely considered his dearth of a sex life; years of dealing with women who just wanted a Gavin de Marco feather in their sexual cap had soured him. It seemed to come with that heady territory, but that didn't mean he had to like it.

That thought, rather uncomfortably, brought him around

to Katie Moore. He didn't want to dwell on her spirited personality or her open, lovely face, because that had nothing to do with the business at hand. And his reaction to her was downright irritating.

He'd wanted to dive right into research last night, but Hayley wouldn't have it. Ty, on St. Louis time, would be up well before them and have it ready before they headed to the office for their meeting. And, she'd pointed out, since he was still on St. Louis time himself, it was two hours later according to his body clock. So she'd fed him and hustled him off to bed at what would have been midnight at home.

Usually, especially when traveling, once he woke up that was it. The brain kicked into gear and there was no turning it off. But now, Cutter seemed to have short-circuited that pattern as the warmth of the dog's presence seeped into him. And much to his own surprise, he went back to sleep.

When he woke the rain had begun again, and Cutter had his chin propped on his leg. He could feel the dog staring at him. Willing him awake? It wouldn't surprise him at this point. He ruffled the dog's fur as he turned his head for a glance at the clock. Still early, barely six, but even though it was still dark here at that hour, he knew he was done sleeping. And he wasn't complaining. He'd gotten more than he usually did by at least an hour.

"Five hours," he said aloud to the dog as he flipped on the light. "Wow. If you brought that with you, thanks."

The dog grinned at him.

Gavin blinked, staring. That was a ridiculous thought. But what else would you call that silly, tongue-lolling, mouth up at the corners expression?

He heard a sound from the other room. Somebody else was up, he thought. Cutter clearly heard it as well and jumped down from the bed. Gavin grabbed the jeans he'd had on last night and tugged them back on; he'd sort out unpacking later. He stepped out into the hallway. He followed the dog out into the great room, where he saw not Quinn—another early riser—as he'd expected, but Hayley. She was in the kitchen, laying out a rather large array of eggs, bacon, ham, peppers, onions, potatoes, cheese and spices. When she heard them she looked up and smiled.

"I thought maybe that was where he disappeared to," she said, nodding at the dog. "He seems to have decided you need his attention."

Cutter trotted over to her and she gave him a quick pat.

"I'm still trying to figure out how he got in without me hearing," Gavin said, not commenting on what she'd said about the dog's decision process; he didn't want that door opened.

"He has his ways." She glanced over at the dog's set of bowls as if to make sure he had food and water. As if on cue the animal walked over and began to lap. "Did you sleep? He didn't keep you awake?"

"Some. Enough. And no. It actually was…" He wasn't sure what to call it.

"He's very comforting. And you," Hayley added, eyeing his bare torso assessingly, "are too thin. You're going to eat while you're here."

"Hey," he protested, "not everybody can be built like Quinn."

She laughed. "He always said you run on nerves and coffee."

"Fuel of the gods," he said. Cutter, finished with his drink and a few pieces of kibble, came back and sat at his feet. He scratched the spot behind the dog's right ear that he knew he liked.

He couldn't help but notice that through breakfast—Quinn's famous scramble that was never the same twice, and which he ate enough of to satisfy even Hayley—and the rest of the early morning, Cutter was never far away. In fact, he seemed to have attached himself nearly at the hip, even following him when he took a shower and dressed.

Before, for a meeting with a client, he would have worn a suit. But Foxworth was a different place, and he was a different man, no longer worried about impressions and the look of success. Yet when he stood in front of the bathroom mirror with his razor in hand, debating whether to bother, it was Katie's image that floated into his mind. Did the local librarian like or dislike stubble? The moment he realized where his mind had drifted, he slapped the razor down on the counter, rather sharply.

When he'd packed he hadn't included one of those suits, telling Charlie that if they needed him in such a rush they had to take what they got. Of course, that had been when he'd thought they'd needed him up here for a case. A case that at the time hadn't existed. Which gave him another thought. When she'd sent him, Charlie had to have known there was no case.

Back in the guest room he picked up his phone and hit the speed dial. As he'd half expected, it went to voice mail. *Probably thinks I'm ticked. As I would be, except—*

The tone cut off his thought. "Okay, Charlie, I get it," he said for the recording. "I'm a bit restless. But now there really is a case, so you're safe for a while. See you when I get back."

He ended the call and put the phone in his pocket.

Then he started to mentally prepare for the meeting with Katie Moore, who was also the reason he wasn't really angry with his boss.

And that realization made him even more restless.

Chapter 7

Gavin gave Cutter, with whom he was sharing the back seat, another head scratch. The dog shifted in the seat, giving up his intent looking-out-the-window to lie down beside him and plop his chin on his knee. Automatically Gavin stroked the dog's head, and was once more struck at how soothing that simple action was.

He seems to have decided you need his attention...

Hayley's words played back in his head. The dog certainly seemed to sense things. Although that didn't explain the stunt he'd pulled last night with the phone. He wasn't sure anything could.

Keep it up, de Marco. Pretty soon you'll be buying everything else they say about this critter.

With an inward laugh at himself, he gave the dog a final pat as they turned off the paved road onto a gravel drive.

He'd forgotten how truly peaceful the surroundings were here at the northwest headquarters. Set back from the road at the end of the drive that curved through thick trees, the dark green, three-story structure sat in a clearing that seemed a world away from city chaos. It was unmarked; as with most of Foxworth, they didn't advertise their presence.

He noticed that the double sliding doors of the warehouse-like building set to one side were open.

"Rafe must be here," Hayley said, clearly having seen the same thing.

Despite the good working relationship they'd developed, Rafer Crawford still unnerved Gavin like no judge or opposing lawyer ever had. He also knew that building was mostly Rafe's bailiwick; the former marine sniper with the deadly eye had a knack for mechanics. He said the two went hand in hand, that the calculation on a long shot was brother to the logic of machinery.

Cutter seemed to know the man was back as well, although he seemed a bit reluctant to leave his self-selected spot at Gavin's side. Bemused anew, Gavin told him to go and shook his head when the dog gave him a final nudge before taking off for the open doors at a dead run, head and tail and ears up, letting out an odd series of barks, a staccato combination of short and long.

Rafe came out through the open doors to greet the dog, who danced around him delightedly. Gavin knew the tall, lean man was a favorite of the dog, as evidenced by the specific bark he used only for him. After a minute or two the animal left his beloved Rafe and came trotting back to attach himself at Gavin's knee. An act they all seemed to notice, including Rafe as he headed toward them.

Gavin was struck by how different the man seemed here. He, as all of Foxworth did, occasionally visited the St. Louis headquarters. Rafe always seemed more guarded there, although dressed like any other person who worked in one of the towering buildings, drawing no notice from people too busy with the bustle of their own lives to see the leashed predator among them. That he was able to go unnoticed at all was testament to his skill, Gavin supposed.

But here he was more relaxed, at ease, as if here he didn't have to hide behind a mask of bland civilization.

"Who's in trouble?" Rafe asked with one brow lifted when he reached them.

"Apparently I was," Gavin answered, not taking offense.

Rafe glanced at Cutter, who was leaning against Gavin's leg. "I see." He shifted his gaze back to Gavin and considered that for a moment. "Getting on Charlie's nerves again?"

"Interesting that that's your first guess," Gavin said drily.

Rafe's mouth quirked at one corner. "You two remind me of a pair of siblings I knew once. So alike they had to pick fights with each other now and then, just to keep life interesting."

Gavin glanced at Quinn; he was, after all, Charlie's brother.

"Don't look at me," Quinn said instantly. "I gave up trying to fight with Charlie long ago, when I realized that in the end I always lost."

"Wise man," Rafe said, without inflection. Then he looked back at Cutter. "Interesting," he said again.

"So it seems," Hayley agreed—although Gavin had no idea with what—and she didn't even bother to try to hide her smile.

"We've got a case?" Rafe asked.

"Just arrived last night," Quinn said, and gave Rafe a condensed version of Cutter's antics and Katie Moore's arrival as a Foxworth case. "She's due here in about an hour, and we'll make the final determination."

"Need me?"

"Not yet, but come on in, so you'll be up to speed."

The dog stayed close to Gavin as they went inside and up the stairs to the big meeting room. He was drawn to the wall of windows looking out over the meadow behind the building. Beyond the clearing the forest stood, the evergreens a backdrop to the brilliant fall color of the deciduous trees as their foliage flamed out before surrendering to winter. Somewhere up there, he knew, a pair of bald eagles had their nest. As a man who had lived his life in cities, he could see the appeal, even as he felt a little out of place. More than eagles roamed the forests in the northwest.

Still, he knew there were those who'd consider the city more dangerous than this place, no matter what kind of wild creatures were out there.

Doesn't take trees to make a jungle.

He smiled inwardly as one of Rafe's observations echoed in his mind. He couldn't argue that. In fact, he could attest that some of the most lethal jungles in the world were those consisting of concrete and steel and people more ruthless than animals driven only by instinct. Win at Any Cost was the motto of too many in those places, as if they'd completely lost the ability to see any view but their own. It wasn't a sense of right or wrong, just win or lose, and the latter was to be avoided no matter what, no matter if the person in the right was forever damaged.

Which was another of the reasons he'd walked away.

He turned from the expansive view and moved to the back corner of the room where Quinn and Hayley were hunched over the bank of computers.

"Ty's research," Quinn explained as the file downloaded. "He had an appointment so he recorded a video for us."

"Where is Liam, by the way?" he asked, referring to the operative who usually handled their computer work. He and Ty had a friendly competition over who could dig deepest fastest, and it made for some amazing—and some-times frightening—results.

"Texas," Quinn said. "Checking on the kids from our last case."

Gavin nodded. He'd done a bit of work on that case, helping smooth the way for the two young brothers who had been struck yet again by tragedy to leave the state for a temporary stay with a well-qualified foster family who also happened to be Liam's parents.

"How are they?" he asked. "Those kids have had a rough time."

"Liam says they're doing great. That's about all I could get," Hayley added with a pleased smile, "because he's a bit distracted. He took his girl with him to meet the family."

Gavin blinked. "That was fast."

"When it's right, it's right," Quinn said, looking at his wife.

As he watched Hayley's smile, Gavin felt a twinge that he hated himself for. He thought he'd long ago accepted that such a connection was not in the cards for him, but being around these two seemed to shake that acceptance.

Cutter's head came up and he gave a rather emphatic bark.

"Katie must be here," Hayley said.

Gavin knew the gravel drive announced a car's arrival to the dog's sensitive ears long before they would hear it. As he listened, Cutter bumped up against him as if trying to nudge him toward the door, and the stairs.

"What?" he asked the animal, who merely looked at him steadily and continued to nudge. He glanced at Quinn and Hayley, who were smothering smiles; apparently they found their dog's odd behavior amusing.

"Go on down and get the door, would you?" Hayley said, a bit too breezily.

"We'll be down as soon as we glance through what Ty turned up," Quinn said. "I'd like to have an idea before we talk to her."

And so Gavin ended up following the dog's urgings and headed for the stairs.

"Coffee's on, and there's some fresh-baked cookies on the counter next to the fridge," Hayley called out, sounding too chipper for the circumstances.

With the feeling he was definitely missing something, he headed down the stairs to play greeter. He'd had enough sleep—barely—to alleviate the jet lag a bit, so he'd be fine. He'd handle this like any Foxworth case, if they indeed decided to take it on. His odd reaction to Katie Moore last night had only been because he'd been tired and jet-lagged.

When they got downstairs Cutter ran to the door and sat expectantly.

"Why don't you just open it?" he muttered at the dog. "That automatic door opener is for you."

Cutter tilted his head back so far he was practically looking at Gavin upside down. He wondered if that was the dog equivalent of rolling his eyes. With a sigh he reached out and pulled the door open. As he'd expected, it was Katie.

What he hadn't expected was the difference from the rain-dampened woman he'd met last night. He took it all in rapidly, noticing details as he had all his life.

This woman was pulled together, leaving little sign of her distress from last night. She wore a bit of makeup—not much, and he'd dealt with enough overdone paint to know—that accentuated her delicate features and made those incredible eyes look even bluer. Her hair fell in loose waves to her shoulders, and the streaks of golden blond seemed warm on this chilly morning.

She was dressed for the temperature in a sweater the same blue as her eyes, with a loose sort of collar that fell softly around her neck and shoulders, worn over a pair of trim black leggings and midcalf boots. No high heels for her, but a solid, block heel and leather that would withstand a northwest winter. But those legs...

His breath jammed up in his throat, his pulse skipped and then picked up speed.

"Hello," she said, and he realized that low, husky note in her voice hadn't just been from her emotional state last night. It sent a tickling sensation up his spine.

So much for being tired and jet-lagged.

Chapter 8

Katie's first thought was that he didn't remember her. She had no such problem. The image of Gavin de Marco—tousled dark hair, dark eyes that seemed to see everything, that air of crackling intelligence—was all etched into her memory. Far too deeply for a man she'd met only once.

But she doubted he forgot much, so her second thought was that he didn't recognize her because she looked so different. Which made her think of how bedraggled she'd looked when she'd gotten home last night. Her first look in a mirror had made her groan at her appearance, hair lank and flat, what makeup she'd had on washed away, eyes still reddened from her earlier crying jag.

She told herself she was embarrassed that any of them—except maybe Cutter, whom she now gave a stroke between the ears—had seen her like that, not just this man. She knew she looked more presentable now, even if her eyes were still red, although this morning it was from lack of sleep, not crying. Gavin, she noticed, had skipped the razor this morning, and to her surprise, since she usually didn't care for stubble, decided on him it looked good.

Of course, what wouldn't?

"Mr. de Marco?" she finally said.

"Yes. Sorry. I didn't mean to… Come in."

The dog was effusive in his greeting as she stepped inside, making her smile, but inwardly she was puzzled. Because Gavin seemed…almost rattled. Not that she could judge, of course, but from everything she'd read last night—and she'd been up until the wee hours, so fascinating was the subject—this man was never rattled.

One report had spoken of how on cross-examination he'd made a witness practically confess to the crime his high-profile client was on trial for. The man had come at him right over the courtroom railing. Even those who had been there weren't sure how he had managed to send the man tumbling to the floor, because he'd barely seemed to move. Through it all he'd never lost his cool. After the bailiffs secured the man, he hadn't even had to straighten his tie.

She'd also read a lot of the speculation. He'd had a career most law students could only dream of. He was, as they said, a rainmaker of the highest order…and yet he simply walked away. Some said it was because he'd made so much money he would never have to work again. Others said it was because he had nothing left to prove. While that was certainly true, Katie didn't quite believe it was that simple. And now that she'd met him in person, she was certain of it. This was a complex kind of man.

He gestured her into the large downstairs space. To her surprise, it looked more like the living room of a comfortable home than the plain, businesslike exterior had suggested. There was a gas fireplace on the long wall, and before it an inviting grouping of sofa, chairs and a large square coffee table. On the opposite wall was a stairway, rather more utilitarian. To the right were a couple of door-ways, one of them partially open and revealing a vanity and sink, so she guessed it was a bathroom. Next to it was another door, closed. Bedroom? she wondered. Did they get so involved in their work that sometimes they didn't go home?

In the back corner was a compact but efficient-looking kitchen, from which she could smell coffee brewing, making the space even smell like a home.

Even as she thought it, he spoke again. "Coffee?"

"Thank you." She meant it; she would need the caffeine after last night.

"Sit down," he said as he went to a control on the wall, flipped a switch, and the gas fireplace leaped to life.

When he had gone into the small kitchen she sank down on the couch and drew in a deep breath, only then realizing she'd barely been breathing at all since he'd opened the door. She'd expected him to be there, obviously, but not to be the one who greeted her.

"Good morning to you, too," she whispered to Cutter as he nudged her hand. She patted the dog's head again, then gave him a long stroke over the silky, soft fur. He gave a happy little whine, then turned as another door at the back of the building opened. A tall, lean, dark-haired man dressed in black walked in. Cutter was there before he shrugged off his jacket, and Katie noticed he paused to greet the dog before he finished. She liked that.

And then the dog darted into the kitchen, just as Gavin was picking up two steaming mugs, and appeared to be trying to figure out how to carry a small basket at the same time. Cutter solved the problem. He rose up on his hind legs and took the edge of the basket carefully in his teeth and walked back toward her. She couldn't help it, she was grinning when the animal came over and with exquisite care put the basket down on the table in front of her. It held, she saw, various packets of sugar and sweeteners, and small containers of milk and cream.

"Why, thank you, kind sir," she crooned to the dog, who gave her a tongue-lolling grin.

Then Gavin arrived with the mugs. He handed her one, then turned, obviously intending to sit in the chair at a right angle to her. But somehow Cutter was there, and they got tangled up as the dog practically pushed him the opposite way, although she was sure it was unintentional. The dog looked rather satisfied, however, as Gavin ended up sitting beside her on the couch. Not too close, but close enough that she was aware of him in a humming sort of way.

The other man, his own mug of coffee in one hand and a plate of cookies in the other, had stood for a moment watching the odd little dance with what seemed rather intent interest. But he said nothing to Gavin, just walked over to them, set the plate down and turned to her.

"You must be Katie Moore. Rafe Crawford," he said, holding out a hand. She took it, noticing a scar here and a nick there, and long, lean fingers. He didn't try to crush her hand, but didn't handle it as if she were fragile, either.

But then she looked at his eyes, eyes that were the color the stormy sky had been yesterday. She'd never seen really haunted eyes before, but she knew she had now. Reacting instinctively, she gave his hand an extra squeeze. "Mr. Crawford."

There was a split second's pause, just enough to tell her he'd noticed, before he said, "Rafe, please."

He sat in the chair Gavin had intended to use, all the while looking at Gavin on the couch. And Katie thought she saw the faintest trace of a smile curve one corner of his mouth for a brief moment.

She straightened. "I hope this isn't a waste of your time."

"We wouldn't be here if Quinn didn't think we might be able to help," Gavin said.

"I hear Cutter brought you in," Rafe said. "That's the seal on it." She blinked. The man looked utterly serious. And his eyes, those haunted eyes, did not speak of a man with a fanciful nature. At her expression, Rafe shrugged. "All I can say is he's never been wrong."

Before Gavin could respond to that—although Katie wasn't sure what he could possibly say—there was the sound of footsteps on the stairway behind them. And then Hayley and Quinn were there. After greeting her they sat in the other two chairs, leaving her and Gavin as the sole occupants of the couch.

Hayley smiled. "Shall we get started?"

At Katie's nod, Quinn picked up a remote and aimed it at the flat screen on the wall. "This is from Tyler Hewitt, from our headquarters in St. Louis. He did some digging first thing his time. Usually we're live with him, but this is recorded because he had an appointment this morning."

"Okay," she said. "What do you need me to do?"

"Just listen, watch. If anything you see or hear doesn't jibe with your perception of things, say so and we'll stop and make a note. Then, when we're all on the same page, we'll proceed."

Katie nodded again. She didn't think anything showed in her face, but Hayley said quietly, "I know this won't be pleasant for you. If you need to stop at any time, just say so."

"Thank you." She'd known she'd have to go through it all yet again, probably in more detail than she had since it had happened and she'd spent hours with the police. She'd been shoring up her mental armor all morning. But the woman's understanding made the ache of anticipation ease a bit, and she realized she really quite liked Hayley Foxworth.

"And fair warning," Quinn said, "when it gets out that Gavin's involved, and it will, there's going to be buzz."

"I'm sure there will be," she said with a glance at the man who seemed absorbed in contemplating his mug of coffee.

"All right, then," Quinn said, and pressed a button on the remote he held.

The young man in the video was a thin, wiry sort, with short, blondish hair that looked perpetually on end. He had a small patch of beard below his lower lip, and alert green eyes.

"Hi, guys," issued from the speaker. "I'll get right to it. Here's what I have on the basics of the crime itself. I'm still digging into the principals. I'll get that to you later today."

And as she had with Gavin, Katie found it easier to listen to Tyler Hewitt's matter-of-fact reciting of the facts of the case than she'd expected. Something about his tone enabled her to take a half step back and listen rationally. It began with images of everyone involved and Ty's voice calmly introducing them. Although she'd been steeled for seeing Laurel's picture and didn't react, Katie winced at the particularly stern photo of herself that flashed on the screen, pulled from her county employment file. There was a shot of Ross on a ferry crossing, grinning at the camera, his hair tossed by the wind. Laurel had taken that one, she knew, and posted it on one of her social media accounts, which she guessed was where they got it.

She smiled at the image of her father, an attractive professional portrait that was one of her favorite pictures of him. She'd spent her whole life with all her girlfriends commenting on how handsome he was, always with a note of surprise she found faintly insulting until Laurel had laughingly explained that no one ever expected a friend's parent to be gorgeous, no matter what the friend looked like.

The video went on to show shots of the neighborhood. It was all painfully familiar, their apartment building, even a close-up of their front door with the apartment number. Over it all came Ty's businesslike recital of what the police investigation had shown. How Laurel had been last seen alive at the market around the corner from the apartment. She'd purchased milk, eggs and some other staples. She'd paid with a debit card, as she usually did, at 8:20 p.m. She'd walked out with two bags and turned left, heading for the apartment. No sign of a car, which roommate Katie had confirmed; she usually walked since it was so close.

The reports indicated there had been no sign of forced entry at the door or any of the windows, leading them to assume that her attacker had a key or she had let them in. Or that Laurel had come home with hands full of groceries, had stepped inside to set them down, and the killer had followed her in. Katie had stated she and the victim had the only keys except the building management. And since the management was a middle-aged couple who were on a late dinner cruise at the time of the murder, they had been cleared.

Then, abruptly, the image changed to a black-and-white video of the front of the market. And into that image walked Laurel.

Katie's calm shattered. She closed her eyes and turned away, trying to suppress a shudder.

Then Katie felt a wonderful warmth, a strong arm coming around her shoulders. Gavin, giving support. She assumed it was just something he did, something he'd had to do before with distraught clients. But she welcomed it nevertheless.

What had she let herself in for?

Chapter 9

Gavin felt Katie suppress a shudder, and knowing she had found her friend's mangled body he could only imagine the images breaking through her calm.

"Katie—" Hayley began.

"It's all right. Just give me a moment." She drew in a deep breath, clearly trying to steady herself. "It's just… seeing her like that, alive and well… I have dreams about it, and I just had a bad one night before last and…"

"And Cutter brought you to us the next day," Hayley said. "That may be what he sensed, your distress."

Distracted for a moment, she looked at the dog and seemed to ponder that. She nodded slowly, as if it made sense. And Gavin realized she was back in control. A quick glance at Hayley and he also realized that had been exactly her intent. Distract Katie until she could regain her composure.

Well done, he thought, and gave Hayley an approving

nod. He fought down the fleeting thought that he was glad she'd done it so he didn't have to. He wasn't doing too well keeping his unexpected reaction to this woman under wraps.

Katie indicated they should go on. Hayley hit a button on the remote, backed up the recording a bit, then let it run. Since he was seeing this for the first time, Gavin continued to pay close attention. It seemed fairly straightforward, as such things go, and he was long used to reading police investigation reports—and reading between the lines.

At some point he realized he still had his arm around Katie. It startled him; that was part of a lawyer's repertoire that he had left to his assistants. She was calm now, so it was no longer necessary. Yet he found himself loath to surrender the contact. Which in turn made him barely manage not to blatantly jerk away, and, when the video ended, perhaps made him a bit harsher than usual. He stood up and turned to look down at her. Intentionally. And his voice was cold when he spoke.

"This will not be easy, or pleasant, Ms. Moore. You will have to go through it all time and again. All the bloody, ugly details. I will ask you questions you won't want to answer but you will have to, and with the truth. I will ask you things that may not seem relevant to you, but you'll answer anyway. I will dig into things you'd rather not share, things you'd rather stayed hidden. You may not look at your friend, your father, or even yourself in the same way when this is over."

She'd grown slightly pale as he hammered his point home, but to her credit she didn't buckle. Instead he saw her jaw set under the onslaught, and his instincts told him she could and would withstand the long haul.

He wasn't totally convinced he would.

A sea of mental red flags surged in his head. He wasn't

even sure what some of them were about, but he suddenly wanted out of here. Away from this, away from her.

On the thought, Cutter lifted his head from her knee and looked at him with a steady, unblinking gaze, a stare really. If he had to put a label on it, it would be *Don't even think about it.*

He shook off the crazy feeling and asked the question he had to ask.

"That said, are you sure you want to do this?"

"Of course I don't want to," she said, only the faintest trace of strain in her voice. "But I will. I have to."

"We go after the truth. Is that what you want, or do you want them to believe your father is innocent?"

She stood up and faced him head-on. Determination came off her in waves. "They are one and the same," she said, holding his gaze without flinching, something supposedly tough criminals had had trouble doing.

In that moment he believed her. He'd withhold final judgment until he met and questioned her father, but for now, they would begin.

"All right," he said. His tone revealed nothing of his own tangled feelings. He'd walked away from the criminal defense arena, intending to never go back. He hadn't been down in those trenches for a long time. This, even if it never ended up in a trial, was as close as he'd gotten, and a lot closer than he'd wanted to get. If it did come down to a trial, her father would have to hire his own attorney.

But he couldn't deny that he liked Katie Moore's spirited defense of her father. And he was here anyway, so why not help? He wasn't really stepping back into the ring, just helping to find the facts of the case. That's what he did at Foxworth.

And, he told himself, the unexpected fact that he found

this woman both quietly attractive and sharply intelligent had nothing to do with his decision.

Nothing at all.

"I'm assuming you don't need me, so I'll go back to earning my keep."

Gavin gave Rafe a glance as they stood alone in the kitchen where he refilled his mug with Hayley's coffee blend of the day. "You earn your keep just by being available to call on."

Rafe gave a half shrug. "Until then, I keep busy. Keeps me from getting bored."

Gavin wondered for a moment what a bored expert sniper might do for entertainment if he didn't have the mechanics he loved to keep him distracted. It was an interesting thought.

"And I," Rafe said as he rinsed his own mug out and put it in the compact dishwasher, "would not want to face you in court. As an attorney, a defendant, a witness or a judge."

Gavin shrugged. "It's a rough game."

"I think she's up for it."

He met Rafe's speculative gaze then, and kept his tone carefully neutral. "Agreed. She's tougher than she looks."

"Cutter thinks so, too," Rafe said. "And his track record's impossible to ignore. In more than just bringing us cases."

Gavin's eyes narrowed, yet Rafe met his gaze easily. It would take a lot more than an accomplished and notorious lawyer to intimidate this man, if it could be done at all.

"Just saying that he's good at more than matching us up with cases," Rafe drawled. "And I think you're next on his radar."

Gavin blinked. "What?"

"That little seating dance that ended up with you sitting next to our client? Not an accident."

"Come on," Gavin said incredulously. He knew the credit this branch of Foxworth gave to the dog for…changes in their personal lives. But him ending up next to Katie had been an accident. Of course it had. It was a *dog*.

"Track record," Rafe repeated. "And a familiar tactic by now."

The idea that he had been maneuvered by a dog who had some idea in his canine brain that they belonged together was the craziest thing he'd ever heard. And in his career he'd heard some very crazy things.

And some of them were true.

"She's a client," Gavin pointed out, his tone resolute. "Nothing more."

"Sure," Rafe said, but Gavin thought he was laughing inside. As much as the man ever did, anyway.

Gavin couldn't deny people had ended up together— quite happily—thanks in part to Cutter's intervention. Apparently anyway, he thought, adding the qualifier because he doubted happy endings a bit more than just about anything in life.

Except the truthfulness of people in general.

Fresh coffee in hand, he headed back to begin what could be a very nasty process.

Chapter 10

Cutter was still by Katie's side, but Quinn and Hayley had left to meet with their friend, sheriff's detective Brett Dunbar, who had apparently picked up some scuttlebutt through his extensive grapevine.

Gavin walked toward her, took a swallow of coffee, set the mug down, then looked at her.

"I think better on my feet," he said by way of explaining why he would be standing while she sat.

"So you're not standing just to try to intimidate me?"

She said it with just a shade too much innocence, enough so that he understood she was letting him know she hadn't missed the tactic earlier. He didn't apologize, but noted her perceptiveness.

"I needed to know if you were up to this."

"Then I'll take the fact that we're proceeding as a compliment."

He barely managed not to smile. He hadn't been wrong

about her spirit. *And I could think of a lot more compliments to add to that.* He quashed the unexpected thought. It had nothing to do with the case, after all.

He was true to his word and made her go through it all again, asking her questions as things came up, and often made them non sequiturs, jumping around in the story, which he'd found sometimes gave him answers that he wouldn't have gotten otherwise.

"When did you last see her?"

"That morning at 7:30. Right before I left for work."

"Why that market?"

"It's close, and she doesn't—didn't—have a car. Hers had quit on her, and she'd been using Ross's."

He noticed the stumble of someone who hadn't managed to completely change a lifetime of thinking yet, but said nothing.

"You believe Carr's alibi?"

"Hard not to. And the police did. There were at least a dozen people who said he was at that party all evening."

"How long had they been together?"

"Off and on, a couple of years."

"He ever hit on you?"

She blinked. "I... He asked me out once, yes. Before he started seeing Laurel."

"Didn't go well?"

"Didn't go at all. I said no."

"Why?"

"He's not my type."

And what is your type? "So there was no chemistry, or you sensed something...off about him?"

"Yes to the former, but I doubt I could give you an honest answer about the latter."

"Why?"

"It would be too colored by what happened. Too easy

to believe I'd seen…something, because of what happened later, when it's clear he didn't do it."

Points for that, he thought. "Let me sort that part out. I need you to give me everything you thought or felt or suspected, whether you have proof or not."

Her brow furrowed. "But if there's no proof—"

"Right now I'm looking for paths, not proof. Directions to go, places to look. Possibilities, not conclusions."

After a moment she nodded. "Then I guess…we had nothing in common. Didn't like the same things at all."

"Books?" he suggested.

She laughed. "I think for him an evening at home in front of a fire with a book would be akin to torture."

"And what is it to you?" he asked softly.

"Heaven," she said simply.

A sudden image of just that, shot into his mind. Katie curled up before a fire, light dancing over her, maybe cuddled in a soft blanket, reading with that intensity only a true lover of books could have. His reaction to the quiet, peaceful image startled him. His mind careened into crazy places, imagining the scene in such detail it seemed almost real. He projected himself into the silly imaginings, walking into that room, stopping and just savoring the tableau.

He yanked himself back to reality. He wasn't prone to mental wanderings like that, and he was a little disconcerted not only that he'd done it, but that it had caused a strange sort of ache inside him.

"What else about him?" He hoped his tone wasn't too sharp, but he needed to get back on track. She didn't seem to notice, or more likely she assumed it was his way, which was just as well.

"He was a little too smooth for my taste." She smiled then, and it held a wealth of emotions, sadness, ruefulness, pain and loss. "And then he saw Laurel and that was that anyway."

"She was an attractive woman," he said neutrally.

"She was more than attractive. Funny, vivid, gregarious, always ready to go and do. She was beautiful, and so, so alive. She was everything I wasn't, so it was no wonder…" Her voice trailed away and she turned back to Cutter as if for comfort.

"That is the first stupid thing you've said."

The words were out before he could stop them, and once they were, he didn't regret them. She was staring at him, but this time he couldn't read anything in that look.

"Some people would much prefer that book before the fire to a merry-go-round of going and doing," he said.

Wasn't he proof of that? No one had gone and done more than Gavin de Marco at his peak, after all. He'd been at the apex of the glittering world so many lusted after. He'd been amid the movers and shakers, the household names from government, business and the entertainment world. There were few of them who, even if they'd never met, wouldn't take a call from him back then. And if they ever found themselves in need of a criminal defense attorney, he would have been at the top of their short lists.

And yet he had never felt more relieved than when he had walked away and left it all behind.

"Do you think," she said slowly, still looking at him, "that it's possible to change from one to the other?"

"I did."

He wasn't sure why he'd admitted that, but it was nothing less than the truth. And no one had been more surprised than he himself. When he wondered if she was wishing she could change in the other direction, he felt a twinge of sadness and had to stifle the urge to tell her she was fine as she was.

But this was not about her, and she likely wouldn't appreciate him making it about her, so this time he stopped himself.

"Tell me about your father."

Her chin came up then. "My father is a good man. He's kind, loving and strong. He's successful now, but he wasn't always. There were tough times, some when I was a kid, especially after my mom died, but he never gave up. And he often did without, so that I didn't have to."

"Textbook-perfect parent?"

Her gaze narrowed again, as if she suspected there was sarcasm behind the words.

"As perfect at it as any human being can get," she answered. "He had his flaws elsewhere, but as a father he was the best."

"What flaws?" For a moment she didn't answer. "I warned you," he said.

"I was thinking, not avoiding," she said, her tone a little sharp. Then, more evenly, she said, "He has a tendency to bite off more than he can chew, and then has to scramble, or put in impossibly long hours to get it done. Or leave half-finished projects all over. His shop—he makes metal sculptures as a hobby—is full of them. And sometimes he's too generous for his own good."

"Meaning?"

"I'm guessing you already know he owns a mailboxes franchise." At his nod, she went on. "What you don't know is that some of the box renters are transient or homeless, so he'll carry longtime customers if they come up short. He has a few disabled or elderly customers, and if they can't get in to pick up their mail, or there's a package too big or heavy for them, he'll hand deliver it on his way home."

"Admirable," he said, meaning it.

"He is an admirable man. One of those who just quietly keeps the world turning."

"And you love him."

"I adore him. But I'm not blind. He floundered a bit—well, a lot—after my mother died. We both did. He loved her so much he changed his whole life because he couldn't bear going on as if nothing had happened. He changed his job, his car, his friends, we moved… He changed everything but me."

He studied her for a moment. "But weren't you the biggest reminder of all?"

She didn't flinch. "Yes. And that's what finally made him realize that he couldn't run from it. That grief was going to happen no matter what he did."

"Were you ever afraid he'd want to change you, too?"

"Never," she said firmly, instantly. Before he even had the chance to wonder why on earth he'd asked that one. "We were a team, the two of us."

"Maybe he wanted it to stay that way. Didn't want a third team member."

Her brow furrowed. "He's always the one encouraging me to get out more, meet people, date, all that."

He hadn't meant that, he'd meant Laurel, but he found it interesting that it apparently didn't occur to her. And he found himself interested in the answer to this, on more than one level. "You don't?"

"I haven't had time, with the new job and moving." She sounded a tiny bit defensive.

"So no boyfriend in the picture, who might get jealous of the time you spent with Laurel?"

"No," she said, sounding relieved now, as if she'd thought he was going to chide her about her social life. Which would be rich, coming from him. He steered her back to the question.

"And your father?"

She blinked. "What?"

"Was he jealous of the time you spent with her? You and he being a team of two all those years?"

She drew back sharply. Her lips parted to speak, and then she stopped. Looked thoughtful. He guessed she had been going to answer angrily, then had reconsidered. Perhaps she remembered what he'd said about asking questions she wouldn't like.

"No," she said, calmly enough. "He was not. Laurel had always been my best friend. Growing up, he included her as if we were sisters. They even threw a surprise birthday party for me together, in April, right before…"

Another layer of pain for her, he thought; for the rest of her life her birthday would be connected to the loss of her best friend. He changed direction again, wondering on some level if he was doing it to protect her. He was usually more ruthless than that, but she wasn't the suspect here, her father was.

"What about your father's social life?"

"He's only now starting to live again himself."

"So he's going out, seeing people?"

"A little, yes. He was too grief-stricken for a very long time. It was nearly fifteen years before he would even think about it. I'm glad for him."

"But he wasn't out that night."

She stiffened visibly. "I told you—"

"I know. The old movie."

"*Casablanca.* Mom's favorite classic film. He always watched it, if it was on. Even though it hurt."

"You don't?" That really had nothing to do with anything, but he was curious. He was curious about too damned much with this woman.

"I'll watch it," she said with a half shrug. "But I don't make an appointment for it, like Dad will."

"Is that—"

The ring of his cell cut him off. He glanced at it, saw that it was Quinn, excused himself and walked toward the kitchen as he answered.

"News?" he asked without preamble.

He listened to Quinn's rapid report with his back to Katie. He was glad of it when an old, familiar coldness began to spread through him.

"Got it," he said when Quinn finished, saying they were on their way back. Just as well, Gavin thought. This could get ugly.

He ended the call with a swipe and shoved the phone back in his pocket. After a moment he realized his teeth were clenched, and purposely relaxed his jaw. Then he turned and walked back, looking down at her.

"I thought we had an understanding," he said, the coldness seeping into his voice.

Her brow furrowed. Even Cutter lifted his head to stare at him, as if he sensed the change in him.

"What do you mean?" she asked, sounding so honestly confused it made the cold bite even deeper. "Which understanding?"

"That you wouldn't lie to me."

Chapter 11

Katie stared up at him. It really was intimidating, having him tower over her, whether that was his intent or not. She stood, but it didn't help much; he was still much taller than her own five-four.

But that was nothing compared to the ice in his voice. Even Cutter was on his feet, as if he sensed the sudden change in mood in the room.

"I didn't lie to you," she said, with as much calm as she could muster considering the accusation. "About anything."

"Lies of omission are still lies," he said, his voice even colder, "and I will not tolerate either. From anyone."

Some part of her mind that wasn't shrinking away from that iciness was telling her there was more than just this case prodding at him, and she wondered why he'd felt compelled to add those last two words. But right now she couldn't spare brainpower to figure it out. This was the Gavin de Marco they wrote about, and she needed all her wits to even begin to deal with him.

She suddenly remembered, in her research last night, watching a video from one of his old cases that had been broadcast across the country. The prosecutor had given his opening statement, sounding convincing if a bit strident. And then Gavin de Marco had risen, slowly, all the while shaking his head in confident amusement as he glanced at the opposing attorney, then the jury. Letting his reputation make the first statement without saying a word.

She was getting her first inkling of what it must have been like to go up against this man.

"What is it you think I lied about? Or since you said omission, what do you think I left out that makes a difference?"

"You neglected to mention your father's history."

She drew back, more puzzled than ever. "What?"

"You didn't think the fact that he used to be a locksmith was relevant?"

Her brow furrowed. "That was nearly twenty years ago. I barely remember it. Why would it matter now?"

"Can you still ride a bike?"

"What's that got to—" It hit her suddenly, belatedly. *No evidence of forced entry...*

"You think he picked the lock."

"A pro can get in without leaving any obvious signs. He was a pro, for over a decade according to Detective Dunbar's source."

Katie sank back onto the couch. Cutter made a low sound, between a whine and a growl; he clearly wasn't happy with things at the moment. And neither was she. It had been difficult enough keeping up with his seemingly random questions; she'd never expected him to jump around from subject to subject like that. Then she'd realized that was probably why he did it, to keep the person he was quizzing off balance and more likely to make a mistake or get caught in a lie.

Lies of omission are still lies, and I will not tolerate either. From anyone.

"Nothing to say?"

She drew in a deep breath. Did he really correlate a simple missed connection to lying? She'd been prepared for him to be suspicious of her father, given the police were, but she hadn't been prepared for him to doubt she was telling him the truth.

"I…it never occurred to me," she said, her voice a bit shaky. "It's been so long, and once he left it, he never went back. I don't think he even still has his tools. It was all part of his life with Mom, and he couldn't bear it."

For a long moment he just stared down at her, saying nothing. Finally, as she was sure he intended, it got to be too much.

"Perhaps I should have held out for a say in this understanding," she said with a grimace.

"Such as?" *God, the man could freeze fire with that voice.*

"Oh, something simple. Basic. Like presumed honest until proven a liar."

He let out a short, compressed breath that managed to sound amused and sarcastic at the same time. "I've found it more accurate to assume the opposite."

"Then I don't envy you your life."

"If you'd lived that life, you'd understand."

"And if you'd lived my last six months, you'd understand I would never lie about this."

For a moment he just continued to stare at her, steady, assessing, but not quite as cold. Or maybe that was her imagination. Or wishful thinking. She'd known this would be uncomfortable, even painful at times, but she hadn't expected this sense of…almost sadness, that he thought so little of her so soon. Quickly she caught herself. What Gavin de Marco thought of her meant nothing, as long as he believed her father innocent.

Which he now clearly had doubts about. Thanks to a job her dad had once done, and admittedly done well, but had left behind long ago. The unfairness of it stiffened her spine and she held his gaze steadily and, with an effort, kept her voice calm and even.

"You need to talk to my father. Once you do, even if you go in with this attitude, I'm sure you'll see that he could never have done this." She let a bit of accusation into her voice. "Unless you've already jumped to your conclusion."

For an instant she thought she saw a corner of his mouth twitch, as if he were fighting a smile. That seemed unlikely, so perhaps he was trying not to laugh at her.

"I intend to talk to him," he said, ignoring her jab.

Maybe she shouldn't have done this at all, she thought. The police couldn't possibly have any evidence, not really, because her father was innocent. They might have been better off leaving it all alone. Especially if de Marco already agreed with the police that her father was the most likely—and she feared the only—suspect.

"If that," she said rather defiantly, rising to her feet again, "is all the police have to go on, then I'd say Dad has nothing to worry about."

"I told you, you weren't going to like this."

"And you were right." She was aware that Cutter had also stood again, now directly in front of her. She kept her eyes on the man who was watching her so intently it made her skin heat.

"Sit down, Ms. Moore. We've only just begun."

What she wanted to do was storm out in some kind of high dudgeon, but he'd probably only laugh at her. And that would really sting. She was calm, even serene by nature, and she didn't like the way this man rattled her. Although she also knew she should have expected it; this was Gavin de Marco, after all.

Cutter whined, then moved, nudging the front of her legs gently but insistently. The dog was urging her to sit back down, she realized when she had to shift to keep from doing just that.

"What if I say we're done?" she asked, her tone even sharper than she'd intended. She was way out of her league with this man, and that irked her.

He shrugged. "Then we're done. Barring misrepresentation, the client decides when Foxworth quits."

She wanted to exclaim she hadn't misrepresented anything, but was afraid that might make him think she was protesting too much. So she went instead with the question his words had planted in her mind.

"And if the client never does?"

His answer was simple, concise. "Then we never quit." He smiled then. "Quinn's got a couple of things he's been chewing on since before I signed on."

"And have they ever solved any of those?"

He nodded. "Several. Eventually. Are you firing us?"

For a moment she just looked at him. Calmer now, she realized the absurdity of it, giving up the chance to have a defense attorney of his stature working to defend her father, just because she didn't like the way he went about it.

And because he hurt your precious feelings.

She chided herself rather fiercely, and pointed out to her roiled emotions that she had no right to feel hurt when he'd warned her she wasn't going to like his tactics. And firmly denying those emotions had nothing to do with how attractive he was. Even if he wasn't way out of her league, this was hardly the time.

Slowly, feeling a bit more in control of herself now, she sat back down. For just a moment she saw an odd expression flit across his face. The kind you wore when you'd just checked something off on a list.

Now you're trying to read his mind? A man renowned for never betraying what he's thinking or where he's really going?

She nearly smiled then. But she managed to rein it in and sat rather primly, waiting for him to start again.

Chapter 12

Katie Moore was definitely tougher than she looked, Gavin thought. He almost hated to start in again, but he wanted everything he could get before he started on her father. And so he would begin with the ugliest parts, because after that, talking about her father again should be a relief.

"Tell me about that day. Step by step from when you got out of your car at your apartment. Every detail, whether you think it matters or not. Can you do that?"

"I could bury you in details," she said. Too sweetly? He nearly smiled again. No, there was nothing mousy about this librarian. He wondered if there was another occupation outside of the police or military—or lawyers—that came with so many erroneous assumptions.

"Try," he suggested.

And she almost did. She gave him every step of the way, from the moment of her late arrival home after a study night at the library, from the smell of the roses, to which lights were on in the building. Her voice trembled slightly when she reached the crime scene on her mental journey.

"I thought something had fallen, spilled somehow on the entry floor, that I'd tracked it into the living room without realizing. Then…" She swallowed and went on. "I realized it was blood."

From there her account matched the reports, and he was amazed at how steady she was as she recounted finding the bloodied, hacked body of her best friend in front of the couch. The only sign she gave of how distressed she had to be was the waver in her voice and the way she wrapped her arms around herself as if she was afraid she was going to fly apart. Not unexpected.

What was unexpected was the urge he felt to sit beside her and put his arm around her again. And how he was having to work harder than usual to keep his brain on track and catalog the details she was giving him. Because that stupid brain kept wandering off into other places that had nothing to do with the case and everything to do with those blue eyes of hers.

When he had finally finished making Katie go through it time and again he felt a bit too much like a mean kid torturing a helpless animal.

Although, there was nothing helpless about Katie Moore, he noted as she simply looked at him, waiting to see if they were going to start all over again.

"Enough," he said, rather gruffly. "We can't go any further until I talk to your father in person."

"That will be the deciding factor? If you believe him?"

"Yes." He left it at that. He knew Quinn would go with his instincts on the case; it was, after all, the big reason he'd taken him on at Foxworth.

"He is innocent," she said yet again. "He was nearly as upset as I was over Laurel. He still is, in fact, just as I am.

She'd been part of my life almost forever. He would never have hurt her. He would never hurt anyone."

Gavin felt the strangest urge to reassure her, even though he had long ago lost count of how many times he'd heard that phrase and it had turned out to be wrong.

He was startled—and unsettled—by how strongly he wanted it not to be wrong for Katie.

Cutter's string of oddly rhythmic and definitely happy barks interrupted Katie's roiling thoughts. The dog leaped from where he'd been close at her feet, as he had been most of this disturbing session. He trotted quickly over to the door, tail up and wagging furiously.

She found herself amused—and thus relieved—as she watched him rise up and bat at the large, square button beside the front door. The door swung open and he squeezed through the moment the gap was wide enough.

"Quinn and Hayley," Gavin said. "That's their bark." At her look, he shrugged. "Don't ask, I don't know. All I know is I doubt they're paying him enough."

To her surprise, she found herself laughing at that, and a bit more of the tension of the past couple of hours eased. She liked his sense of humor, when it snuck out. That a sense of humor was high on her list of desirable traits in a relationship in all those silly quizzes Laurel used to make her take was incidental.

She stood up as the door swung open again. Hayley was the first in, Cutter dancing around her feet.

"And have you kept things under control here, my fine boy?"

Quinn glanced at Katie and Gavin. "Everybody looks intact and unbattered, so I'd say yes."

The greetings complete, the dog promptly returned to his selected place at Katie's feet and sat, leaning against her leg. But he kept looking at Quinn and Hayley. He seemed to wait until he was sure he had their full attention before letting out a distinctive sound that sounded half whine, half growl.

"Oh?" Quinn said, as if the dog had spoken. He looked at Gavin then. "What's the problem?"

Katie was sure she was gaping at this canine communication. Gavin only shrugged, so although she felt a bit silly being directed by a dog, Katie answered. "Your attorney thinks I purposely kept a big secret from him."

Quinn's gaze narrowed, as if he knew quite well what that would mean. "Did you?"

"I didn't tell him something from twenty years ago because I haven't even thought about it in that twenty years."

"The locksmithing?" Quinn asked. Katie nodded.

"That's a bit over-the-top even for you, Gav," Hayley said. She glanced at Katie. "You were what, nine years old when he changed professions?"

"Ten," Katie answered. "I thought he just helped people who locked themselves out of their cars. But then he quit and bought the mailbox place, and I never really thought about it again."

"What ten-year-old would? Especially with everything else you were dealing with." Hayley looked at her dog, who was leaning into Katie's leg even more. Then she looked at Gavin. "Cutter's giving you his opinion. He trusts her. And we've never gone wrong trusting his judgment."

Quinn looked once more at Gavin, who hadn't said a word since they'd come in. "Where do we stand?"

"I'm done with her for now," he said, not quite dismissively. "Next I need to interview her father."

Katie felt a stab of irritation at the way he said it, but quashed it. This wasn't personal. He was a lawyer approaching a case, and she was just an aspect of that case.

She'd best remember that and rein in her own silly reactions to this man. Even if he was exasperating.

"In case you forgot," Hayley said, giving Gavin a pointed look, "she's standing right here. Talking about her in the third person is rude."

Katie's gaze shifted to Hayley, and the other woman winked broadly at her.

"Sorry," Gavin muttered, but he didn't look at her, or Hayley.

Something sparked in Katie, and her chin went up. "That's okay," she said blandly. "I'd rather he save his energy for helping my father than waste it on being polite to me."

His gaze shot to her then. She thought she saw a sort of startled amusement in his eyes. "Touché," he said with a small nod.

"I'd suggest you not underestimate this one," Quinn said, and there was no doubting his amusement.

"Point taken," Gavin said.

"Before you leave to talk to Katie's father, there's more you should know," Quinn told him. "Brett talked to a guy who's got a brother on the PD down there. He said they're pretty set on Steven Moore as their suspect, but he thinks it's in part because every other lead has been a dead end. Moore's got the weakest alibi, but the rest is all circumstantial, and flimsy at that."

Katie didn't know whether to feel more concerned or relieved. She had faith in the system, generally, but it had miscarried justice often enough that she didn't trust it when it came to someone she loved as much as she loved her father. When it came to her father, she wanted the best help she could get.

And that meant Gavin de Marco.

Quinn went on. "The only solid thing they have is his

phone records. Regular calls to Laurel's number and vice versa for several weeks before she was killed."

Katie looked at Gavin. "My birthday party," she said. "I told you about that."

"You did," he acknowledged with barely a glance at her. Quinn looked curious, but let it go. "And what are they chewing on as motive?"

Quinn shook his head. "They're really short on that, too, Brett said. I told him to call you direct with anything else, now that he's read in on it."

Gavin nodded. Katie supposed he and their detective friend had worked together before, on the big, statewide political scandal if nothing else.

"And," Hayley added with a smile at Gavin, "Brett seems to think that just dropping your name into the mix, if you decide we're taking this on, could shift the direction a bit."

Gavin's jaw tightened. It seemed that he wasn't particularly happy with that. She would have thought he'd be delighted to still have such influence, even years after he'd walked away. She was certainly delighted; anything that turned police attention away from her father was a good thing in her book.

"I'll call my father, let him know we're coming," she said, reaching for her phone.

"You will not," Gavin said, not quite sharply but with a definite edge. "I don't want him warned."

She frowned. "You think…what, you're going to trick something out of him with some kind of sneak attack?"

His mouth quirked. "I hope I have more finesse than that, but essentially yes. Which," he added, "I could only do if it's there to come out in the first place."

She steadied herself, held his gaze, then echoed his words. "Point taken."

"And I need to talk to him alone."

If he'd meant that to rattle her, it didn't. At all. "All right."

She could almost see him register her lack of concern. Good, she thought. That should prove how utterly certain she was of her father's innocence. And Gavin would be, too, once he talked to him. And maybe that weighty name really would make the police rethink. Despite all her worry, she dared to hope.

He glanced at his watch. "Will he be home now?"

"Should be. Sunday's his workshop day. Or football. Shall I drive, since I know where we're going? It's not far."

He hesitated for a moment, then said, "I'll follow you."

She arched a brow at him. "Aren't you afraid I'll call to warn him?"

Something flashed in those dark eyes again. "Maybe I'm more worried you'll want to drive me into a pole when we're done."

Her mouth quirked upward at one corner. "Sorry, can't afford the damage that would do."

"To your car or your driving record?" he asked wryly.

"Yes." She smiled, with a little too much cheer. "I know a lawyer, though. Whether he's good enough remains to be seen. Shall we go?"

He drew back at that. Quinn laughed out loud.

"Nicely done," Hayley said. "He needs taking down a peg now and then."

"Thanks," Gavin said with a glance at his friends.

Katie was still smiling when she got to her feet. The sooner this was over with, the better. Then Gavin would be convinced her father was innocent, and he could put that prodigious brain and reputation to work proving it.

Chapter 13

I'd suggest you not underestimate this one.

Gavin recalled Quinn's statement. Truer words had never been spoken, Gavin thought as he followed Katie's car. As if he'd heard the thought, Cutter woofed softly. Gavin let out a slight sound of disbelief, shaking his head, wondering how he'd let himself get roped into taking the dog with him.

"Take Cutter," Quinn had said cheerfully. "He'll assess things for you."

"Do bring him," Katie had agreed, sounding happy about it. "Dogs love my dad. They have good judgment about people."

"Right," he'd muttered, trying not to notice that Cutter had gotten to his feet and was already headed for the door, as if he'd understood every word.

"Trust him," Hayley had said softly as he stood up.

So now here he was, with the too clever dog opining

from the back seat, wondering how it had happened. But the farther they went, the more he began to think perhaps it was a good thing. The dog would be a distraction, perhaps make Moore feel this was more of a social visit, friendly, so his guard wouldn't be up.

Katie was driving rather sedately, not speeding or rolling through any stop signs despite the lack of traffic. After a final turn onto a small cul-de-sac, she pulled into the driveway of a tidy, bungalow-style house. The driveway was delineated by a row of metal sculptures, birds, fish and some more whimsical, like a curious-looking dragon. The hobby Katie had mentioned, he guessed. Next to the house was a wide carport, extended to provide shelter up to a side door of the house. A silver coupe sat in one spot. Katie pulled in next to it.

He stopped behind her bright blue sedan. A practical four-door, but a flashy color, he'd thought when he'd first seen it. He wondered how much of herself was reflected in the choice.

He watched her through the back window of the car. Katie Moore had proven more than once she could and would stand up to him. If she'd been an attorney, he would have relished taking her on in a courtroom. As it was, he was relishing the thought of taking her on in very different ways. And that rattled him. He hadn't had a response like this to a woman in…forever? Or had it just been so long it seemed like forever?

He'd written off having any kind of permanent relationship. The kind of women he would want for that couldn't— and wouldn't—tolerate him for long. He didn't blame them. His last attempt had been Jessica, who had left him after a mere three months, expressing the rueful hope that he one day find someone who could take his skeptical nature and hell-on-wheels, 24/7 brain.

At this point he doubted such a woman existed. He hadn't been drawn enough to anyone to test the supposition.

Until now.

If thoughts really did come with hazard flags, this one would be big, bright and with a siren attached. It came from a different place than his instincts about people and liars, a place he hadn't heard from any time in recent memory. And it was swift and personal, warning of a steep drop off a cliff and churning water below.

Cutter gave him a nudge with his nose, startling him out of his strange reverie. He put the rental car in Park, but didn't immediately get out. Nor did Katie, and he wondered if she was having to gear herself up for this. He reminded himself that she and her father had been all each other had had for over two decades, so they were very likely to provide a united front. United in a kind of grief he'd never experienced.

Because you never let yourself get that close to anyone.

That little voice that often guided him in an interrogation or in a courtroom had recently taken to personal jibes he could do without. Besides, could he be blamed for finding it hard to trust when he'd spent years around people who lied without a thought?

Of course, all that had been before he'd learned his entire life was built on a lie.

A side door on the house opened. He stayed put, watching, wanting the chance to observe. Katie quickly got out of her car the moment a man stepped out onto the small landing two steps up from the driveway.

The man was smiling widely. No nerves there at an unexpected visit from his daughter. Assuming it was unexpected, of course, that she hadn't called him while en route despite her promise.

A promise he'd believed.

...presumed honest until proven a liar.

He shook his head again, keeping his gaze focused on the pair, assessing as Steven Moore gave his daughter a hug. Her father was, likely by any standard, a handsome man. Tall, broad-shouldered, with the same sandy-blond hair as Katie's, only his was just touched at the temples with gray. His good looks were more dramatic than Katie's quiet attractiveness, and Gavin guessed he could have had more than his share of feminine attention if he'd wanted it.

Was it really possible to grieve so much and so hard that a man who could probably have his pick of attentive ladies would forego all that for so long? Was it even possible to love someone that much?

There was no doubt about the love between father and daughter; it fairly radiated from them. He knew that kind of parental love existed, had observed it often enough. And it put a furrow in his brow as he wondered if that kind of love could run to lying to that daughter's face.

To protect her? Absolutely. To protect himself? To ensure her love for her father stayed unchanging? Because if he'd murdered her best friend, that would surely destroy what they had.

But he was, as were the police, hard aground on the lack of motive. And the man certainly did not look like a killer, but then they often didn't. Who knew that better than he? But he also knew that when desperate to solve a case, it was human nature to start searching for evidence to prove your suspicions instead of continuing to search for an elusive truth. Cops had gut instincts they trusted just as he did. Only, theirs were aimed at a different goal—a conviction in court. Most of the time their two goals coincided, but sometimes...

Katie gestured toward him, and her father looked his way. Something wary came into his expression. Gavin noted it, but didn't chalk it down in a column yet, because people were often wary upon meeting him, simply because his reputation so often preceded him.

And yet there was a touch of the excitement he also sometimes saw. Again human nature, meeting someone they'd read about or seen on TV was somehow different than meeting any other stranger.

He opened the car door and got out. He realized, far too belatedly, that he hadn't really considered what approach to take. He'd been too busy dwelling on the man's daughter and the weird effect she had on him.

And then Cutter was out of the car and trotting ahead, leaving him no time to ponder the matter. He was truly out of it, Gavin thought. To be honest, he'd been off stride ever since he'd opened the door to see a wet, bedraggled Katie Moore standing there. It was time he got over it and got back in the game.

The dog came to a halt in front of Steven Moore, and sat. He looked up at the man, head cocked at a quizzical angle, as if he couldn't quite figure him out.

"Well, hello there," Moore said, bending to pet the dog's dark head.

Cutter allowed it, but he didn't react with the instant warmth and affection he'd given Katie. Of course, he knew Katie from the neighborhood.

"This is Cutter," Katie was explaining. "He belongs to the Foxworths. He's quite the judge of character, so he's here to show Mr. de Marco that you're honest."

She said it with obvious amusement. But watching her father's face, Gavin was certain he'd seen a flicker of... something in his eyes. Worry? Nervousness?

Guilt?

Cutter had remained in place, sitting in front of the man. But now he was looking back over his shoulder at Gavin with the oddest expression. In a person he would have said it was a maybe, or a tentative yes, with reservations.

Trust him.

Hayley's words echoed in his mind. And he found himself wishing the dog could explain those reservations.

Laughing at himself inwardly, he walked up to the trio.

"Mr. Moore," he said, holding out a hand.

The man took it, and they shook. Good, solid handshake, not too weak, not overdone to impress him. One small box checked off.

"Mr. de Marco," Moore said. "It's an honor to meet you. I just wish my girl didn't think it was necessary."

"You don't think it is?"

The older man—Gavin figured he had to be early to midfifties at least, although he looked much younger—let out an audible sigh.

"Since I didn't do it, I don't want to think it is," he said, "but if it will make Katie feel better, I'll go along."

The denial was issued calmly, not an insistent declaration but merely as if it were a statement of fact. And Gavin found himself believing it. Which was odd, since he usually didn't reach that stage so soon.

That had him wondering even more about what the dog's apparent reservations were.

Which in turn made him think, ruefully, that he'd completely lost his mind.

Or, he added silently with a look at Katie, something else entirely.

Chapter 14

"As I explained to the police, those calls to Laurel—" his voice changed slightly with her name; definite sadness there, Gavin thought "—were us arranging Katie's birthday party. And as I also told them, we met several times to go over the arrangements."

Gavin got no hint of a lie in the words. "Whose idea was that?"

"Laurel's. She wanted it to be ginormous, she said. She teased Katie because Katie was going to turn thirty before she would."

They'd been at this for nearly two hours, Gavin doing his usual pacing while keeping a close eye on Moore. He'd begun with small talk, casual, lulling the man a bit with ordinary things before hitting him with a sudden, unexpected question about Laurel and her death. The technique had somewhat backfired on him this time since the topic had, inevitably, veered to Katie. It had been all he could do to stay mentally here in this room when she was right outside, working in the sizable vegetable garden in the back. Doing what, he wasn't sure, as his skills didn't run to such things. Something to do with the coming winter, he supposed.

She'd pulled her hair back and secured it in that pony-tail that bounced when she moved. To keep her hair out of the way as she worked, he supposed. He was supposing too much and too often, he chided himself. But it was difficult not to when Moore had spoken of her with such pride and love. There was absolutely no doubt in Gavin's mind that the man loved his daughter. Or that he had cared a lot about her best friend.

He'd been open and calm about answering questions, although he did blink a time or two when Gavin would jump to a new subject. But he always answered, sometimes with thought, but most times with the ease of someone who'd either thought about it a lot, or answered the questions before. In this case Gavin thought both probably applied.

In fact, everything Moore said felt genuine. Yet the old instincts were firing. He couldn't put a name to the rather vague misgivings he was feeling, but something was off. He was usually able to tell when someone was lying, but as with Katie, omission was something else. In her case, he now thought she'd honestly forgotten about the locksmith thing, since she'd been so young. And he shoved aside the feeling of relief it gave him to no longer think she'd been trying to hide it from him. She was clouding his judgment, and he shoved that realization aside as well, even as he noted he was doing a lot of that since last night when Cutter had practically dragged her into his life.

But in her father's case…

He just couldn't pin it down. He didn't think the man was outright lying, but something was triggering those old

gut feelings. He had the sudden thought that he was agree-
ing with the dog. Yes, but with reservations.

*Maybe you've been out of the game too long. And while
the media used to trumpet that your judgment is flawless,
no one knows better than you that it's not. It's very, very
flawed, and always has been.*

He heard Cutter bark from outside and stopped his pacing and turned to look. He'd kept his gaze away from the
large window that looked out on the garden, since Katie
puttering around out there was apparently more of a distraction than his suddenly unruly mind could handle.

Right now, the dog was crouched in front of Katie in that
universal, front end down, tail wagging in the air posture
of canine play. She was holding up a stick about a foot and
a half long. Cutter barked again, happily. He couldn't hear
it, but Gavin knew she laughed; he could see her face. It
sent a bolt of heat through him that was out of proportion
to the simple vision of a woman playing with a dog.

She raised the hand with the stick and leaned back, that
ponytail swaying. He had a sudden image of pulling away
whatever held it, and watching her hair tumble back down
to her shoulders, and heat jammed through him again. He
sucked in a breath as he watched her throw the stick, following through with the swing of her arm and sending it
a decent distance toward the trees at the back of the lot.
Cutter took off after it in clear delight.

"I should have gotten her a dog, after her mother died."

The quiet words came from barely a foot behind him.
Gavin stiffened, barely managing not to jerk around. He
hadn't even heard the man move, he'd been so focused on
the tableau outside. So focused on the woman out there that
he'd lost all sense of his immediate surroundings.

Great. You've got your head so far up your backside

you let a guy who might be a murderer completely get the drop on you.

"But I was too deep in my own pain. There are so many things I wish I'd done for her. She was so young and hurting so much. But I just wasn't thinking clearly at the time."

There was, Gavin thought, no denying those emotions were heartfelt and real. He knew that without even looking at Moore's face, because it was all there in his voice. And a sudden image of a nine-year-old Katie, maybe with that same ponytail, broken and weeping inconsolably sent an entirely different kind of jolt through him. Pain, sympathy and a sudden wish that she never again have such a horrible ache in her heart.

If her father took the fall for Laurel's murder, her pain would be unbearable.

He turned then, and stood face-to-face with the man. They were almost the same height, and he found himself looking into eyes exactly the same shade of blue as Katie's. It was disconcerting for a moment. But then he asked, his voice low and intense, the question he had yet to ask.

"Did you kill Laurel Brisbane?"

The answer came immediately, firmly. "No, sir, I did not."

Whatever Moore was lying about, Gavin couldn't convince himself it was this. His misgivings were too vague to even hang a name on. For all he knew, they could stem from something else entirely. There had been a time when he would have trusted them without hesitation, but that time had ended four years ago. December 21, to be exact.

"And if you think I did," Moore added quietly, "then you should leave. I know your reputation, Mr. de Marco. And what it can do. Don't get my girl's hopes up any further."

For the first time Gavin saw concern in the man's expression. And he realized Moore wasn't quite as casual about being a murder suspect as it had seemed. He was putting on a good front for Katie, Gavin thought. He didn't want her to worry. In a way this relieved him; he'd been afraid the man didn't understand the gravity of his situation.

And then another realization struck him. That on some level beneath conscious thought, he'd already decided.

"Sit down, Mr. Moore," he suggested. "We have a lot of work to do."

Chapter 15

"That de Marco is really something."

Katie looked across the table at her father. It was the first time he'd paused in eating the meat loaf she'd fixed for his Sunday dinner and lunches next week. The dish was his and her favorite, from her mother's recipe she'd found in a box shoved in the back of a closet where he'd put many of the painful reminders he'd moved with him from the old house but hadn't wanted on daily display.

"Yes, he is." *And isn't that the truth*, she added silently. Although now, away from him, she could think of him much more rationally. She wondered what it was that gave some people that kind of overpowering charisma. Was it something in them, some quirk of genetics or chemistry? Or was it something in the people around them, making them react that way? She'd have to research that, see if anyone had ever come up with a plausible theory.

"And that's really the story, how you met him? The dog?"

She nodded, smiling now although she hadn't been then. "Cutter's quite something, as well."

"He sounds scary smart."

"Yes." She wondered if he'd meant the dog or Gavin, but since the same answer applied in either case, she left it at that.

She hesitated before speaking again. It had been a long day, for both of them, but particularly him because he'd spent those hours getting, as he put it, "grilled." But since she'd been exiled to the garden, she was beyond curious.

"So…did he ask you anything unexpected?"

Her father shrugged. "Some questions I couldn't see the relevance of."

"He did that to me, too. I suppose it must mean something to him, or else leads to something else."

"You know, usually I can figure a man out, after a while. But I have no idea how this one's mind works."

"Maybe that's partly why he was so good at what he did."

Her father looked at her curiously now. "Do you have any idea why he quit?"

"No, other than to work for Foxworth."

"I never heard any rumors that he was in trouble or anything."

Katie was surprised at how much just the idea of that shocked her. She hadn't found anything in her research to indicate he'd left under a cloud, but she didn't think she would have believed it if she had, now that she'd met him. Gavin de Marco was intense, brilliant and charismatic, but if he was ethically challenged she'd eat the plate the last bit of her meat loaf sat on.

"I can't imagine him working for a place like Foxworth if he was that type," she said. "Quinn Foxworth appears to be the straightest of straight arrows."

"But de Marco is a lawyer."

"I think he's more of an advisor now," she said.

"Seemed like a guy in charge to me," her father said drily. He leaned back in his chair, took a sip of the small glass of wine he allowed himself in the evenings, and studied her. "You seem…quite impressed with him."

She managed not to flush, but it took a very deep breath and great effort. "I've never met a household name before."

"He's a good-looking man, wouldn't you say?"

The flush won that time. "Are you asking me or telling me?"

"Aha!" her father exclaimed. "I always know I've got you when you answer a question with a question."

"I'm just trying to figure out what that has to do with anything. And how you can tease me when…when…" She couldn't finish, and lowered her gaze to that last, lonely bite of meat.

"Baby," he said, instantly contrite, "I'm just trying to cheer you up. You're so worried, and I keep telling you there's no reason. The truth will out eventually. Or maybe sooner, now that Mr. Gavin Household Name de Marco is involved."

Her gaze shot back to his face. "Then you're not upset with me for talking to him? You seemed less than excited about it at first."

"I was," he admitted. "Maybe I just didn't want to admit that I might need a lawyer. I'm still not sure I do, mind you, but if I'm going to have one… Well, damn, Gavin de Marco!"

She laughed at both his tone and expression, feeling much better now. Because it was true. Having Gavin on your side was a very big deal.

And given her silly reaction to him, having to deal with him herself was going to be a huge task.

* * *

"Damn, that was fast."

At Quinn's words Gavin looked up from the legal pad he was holding. He was sitting beside the fireplace at the Foxworth headquarters, the flames casting a flickering light across the page. Cutter was curled up before the fire, no doubt still a bit damp from his romp in the meadow earlier.

"What?" Gavin asked, lifting the fountain pen from the page. He still took notes with pen and paper because he'd found there was something about the process that got his brain into that zone he needed. Even when he did record an interview, he made written notes, adding to them as he listened to it later, usually with his eyes closed to summon up the memory of how a person had looked or spoken, which was sometimes as important as what they'd said, or more so.

Quinn held up his phone before sliding it back into a pocket. "That was Brett. Word's out that you're involved, and already the police are rethinking. Or at least questioning their assumptions."

"Question is, are they angry?"

"Brett says they'll get over it. They knew they'd settled on Moore because every other lead washed out," Quinn said. "Brett gave me the name and number of the lead investigator, who by the way wasn't at all interested in talking to Moore's attorney until he mentioned your name."

Gavin's mouth tightened. His reputation was the biggest double-edged sword he'd ever dealt with. It sliced through protocol and often reluctance, but it also affected things in ways he wasn't comfortable with. No one should ever have been negatively impacted just because he was too busy or didn't want to handle their case. And yet he knew it had happened. It was one of the other reasons he'd walked away.

"If I haven't said so lately, thanks for taking me on," he said, not exactly sure why.

Quinn looked startled, then smiled. "I think you have that backward."

Gavin shook his head. "No. I come with a lot of history, not all of it good, and I know I'm sometimes tough to work with."

"Tough to keep up with," Quinn said. "Entirely different thing."

"Speaking of which, now that we're rolling I'm going to stay here," Gavin told him. At his announcement Quinn lifted a brow quizzically. "It'll be easier on everyone if I'm out of your place," he explained. "You know how I get."

He didn't sleep much anyway, but when he had a case he was up at all hours pacing and going over things, sometimes talking things through out loud.

"Hayley wouldn't mind, and you know I don't."

"But I do. Besides, worrying about disturbing my hosts affects my focus."

Quinn shrugged. "Well, this is now your baby, so you're the boss. How did it go with Moore?"

Gavin's mouth twisted. He stared into the fire, wishing he could let go of that tiny, nagging instinct that said Katie's father was hiding something. "I quizzed him up and down for nearly three hours. I couldn't shake him off his story, and I used every interrogation technique I know."

"Short of torture, I hope?"

His gaze shot back to Quinn's face. He was clearly joking, but it always rattled him a little to remember that this man had been one of the most elite operators in the military, one who had no doubt been trained in just that sort of technique. He was glad Quinn was on the side of the angels; he shuddered to think what the man could do if he'd gone rogue. But nothing could ever shake the core of who Quinn Foxworth was. Having Hayley in his life now had only solidified that, made him even stronger.

I envy him.

The stray thought flashed through Gavin's mind. How those in the world he'd once inhabited would laugh at the idea of Gavin de Marco envying anyone, he who had it all. But he did envy Quinn, and what he'd found in Hayley.

He quashed the thought, and the odd shiver that had gone through him when he'd acknowledged it. He was here to work, not indulge in idle musings. And certainly not to have Katie Moore pop into his head every time it happened.

"What does your gut say?" Quinn asked.

"That he's hiding something," Gavin admitted.

Quinn cocked his head to give Gavin a curious look. "But we're taking the case anyway?"

"He's hiding something," Gavin repeated, then added, "but I can't buy that the guy's a murderer. Especially not of his daughter's best friend."

"All right. Need anything from us?"

"Not yet. I'll be contacting the cops tomorrow, and the victim's family. Ty's running down data on them for me."

Quinn nodded. "Another session with Moore?"

Steven or Katie?

Damn, he needed to get this crazy reaction under control. "Probably. Go home to your wife."

"Always," Quinn said with a grin that made that envy spark again.

Quinn headed for the door, then turned to look at Cutter, who hadn't budged an inch from Gavin's side. The dog stared back, and Gavin had the craziest feeling they were communicating somehow.

"Not coming?" Quinn asked lightly.

Cutter gave a low woof. Quinn's gaze shifted to Gavin.

"Well, well. It seems you have a roommate."

Gavin blinked. "What?"

"I'd say he's appointed himself your guardian."

Gavin stared at the dog, who looked up at him with eyes full of utter innocence. "Guardian?"

"He saw you in the aftermath of the whole governor thing. I'd say he knows you'll bury yourself in this and forget to eat and sleep without someone around to remind you."

He looked back at Quinn, but saw no trace of a joke in his expression this time. "Seriously?"

Quinn ignored the question. "His food's in the cupboard next to the sink. Just keep it topped off. He'll self-regulate. He'll let you know when he wants out, and he'll stay close, especially now that he's adopted you. Oh, and his carrots are in the fridge. Not too many of those, though, or you'll be sorry one way or another."

"You're really going to leave him here, to…what, baby-sit me?"

Quinn grinned. "Consider yourself a dog sitter, if it makes you feel better."

Before he could even formulate a response to that, Quinn gave him a mock salute and was gone. Cutter jumped up on the couch beside him, avoiding his loose papers with delicate care. He settled down against the back cushions, and plopped his chin on Gavin's leg. He looked utterly at home and satisfied.

Gavin looked down at the dark head, and into the amber-flecked dark eyes looking up at him. With a sigh he picked up his pad again and uncapped the fountain pen.

But when he started writing again he was smiling.

Chapter 16

Gavin awakened in the headquarters bedroom with Cutter once more curled up beside him. He couldn't deny he again had slept better than he usually did, but he was hesitant to ascribe it to the dog's presence. But then, Cutter wasn't your garden-variety dog.

Uncharacteristically, he spent a few minutes petting the dog before getting up. Cutter waited until he was upright, then went and politely sat at the back door. Gavin took the cue and let him out, stepping out himself into the crisp, predawn chill. It felt wonderful to someone used to the frequent humidity of St. Louis, and he breathed it in deeply.

The motion-sensor light came on as Cutter came trotting back. He paused at a basket beside the door, nosing at it. He came up with a grayish-yellow tennis ball and sat before Gavin hopefully. He couldn't stop the memory that shot into his mind of Katie happily and fairly efficiently throwing a stick for the dog. He shook it off.

"It's too dark to see it, isn't it?" He wasn't used to being this far north this time of year, where it was still dark at this hour. But then, he'd also usually been up and working for a couple of hours by this time, so he'd better adjust.

Cutter cocked his head at an angle, ball still in his mouth.

"I get it. No problem for you, right?"

He hesitated, but figured if it got lost they'd find it once it got light. So he took the rather grubby ball. Cutter, seeing that the human had apparently figured it out, came vibrantly alert, his gaze fastened on the hand that held the ball. Gavin threw it, somewhere between a casual flip and giving it everything he had. The dog raced into the darkness, vanishing the moment he left the circle of the motion light, and Gavin had the sour thought that if he didn't come back he was going to have some difficult explaining to do to some people he really liked.

A moment later the victorious animal came trotting back, dropped the ball at his feet and spun, clearly ready to do it again. And something about the dog's playful posture made it impossible to resist. It was thirty minutes later that he finally called a halt. The sky was just beginning to lighten when they went back inside.

He put on a pot of coffee, a little surprised at how much company an animal could be. He waited for the coffee to finish, stifling a yawn, anticipating that first hit of caffeine. And when it came it was worth the wait, and the groggy morning feeling started to slip away.

Cutter nudged his knee. He looked down. The dog started toward the patio door, pausing to look back over his shoulder. That, Gavin thought, was a dog signal anybody understood.

"Already?" he asked. Maybe the ball chasing had distracted him from the real business at hand. He followed obediently, laughing inwardly at himself as he did so.

They stepped outside, but instead of heading off into the meadow the dog stopped, then turned sideways to the building, looking toward the drive. Gavin turned to look, but saw nothing but the empty gravel approach and the thinner stand of trees between them and the road.

"Waiting for Mom and Dad?" The inner laugh was sounding in his voice now.

As if in answer Cutter sat at his feet. Gavin was wondering what to do with him when a brilliant blast of golden light burst through the trees. Cutter stayed still as Gavin stood there watching the sunrise flare, lighting up the sky and clouds in an explosion of gold, orange and pink. He could see the rays as they backlit the branches of the evergreens, and above the treetops the undersides of the clouds fairly glowed with color. It was a show to rival anything he'd seen in any of the myriad places he'd been. He could see that it would soon disappear behind the heavy, hovering cloud layer, but right now it was a glorious stripe of brilliant light and color play along the horizon. And all the more precious for being fleeting.

And when did you start getting philosophical about things like the sun coming up in the morning?

Cutter woofed softly and Gavin laughed because he was the one who'd gotten him out here to watch this amazing show. Of course, that couldn't really be why he'd done it. Dogs couldn't even see in color, could they? And did it really matter, when it had worked, had gotten him to stop and watch something he probably would have ignored or been completely unaware of?

"Maybe you should take credit," he said, and got another quiet, approving woof. "How about some carrots, dog?"

Cutter jumped to his feet eagerly. When Gavin opened the door he darted inside, raced to the kitchen and sat expectantly while Gavin retrieved the treats.

He headed for the shower. In twenty minutes, he was back at the kitchen counter pouring another mug of the strong brew he preferred and checking his phone, planning out his day. Since it was later there, he first called Ty for anything new. There wasn't much on Steven Moore, who had apparently stayed out of trouble most of his life, except for a couple of speeding tickets when he'd been a teenager. Having had a couple of those himself—one embarrassingly recently—Gavin wasn't going to hang the man over that, but he told Ty to keep digging.

"I will. Oh, and the ex-boyfriend is apparently out of town, since Friday. San Diego, some seminar for his job starts today." Gavin made note of that, since he obviously needed to talk to the guy personally, cleared by the police or not.

Then Ty added the unexpected news that the victim had an arrest record. "Minor, but I know you want everything."

"Yes. What for?"

"For driving under the influence when she was eighteen."

"Any record of an accident or anything involved with that?"

"Not yet, but I'm still looking."

"Thanks, Ty."

Well, now. Gavin thought for a while as he sipped his coffee. No one had mentioned that fact. Was it possible they didn't know? Didn't seem likely. Perhaps they thought it of no importance, being so long ago. And maybe it wasn't.

Like Katie thought her father being a locksmith unimportant?

He grimaced inwardly. He glanced at his watch, saw that it was now after eight and made another call to the number that Detective Dunbar had provided. The man he reached, a detective named Davidson, clearly recognized his name. And that of Dunbar and Foxworth, both of which were apparently worth a lot in law enforcement circles here. He was clearly wary but cooperative enough, and agreed to meet with him this afternoon, after he completed a court appearance.

Which left Gavin a bit at loose ends at the moment. He planned on speaking to Moore again, but wanted to observe him at work, so he needed to give that another hour. He pondered fixing breakfast; there were eggs and plenty of other things available. In the end he settled for a couple of pieces of buttered toast made from bread from the local bakery, something he'd had last time he was here and liked. Cutter munched on some kibble from his bowl, but as Quinn had said, stopped on his own while it was still half-full.

When he was done and had tidied up, he stood for a moment, thinking. Or rather, trying not to think about a particular person.

He could get what he needed from the police detective this afternoon. He was certain they must have looked into that old arrest; since it was a murder case they'd dig deep. Given how long ago it had been it likely had nothing to do with her murder, but he hadn't become a success leaving unturned stones.

But right now he was more curious why Katie hadn't mentioned it.

Shoving those inner warnings into a mental box, he put his phone in his pocket, gathered up his keys and jacket and headed for the door. Cutter beat him to it and slapped the button to open it. Gavin realized with chagrin he'd forgotten to lock the front door last night. Lucky for him he was here, and not at home in the city.

Lucky, too, that he had a self-appointed guard dog in Cutter.

He was a little surprised when the dog raced out to his rental car, clearly intending to come along. Gavin wondered if the dog expected to go home now, like a kid after a sleepover. Well, if he did, he was just going to have to wait. Gavin wanted to get to his own destination.

The new community center hadn't been open when he'd last been here, but it had been under construction and he knew where it was. He found it without the help of GPS and pulled into the parking lot. He spotted Katie's blue sedan parked in a far corner, out of the way of patrons, so he knew she was here.

He'd planned on leaving Cutter in the car but the dog had other ideas and was out the moment he could squeeze past Gavin. The dog trotted over to the door of the library as if he'd been there dozens of times. Maybe he had been. Gavin hesitated, fairly certain the dog wouldn't be allowed inside and wondering how he was going to convince him of that. But then Cutter plopped down beside the library sign, seemingly perfectly happy to wait there.

"So what, dog?" he asked as he caught up. "You know you're not allowed in?"

The dog glanced up, and Gavin suddenly noticed that behind the library sign—and directly over Cutter's head—was another sign advising that only service animals were allowed inside.

"If you're telling me you can read, I'm not buying it," Gavin said, but he was chuckling inwardly. The dog put his head down on his front paws as if settling in. Gavin sighed. He was trying to think of the last time he'd been in a public library as he pulled open the door. And trying not to think of the woman inside, the real reason he'd decided to come here.

* * *

Katie hung the last floaty, cloth ghost from the beam over the library information desk. It matched the one in her office window and completed the library's Halloween decorations. This had been a huge success at the prior library she'd worked at, with parents happy to have something else for their kids to do than go door-to-door. Especially given that so often the end of October meant a rainy if not downright stormy night. She had hoped it would be the same here, but hadn't expected the number who had signed up for this first ever event at the new building tomorrow. She'd planned on getting all ready earlier, but the news about her father had disrupted everything.

She leaned back on the short stepladder to see if she liked the arrangement of ghosts and jack-o-lanterns alongside orange and black streamers.

"Nice."

The deep, masculine voice startled her, both because it was so close and because she recognized it.

But when she twisted on the ladder to face Gavin de Marco, he wasn't looking at the decorations. His eyes, those dark, smoky eyes, were fastened on her. And again he hadn't shaved, the slight stubble giving him the rakish air it usually only gave celebrities who studied the effect in the mirror before stepping outside to be seen. She was certain Gavin had merely not wanted to take the time.

She was suddenly aware that her backside was about at his eye level and wished she'd worn something a bit less snug than leggings. But she'd known she'd be up and down the ladder today, and had gone for comfort. She felt her cheeks heating, and quickly scrambled down the ladder. By the time she hit the floor she'd recovered her poise.

She waved toward the line of ghosts and pumpkins. "I'm glad you like them," she said, quietly as always when she was out on the floor. She wasn't sure if she hoped he'd say he hadn't been talking about the ghosts, or not. "The kids seem to, and that's what it's all about. It's for the story night tomorrow. You probably saw the sign out front. It's the first time here, so we're going all out."

God, she was rambling like an idiot. So much for poise. *Shut up, Katie!*

She waited, half expecting him to laugh at her. Instead he said, keeping his own voice low, "What Halloween story?"

Did he really want to know, or was he politely trying to save her from her own jabbering? Odd in itself, since she didn't tend to that. At least not so mindlessly. But the thought of him whispering had somehow derailed her efforts at composure.

Fortunately she'd had to answer this before, so she had a response ready. "It's a collection of short stories I've put together over the years. Just scary enough but not too scary for kids. Then we top it off with a movie based on one of the stories. It's good fun for adults, too. If you wanted to come, I mean."

You did not *just say that.*

But one dark eyebrow lifted, and she knew she had. If he laughed at her, at the very idea or the unintentional double entendre, she would be more embarrassed than she had been in her adult life.

And if he didn't, she would be one step closer to deep, deep trouble with this man.

Chapter 17

Katie gave herself an inner shake and put on her most professional, library sound-level voice. "What can I help you with? Not looking for a book, are you?"

Gavin's dark eyebrow arched up again. "What would you recommend if I was?"

"Depends. What was the last book you read?"

"The *U.S. Patent Prosecutor's Desk Reference*."

She blinked. "Wow. Case-related, or was that for fun?"

"Not much fun in it. But some of it is more interesting than you might think."

She looked thoughtful for a moment. "The case histories, and SCOTUS decisions?" He seemed surprised at her words. Or perhaps her familiarity. Her mouth quirked. "You're the most famous, and probably the best, but you're not the only lawyer in town."

He chose to answer her original question, ignoring the rest. "It was research. We were helping a kid who had his invention stolen. No one would take him seriously because he was only fifteen."

"Good for you," she said, meaning it.

He shrugged. "Foxworth" was all he said, as if that answered it completely. As, perhaps, it did.

"I assume you didn't really come here for a book recommendation," she said.

"No. I needed to ask you about something."

"All right." She gestured past the information desk. "Let's go to my office." When the door had closed behind them, she turned to face him. He was looking around the room.

It wasn't huge, although it was bigger than her old office. There was plenty of room for her desk and the credenza behind it, a couple of chairs for visitors, and—of course— the big bookshelf on the opposite wall. It held all her very favorite books in different genres, so that she could hand one to someone and have them read the beginning to see if they'd like it. Then she could get them either a print or ebook copy to check out. The rest of the wall space held framed book covers, of everything from Mark Twain classics to the world-famous wizard series, all stories she'd read repeatedly and loved.

She watched him, guessed there wasn't much he missed in his perusal. Now that they were in the semi-sound-proofed environs of her office, she spoke in a normal voice. "What did you want to ask?"

He took her cue and spoke normally now. It wasn't much of a relief, Katie noticed with an inward grimace. "I need contact information for Laurel's family."

"Of course. They're in Arizona now," she said, reaching for her phone on the desk, and brought up the info. Then she looked at him. "Is it all right if I call them to say you'll be in touch?"

"You've talked to them recently?"

"Last week." She didn't mention that the call to Laurel's mother had ended with them both weeping inconsolably. "They're still pretty broken up."

He studied her for a moment before saying softly, "And so are you."

"Yes." She didn't bother to deny the obvious. She would never deny how much she loved and missed her friend. "Laurel was the closest thing I ever had to a sister. I will never get over losing her. It would belittle our relationship if I did."

"Then you knew about her arrest record."

The unexpectedness of the words, which she was sure was planned, put her on edge, as did his tone. Something in his voice reminded her of how he'd sounded about her father having been a locksmith two decades ago.

"Of course I knew."

"Why didn't you mention it?"

"I'd completely forgotten. And," she said before he could speak, her voice rising a notch, "if you're thinking about saying something about me forgetting something important again, like it's a pattern, don't."

He said nothing, just looked at her the way she imagined he stared down a hostile witness in a courtroom. Or an opposing attorney. So what chance did she have to withstand him?

She was sliding beyond edgy into angry. "I probably wouldn't have mentioned it even if I had remembered."

"Because?"

She ticked reasons off on her fingers. She needed both hands. "It was twelve years ago. She was eighteen. In fact it was her eighteenth birthday, and her first time to drink alcohol. First and only time she ever broke a law. She didn't have another drink until she was twenty-one, and never more than two. She didn't have an accident. No one was hurt. She never got in trouble again. She was the textbook case of being scared straight."

Again he said nothing, didn't even acknowledge her list. He just looked at her in that same unsettling way, as if she were that witness on the stand, and that irked her even more.

"But mostly," she added, her voice tight now, "I wouldn't think to mention it because I don't think that way. I don't waste my time dwelling on old, meaningless mistakes. She's my—she was—my best friend."

"Even friends can betray you," he said, and she had the oddest feeling that mind of his had gone somewhere else for a moment. Something about the suddenly distant look in those smoky eyes. But the words themselves sent her mind racing down an ugly path, as if he were accusing Laurel of something. And that, when she wasn't here to defend herself, made Katie snap.

"If all you do is look for lies, I'm not surprised you find them. Or what you think are lies, but are in truth honest mistakes or omissions. What an awful way to live."

For a moment his eyes closed. "Yes." His eyes opened again, and she knew she wasn't wrong about the pain there. As he went on, his voice was whispery, ragged. "It is."

Her anger evaporated as she stared at him. It was replaced by an aching empathy, because in that moment he reminded her of some trapped creature, helpless. She didn't know what to say. Instinctively she knew this was a side of him he rarely let show. It would never do for the stellar defense attorney to show such weakness.

Unless it was intentional, to lure someone in, so he could get what he wanted.

And now he's got you thinking like that, suspecting ulterior motives in everything.

She heard the sound of rain hitting the window to her right. The promised storm had arrived. And just in time, she thought. Gavin must have heard it, too, because he turned toward the window. And the pain she'd seen vanished, disappearing behind what had to be a formidable wall.

"Cutter," he said suddenly, rising.

"What about him?" she asked, also getting up.

"He's outside."

She blinked. "You mean outside here?"

He was already headed for the door. Katie followed, pausing only to grab one of the towels she kept in the cupboard behind the information desk, in case of spills or damp kids dripping water on the floor.

"Why is he with you?" she asked as they walked past the nonfiction section toward the door.

"He seems to have…attached himself to me. I don't know why."

He seems to know, somehow, who needs him most…

Hayley's words, when she'd been speaking of the dog's visits to hospitals and nursing homes and a children's shelter, came back to her now. Ordinarily she'd laugh at the idea of a man like this needing the help of a therapy dog.

But she'd seen him just now, seen that look in his eyes. Maybe that was what the dog sensed, whatever had caused that pain.

Cutter was tucked up neatly near the front door, patiently waiting in the shelter of the eave, and wasn't wet yet. He jumped to his feet to greet her effusively, making her smile.

"Did you move back there because you knew it was going to rain?" she said to the dog as she bent to stroke his head. Cutter nuzzled her hand, his tongue swiping over her fingers in a doggy kiss.

"Wouldn't surprise me," Gavin muttered. He looked at his car, as if measuring the distance to it in the downpour.

Katie straightened, looked at the steady rain hitting the walkway inches away. She held out the towel, but Gavin shook his head.

"You'll both be wet by the time you get to your car," she pointed out.

"We'll dry."

"You might not like how he dries himself," she said, picturing a hearty shake with water spewing everywhere once the dog was in the car. "You can bring it back later. Or I'll pick it up from Hayley."

There was a second's hesitation, but then he reached out and took the towel. Then he said, "I'm not staying there."

"Oh? Who got tired of whom so fast?" she asked, teasingly.

"Nobody." Then, with a wry smile, he added, "But they would have. I'm...kind of a pain when I'm on something."

"I hadn't noticed. Tell me," she asked conversationally, "does that brain of yours ever shut down, or even slow down?"

He grimaced. "Not really."

"How do you sleep?"

"Not well."

"I'm not surprised."

A man with two young children approached the library.

"Hi, Miss Moore!" one of the kids called out, and she recognized him as the boy she'd steered onto a series of adventure stories about a boy around his age. He'd loved them, which to her was her job well-done. The town was too small to have a dedicated children's librarian, so she worked to keep her hand in there with current stories along with the classics.

"The new one's here," she said to him, and he lit up. "I set it aside for you."

The trio went inside. Katie hung back for a moment, giving Cutter a final pat.

"Nice," Gavin said. In an entirely different tone than he'd said it earlier.

"It's my job, and I love it."

"It shows." He gestured with the towel before tucking it inside his jacket; the rain was getting heavier now, and they were getting splashed with the bounce. "I'll likely be grateful for this. I'll get it back to you."

"When you can," she said, and watched the man and dog bolt for the parking lot through the downpour. Water was flowing over the concrete walkway in sheets now, headed for the drain just outside the doors.

And speaking of drains, she thought as she turned to go back inside, just being around that man was draining.

But he'd be gone soon, hopefully after helping to remove that cloud of suspicion from over her father's head.

She wasn't sure if she'd be relieved, or sad.

Chapter 18

Gavin fingered the damp towel as he sat and watched the man inside the business. He'd parked far enough back to be inconspicuous, and used the small pair of folding binoculars he'd brought from Foxworth. He'd wanted to see him in this environment, watch him interact without being aware of observation, which in itself tended to change people's actions.

He'd already noticed several things. One, Steven Moore had a comfortable smile and manner that appeared to put people at ease. Many of his customers—and there were several this Monday morning—smiled and greeted him like a friend. And those who came in looking around, obviously unfamiliar with the place, he called out to but didn't swoop down on, letting them look at their leisure.

He wondered if any of them had heard that he was a murder suspect. Perhaps they had, and didn't believe it. Or maybe they thought it was a different Steven Moore; it was hardly an unusual name.

Gavin especially paid attention when there were no cus-tomers inside, but Moore seemed to busy himself, sorting mail and checking the various machines. When he disap-peared into the back, he always emerged with something, be it copy paper or a stack of mail. A few times he answered a phone on the counter, beside a large scale for weighing packages, and smiled then as if the person speaking was in the room with him.

All in all, it was a fairly busy place on this Monday. If being a murder suspect was weighing on him, it didn't show.

For a while Gavin sat chewing on that largest piece of the puzzle—motive. Hopefully he would get an idea at his meeting with the detective this afternoon. They must have something. Or maybe it really was just a Sherlock sort of stab, that they'd eliminated everything else as impossible and so were left with Moore.

At a little before one, Moore walked to the front and reached for the open sign on the door. Gavin guessed it was one with a clock on the other side that would show a "back at" time, and that he was going to set it for a lunch break.

He had time, he calculated quickly. His appointment with the detective wasn't until two, and his GPS had said it would be a half-hour drive at most. He slid out of the car, tossed a "Wait here" back at Cutter, who this time seemed content to stay in the car. He reached the door just as Moore was ready to drop the sign back down with the indication he'd be open again at one thirty. Moore pulled the door open despite the sign and, Gavin noted, before he even looked at him.

"Come on in, we'll get you handled—" He'd looked at him now, recognized him. "Mr. de Marco."

Gavin nodded toward the sign. "Short lunch break."

"I'm eating here. Katie made me lunch for today. I usually just go next door."

Gavin had noticed the pizza place earlier.

Moore backed up and held the door open. There was a tiny bit of tightness in his smile, but Gavin had expected at least that; no one liked getting grilled, even if innocent. Or maybe he didn't like the lunchtime interruption.

"I'll leave the sign down, shall I?" Moore said as Gavin stepped inside.

"Nice place." He didn't comment on the subtle question of how long this would take, but noted the man had the presence of mind to not ask outright.

"I like it."

"Profitable?"

"Some months better than others. I'm not getting rich, but I don't hate coming to work every day, and that's worth a lot."

He could not, Gavin thought, agree more. Foxworth had given him that, and he valued it above any amount of fame or fortune.

"Your daughter told me about it. That you're very kind to people, carrying them sometimes, and making personal deliveries if there are special circumstances."

The man shrugged, but looked pleased. "I just try to be a good guy," he said. Then, meeting Gavin's gaze steadily, he added, "And of course, Katie wants to paint me in the best light, given why you're here."

Gavin smiled. He liked the guy. And that made things a bit difficult, because even though he wanted to take him at face value, his job here was to find the truth. And the truth might not be on the surface. When he got involved, it rarely was.

"Go ahead and have your lunch," he said. "You can eat while we talk."

He wanted the man at ease. And it was only a slight, passing thought to wonder what kind of lunch Katie had fixed for her father.

They went into the back room that took up the entire width of the shop. Full of metal shelving, boxes and stock items and bins that Gavin guessed were for mail on three walls, and the back door. Along the side wall was a tiny kitchenette, and in the center of the room was a large, high table with stools.

Moore went to the fridge and got out a reusable type of grocery bag.

"Are you hungry?" he asked as he took out several plastic storage containers and a round, foil-wrapped bundle about three inches high. "There's way too much, as always. One of Katie's lunches usually lasts me two days."

"No, thank you." So Moore had self-control, Gavin thought. He wasn't one to eat just because it was there. It wasn't always a sign of control in other areas, but he noted it just the same. You never knew in the beginning what might be useful by the end.

He waited until the man had taken a bite of a meat loaf sandwich that had been in the foil.

"She makes a mean sandwich," Moore said, wiping a trace of grainy mustard from the corner of his mouth with the napkin from the bag.

"Have the police told you what they think your motive for killing Laurel is?"

The man reacted visibly to the abrupt question, his mouth and the muscles around his eyes tightening. He set the sandwich down. "No. Because there isn't one. There's nothing on this earth that could have made me hurt that girl, let alone do...what was done to her."

He wondered if the police had identified a motive after

all, and maybe they just weren't tipping their hand yet. He took a stab at some possibilities.

"She didn't make you angry? Or jealous of the time Katie spent with her?"

The incredulous look Moore gave him seemed genuine. "The only thing in my life I've been that angry about is that Katie's mother didn't get to live to see the amazing woman she's become."

"And Laurel? What did you think of her?"

No tightening of his mouth this time. But something flickered in those eyes so like Katie's. Pain? Regret? Or was it simply a tell, that he was about to lie?

"I think that losing her hurt my girl more than anything has since her mother died. And anyone who thinks I would do that to her is vastly, vastly mistaken."

Gavin let the answer hang in the air before saying, "That's not what I asked."

Moore grimaced then. He lowered his gaze to the sandwich with one bite missing. He swallowed as if he'd taken a second bite before speaking.

"Laurel was sweet, kind and incredibly generous. I was glad she was Katie's best friend. She chose well."

He meant it, Gavin thought. But he didn't—or couldn't—look at him when he said it.

A few minutes later he left the man to his food and returned to his car, knowing he needed to leave to make his meeting with the police detective. Cutter's greeting was somewhat restrained, as if he sensed Gavin's mood. It seemed likely, given what else the dog had done so far.

For a moment he sat, pondering what he'd learned. By all appearances Steven Moore was what his daughter thought he was. Kind, gentlemanly, hardworking, all of it. And he loved his daughter deeply; it fairly echoed in his voice every time he spoke of her. Gavin couldn't quite make himself believe, at least not without a lot more evidence, that a man capable of such a brutal murder could have raised a daughter like his.

But he'd lied.

Moore had meant what he'd said, but he was hiding something. Something about Laurel. Not necessarily in so many words, but as he'd told Katie, lies of omission were still lies.

If all you do is look for lies, I'm not surprised you find them.

Oh, she had some fire, did Katie Moore. He'd already been singed by it. In more ways than one.

Was that it? Was his unexpected and unwanted attraction to her clouding his judgment? Was the fact that he was reacting to her as he hadn't reacted to a woman in a very long time messing with his perception, stifling his instincts about people who lied to him, because he wanted to believe for her sake?

He wanted to dismiss the idea as ridiculous, as it always would have been. Gavin de Marco never let the personal interfere with a case.

But he'd also never met a woman quite like Katie Moore, either.

Chapter 19

"So who *was* that this morning?"

Katie turned to see Heather Burns, the assistant library branch manager and bookkeeper, looking at her with both eyebrows raised. Gavin hadn't said anything about keeping his presence and involvement a secret. Not, she thought wryly, that that would be possible. He was bound to be recognized. And he certainly was the kind of man people noticed.

"He's an attorney," she said. "He's helping with the murder case."

She was almost proud of how even her voice was; she'd gotten to where she could say the words without her throat tightening or her eyes pooling with tears. But it was an effort, a battle every single time, and she wondered if that would ever change.

"I heard about them suspecting your dad," Heather said, making Katie's chest tighten. "That's silly."

"Yes," she said. What else was there to say?

"I was kind of hoping he was somebody you'd met. You know. You need somebody in your life."

Katie managed a credible scoff. "Does he look like my type?"

"Honey," Heather said in a tone that matched her arched eyebrow, "*that* was any woman's type. Makes you think of long, slow nights and lingering looks over morning coffee."

Katie felt the heat rising to her cheeks at the images that tumbled through her head. "He is way out of my league."

"Uh-huh. I saw the way he was looking at your cute butt on that ladder. That was not an uninterested man."

"Heather!"

"And speaking of cute butts," Heather began, undaunted. "His is—"

"Let's not," Katie said. "I need to order cupcakes for tomorrow night."

She headed for her office to do just that, but nothing could keep her from hearing Heather's laughing voice. "You not talking about it doesn't change it!"

She closed the door behind her and only realized when she got to her desk and sat down that she was actually trembling slightly. She shouldn't have skipped lunch today; she was just wobbly, that's all.

But that didn't explain the images racing through her mind.

Makes you think of long, slow nights and lingering looks over morning coffee.

Oh, yes. And cute butts.

"He's only here for the case. Then he'll leave, go back home."

She said it aloud, with more fervor than she was feeling. She didn't stop to assess whether she'd convinced herself. Instead, she picked up her phone and pulled up the number for the local bakery. She'd spoken to them before, so now it was only a matter of confirming the numbers. Ordering three dozen cupcakes got her mind back to business, where it belonged.

Detective Greg Davidson was an old hand. Gavin had suspected that from the moment the man had suggested they meet at one of the more expensive coffee outlets in his town. After all, he was doing Gavin a favor by meeting with him, so obviously Gavin could pick up the tab. Sitting across the small, round table from him now, Gavin sensed he was more than an old hand, he was good. He looked to be midforties, had a lean, wiry build, and a manner that put Gavin in mind of a hunting dog, never to be diverted once he was on the track.

"So," the man said, leaning back in the chair and looking at Gavin assessingly, "it really is you. The famous Gavin de Marco."

"Guilty," Gavin said with a shrug.

"Nothing less would get me to meet with a prime suspect's defense attorney."

Gavin shook his head. "I'm not. I work for Foxworth, who was approached by his daughter."

"Heard good things about them."

"All true. And then some."

"You're making my life harder just by being connected to this," Davidson said. "Your reputation is making everybody second-guess every step we take. Dunbar's rock solid, or I wouldn't even be here."

Gavin knew the sheriff investigator's stellar reputation was well earned, after working with him on the governor's mess. "He is."

"If you're not Moore's lawyer, what are you doing here?"

"What Foxworth does. Looking for the truth."

Davidson studied him for a long moment over the rim of his cup of double espresso, which the barista had turned to get the moment she saw him; obviously the man frequented the place. The potent brew was the fuel of many cops, he thought, to cope with long hours, ugly memories and the high risk of carrying the badge.

"Funny," Davidson said, "I didn't think defense attorneys cared all that much for truth, only getting their guy off."

"Some don't," Gavin agreed, his tone neutral. *One reason why I quit.*

"Well, you've sure got things hopping," Davidson said, and he didn't sound happy about it. "We're averaging a couple dozen media calls a day since it leaked you were involved."

"Not my intent." He looked at the detective, whose weary eyes looked like he could use every bit of the caffeine in that espresso. "And probably the less time we're seen together, the easier it will be on you."

"Thought about that. About suggesting we meet somewhere more...discreet."

Gavin glanced pointedly around at the very public, busy place in which they were sitting. He'd been aware since shortly after he'd walked in that the buzz of conversation in the room had picked up, and soon after that a few phones had appeared, no doubt with cameras activated.

Davidson grinned suddenly. "Why have a meeting with the famous Gavin de Marco and not get the perks?" Then he turned serious. "What is it you want?"

"Knowing you can't discuss details of an open investigation, just some answers. Starting with these. Is there a reason, beyond the fact that there's no one else, that made you settle on Moore? And what's the theory on his motive?"

Gavin watched the detective consider his words. Carefully, likely deciding what he could and couldn't say, and filtering what he wanted to say to a man on the other side.

"What," Davidson asked after a moment, "are the odds you're going to end up representing Moore down the road?"

"Zero," Gavin said flatly.

Davidson drew back slightly. "That was pretty definite. Don't like the guy?"

Gavin wasn't out of practice enough to miss the sudden interest. "In fact, I do. But it has nothing to do with him. The only way I'll be in a criminal court again is as an observer or a witness."

"I wouldn't like it much if you ended up testifying to what I tell you," Davidson said. "Assuming I do tell you anything."

Gavin understood that. "How about I provide the information, and you just say yes or no. That way you haven't told me anything."

"Spoken like a true lawyer," Davidson said with a wry smile. "Go ahead. But I reserve the right not to answer."

"A given," Gavin agreed. "First, are you working on the assumption that the victim's one brush with the law when she was eighteen has no connection?"

"Yes."

He had to take a moment to fight back the image of Katie's face when she'd lit into him about that subject before he moved to his next question.

"The boyfriend's alibi is truly solid?"

Davidson apparently felt confident enough to go beyond yes or no on this. "As solid as multiple witnesses can make it. They all saw him at a party, a good ten miles away from the scene, and the host swore his car never moved. It was blocked in by a couple of others."

Gavin nodded before proceeding. While he knew better than most the unreliability of the fabled "eyewitness," this seemed fairly straightforward. "Do you have anything on Moore beyond his regular and frequent contacts with the victim for several weeks before her death, and that his alibi is unprovable?"

"Yes."

Gavin knew there was no point in asking what; Davidson wouldn't tell him, nor should he.

"Anything that's not circumstantial?"

Davidson studied him for a moment before saying, "Not answering that."

Which was, Gavin thought, an answer in itself.

Davidson was getting restless. Gavin could see it in his tapping of his finger on the rim of his cup, and the way he slid the insulating ring up and down repeatedly.

"Do you have a motive?"

There was a moment's hesitation before Davidson said, "Yes," but it was enough to tell Gavin what they had was questionable. At least in Davidson's mind.

"Do you believe it?"

Davidson gave him a sideways look. "Not answering that."

Also telling.

"So how about a little quid pro quo, de Marco?" the detective asked. "What do you think? You're famous for your instincts. What are they telling you about Moore?"

Now he was the one in the tough spot. Were he representing Moore, he would have answered one way. But he was not. But in this case, the truth would do nicely.

"I'm not sure yet. But something."

And that, he supposed, was as much an answer to the obviously sharp detective as the man's responses had been to him. He sensed Davidson was on the verge of calling a halt to this meeting, and he had one more question to ask. And it had nothing to do with Steven Moore's guilt or innocence.

"How certain are you that Laurel Brisbane was the intended victim?"

Davidson studied him for a moment before asking, "Wondering if your…client, the daughter, might have been the target?"

"It occurred to me," Gavin said, his voice even, despite the roiling in his gut at the idea, which should have been another kind of warning in itself.

"We considered it, since it was her apartment. The multiple stab wounds could have been frustration at not being able to get to his real target."

Gavin had read Ty's thorough research, and with Dunbar's help the public copy of the reports, but the cold recounting still made him wince inwardly. In his previous life he'd learned to dissociate himself enough to avoid that reaction, but since coming to Foxworth he'd lost both the need and the knack.

"But you decided not to pursue it," he said.

"We dropped it," Davidson said. "Because there were indications in the locations of the wounds that it was personal. Angry. Enough to strongly suggest the killer knew the victim, or at least his target. And Ms. Moore had a routine. She worked every day, the same hours, including those study nights. There was no reason for anyone who knew her to assume she would be home at that time on a Thursday because she never was."

Gavin nodded. It made sense. So why wouldn't that knot in his gut loosen up?

"And that also," Davidson added, "points more toward Moore. He knew his daughter wouldn't be there."

"But it still doesn't tell you why."

"Right now I'm more worried about who," Davidson said, and stood up. "Thanks for the coffee."

They'd reached the end of the interview, Gavin thought. He got up more slowly, accepting that he would gain nothing by trying to extend this except to put the detective in a more uncomfortable position, and he didn't want to do that. There had been a time when he wouldn't have hesitated to hold the detective's feet to the fire, but that had been when he was a practicing attorney representing a client and had standing in a case.

His outlook had been different then.

"My pleasure," he answered. Davidson looked a little surprised, and Gavin supposed that he'd given in easily. "I'm not the enemy anymore, Detective. Unless you're hiding the truth."

Davidson's mouth twisted upward. "Can't hide what you don't know."

The man tilted his cup in a mock salute, then left the shop. Gavin sat back down, taking a minute to process what he'd learned. Which was more than he'd expected. Most important, that while the police were focused on Moore because they had little else, the lead detective wasn't convinced.

So at least he could tell Katie her father wasn't, at the moment, being railroaded.

He tossed his empty cup in the bin and walked back out to the car, telling himself he wasn't feeling that kick of anticipation at that thought of talking to her again. A text would do, he told himself firmly.

When Cutter greeted him with a soft woof, he had the crazy thought that had it been allowed, he would have liked to take the dog in with him, and get his assessment of Detective Davidson.

He nearly laughed aloud at himself. Gavin de Marco consulting his partner, who happened to be a dog. Now that would be a headline, most likely coupled with speculation that he'd gone completely off the rails.

At the moment, he wasn't certain they wouldn't be right.

Chapter 20

"**W**ell, at least it's not midnight yet," Katie muttered to herself as she got in her car to leave the library. She couldn't blame the late hour entirely on finishing the Halloween decorations in the meeting room, after the library had closed.

No, a good half of that time she could blame entirely on Gavin de Marco. Well, and her own need to know. She'd set up an internet alert on him after he'd left this morning, setting the date parameter at when he'd arrived here to weed out the countless references and stories from his headline career. It had surprised her to see how much had popped up. Even now, Gavin de Marco being in town was apparently a big deal.

That he was looking into a local murder case was a huge deal.

Quinn and Hayley hadn't understood what would happen, that his presence here would somehow leak and that when it did the speculation would run wild. But Katie hadn't expected it to happen this fast. He'd only arrived Saturday evening, and now, by Monday night, news sites and blogs were abuzz with possibilities. Not to mention the photos that had turned up on social media, of him sitting in a coffee place, across from Detective Davidson, a man she remembered all too well from the ugly chaos of that night and the days after.

Her heart had jumped in her chest when she'd come across the first report, suggesting this meant a turn in the case, that if de Marco was here on the side of Steven Moore perhaps the police were on the wrong track. Exactly what she had dared to hope for.

We go after the truth, and there's always a chance you won't like it.

Quinn's words, which she knew had been a warning, ran through her mind. It didn't matter, she thought, because she already knew the truth. There was no conceivable way that her father could have had anything to do with Laurel's murder. Her heart was still buoyed because Gavin's presence had already accomplished her main goal—to get the police to question their assumptions and look in more than her father's direction.

The traffic signal up ahead—one of only three in town—turned red and she began to slow the car. She realized with a little jolt where she was; she'd been so lost in thought that she'd apparently been driving on autopilot.

But some part of her had already decided something, because without even thinking about it she found herself sliding into the left turn lane. The turn that would take her right by the Foxworth building.

He'd told her he was staying there, and though she didn't understand why he would forego the chance to stay with the Foxworths, given they were obviously friends, she took him at his word that it would be easier on everyone.

Does that brain of yours ever shut down, or even slow down?

Not really.

How do you sleep?

Not well.

He might be up now. It couldn't hurt to just drive by, could it? He'd texted her, rather tersely, about his meeting with the detective, saying only, He's not locked in. It was good news, but her worried mind needed more than just that.

She couldn't see the building from the road so she turned onto the gravel drive. The crunch of her tires seemed way too loud and she cringed a bit; if he was asleep, this would likely wake him up. She thought about turning back, but there was no room on the narrow, tree-hemmed drive. Then she saw the building. And a light glowing through the glass in the front door.

The front door swung open before she'd even come to a halt in the parking area adjacent to the building. At first glance she thought no one had come out, but then movement caught her gaze and she saw Cutter racing toward her. He could, she remembered now, open the door himself. She hoped he recognized her and wasn't coming at her in full guard dog mode. She was feeling a bit easier about stopping by at this late hour if the Foxworths were here. Hayley, she was sure, would understand her need to know the details of what had happened in Gavin's meeting with the police.

Cutter had reached her, and she judged it safe by his body language, a dancing sort of step with his front paws, accompanied by an almost musical whine that sounded like he was happy to see her. She opened the door, glad the rain had at least paused, although the respite was likely only temporary. She bent to greet the animal, marveling at the way her anxiety seemed to ease as she stroked the soft fur.

"You're so good at this," she crooned to the dog, who lifted his head and gave her a doggy kiss on the cheek. She laughed, and when she heard footsteps approaching she was able to straighten and smile at Gavin as he came to a halt next to her open car door. He was looking her up and down almost apprehensively.

"Why are you here? Are you hurt?"

That was very specific. He wasn't just asking if she was all right. And there had been an edge in his voice. Her brow furrowed. "No. Why would I be?" He didn't answer. After a moment she felt compelled to explain her presence. "I was late leaving the library, then I was going by and took a chance you'd be awake. I would have kept going and not bothered you if there hadn't been a light on."

"I told you, I don't sleep much."

"I know. That's why—" She stopped, not liking this need to overexplain such a simple thing. Cutter nudged her hand, and she automatically moved to pet him again. "So the Foxworths are up late, too?" She gestured at the dog. "They're here, right?"

"Sorry. No."

She looked down at Cutter, then back at him. "Wait, when you said he'd attached himself to you, you meant he's staying with you? All the time?"

"So it appears." His mouth quirked, as if he were bemused. "Hayley seems to think he's here to remind me to do things like eat and sleep."

"So he's your...keeper?"

"Implying I need one?" he asked, lifting an eyebrow at her.

"I'm sure the Foxworths know better than me," she said, rather primly.

He almost smiled, so she knew he'd noticed the tone. But then, she didn't think there was much he didn't notice.

"You'd better go or come in," he said, and only then did she realize it had begun to rain again, softly. Which told her where she was on the noticing things scale, she thought wryly. What was it about this man that distracted her so? Besides that he was dynamic, charismatic and sometimes downright dramatic.

"I did want to ask about your meeting this afternoon," she said.

"Come in, then," he said.

It was raining harder by the time they got to the door, which Cutter had raced ahead to open again.

"He really is remarkably clever, isn't he?" she said as she stepped inside, into the warmth. She could see the fire was going, and the room was quite pleasant. She began to shrug off her jacket.

"I think the word you want might be *frighteningly*," he said, his tone dry.

"Or *extraordinarily*."

He helped her with a recalcitrant sleeve. "Or *uncannily*?"

"Amazingly."

"Eerily?"

She grinned as he took her jacket and hung it on a rack just inside the door. "Thank you. I'll grant you *astonishingly*."

"And I'll see you an *unsettling...ly*." She laughed, and he chuckled himself as he shook his head. "Never get in a word fight with a librarian."

"Especially an adverb fight."

"Agreed."

He led the way into the living area, where Cutter was already drying before the fire. On the rug were spread out papers of various sizes, both printed and handwritten, and a pad that held the same kind of yellow lined paper the hand-writing was on. A legal pad, of course, she thought. He'd clearly been sitting on the floor, because even the large coffee table didn't have enough space for all of it.

He said nothing about her looking at the papers, so clearly he didn't mind. She focused on the bold, sharp writing on those handwritten pages. She noticed the pen lying on the pad, a substantial, heavy-looking fountain pen. She'd always loved them herself, but had never quite mastered the knack of not ending up with ink-stained fingers. She bet no ink would dare misbehave with him.

He gestured for her to sit down. Cutter whined faintly, so she sat on the floor next to the dog, who gave her another swipe of his tongue in apparent approval. She dug her fingers into the thick fur of his ruff and scratched. The animal leaned into her hand, clearly enjoying it.

For a moment Gavin didn't move, and when she looked up at him he was staring at her rather oddly. But after a moment he sat next to the writing pad, where she assumed he'd been before.

"What did you want to know?" he asked without preamble.

Everything.

The word slammed through her brain, and she bit her lip to keep it from escaping, afraid of how it would sound. She seized on something else, the only other thing that came to mind.

"Why did you ask if I was hurt?"

He drew back slightly. "I'm not sure you want the answer to that."

"I told you, I want the truth."

His jaw tightened slightly, as if he weren't sure this was the right thing to do. But in the end, he answered her.

"The killer is still out there. Until we know why Laurel was murdered, we don't know that you're not in danger, too."

He was right. She didn't like it.

Chapter 21

"Why would I be in danger? I know it was my place, but the police said Laurel's murder was personal—"

"I know what they said," Gavin answered. "I'm not saying you are, just that we don't know for sure you're not."

"But...after all this time?"

"You moved, almost immediately after."

"I had to. I couldn't live in that place anymore." She suppressed a shudder, fought the images that wanted to roll through her mind like some horror film trailer.

"Of course not."

She studied him for a moment, trying to gauge the level of—and the reason for—his concern. Some part of her wanted to think there was a very personal reason, but her common sense screamed otherwise. "You think he just hasn't found me yet?"

He gentled his tone; he clearly hadn't meant to upset her. "Katie, the police are probably right, but until they break the case, you can't be positive. I'm just saying be a little aware of that."

In other words, don't assume you're safe. Now that was unsettling. And it was an effort for her to steady herself.

"Was Detective Davidson chatty?" When he lifted an eyebrow at her she added, "Gavin de Marco having a cup of coffee with a local cop is worth several posts, with photos." He grimaced. She persevered. "Did you learn anything new?"

"Nothing he would say officially, no."

"And unofficially?"

He seemed to hesitate. "They have something. But Davidson's not completely convinced. Are you sure nobody else knew that Laurel had moved in with you?"

"No," she said, earning a look. "I mean, Ross knew, because she told him. And my dad knew, because I needed his key for her. And my landlords knew, because they needed to. They could have mentioned it to someone. All I know for sure is that I didn't go around telling anyone else."

"What about Laurel?"

"I can't be positive, of course, but I doubt it. She wasn't happy about the breakup, didn't want to talk about it, so I don't think she would have advertised that she'd moved out."

"But as you just pointed out, she wouldn't have had to advertise. One mention to an oversharer and it's all over the internet."

She couldn't argue that, not when his photograph—in which he had looked darkly handsome and very, very intense—had shown up while he was still sitting in the place with Detective Davidson.

She shifted her gaze back to the papers spread around the floor. The pages of bold handwriting drew her eye first, and she noticed the flair of the question marks after several entries, and the intensity of the underlining in other places. She wondered what a graphologist would make of it, and guessed it would be what hundreds of articles had already said: Gavin de Marco was exactly like his writing—bold, confident and intense.

She scanned the other papers, copies of reports, lists, some other kind of official file that looked like a short list of offenses, a map printout, a stack of photos with Ross Carr's image on top, a copy of the picture that Laurel had always had in a frame on her nightstand. She had taken it, Katie knew, and Ross had been smiling widely at her.

Instinctively she reached for it, wondering how a man could smile at a woman like that and then cheat on her.

Gavin grabbed her wrist, stopping her. She was startled by the act, but more startled at how her pulse leaped under his touch, so fiercely that if his fingers had been another inch closer to her wrist she didn't think he could have helped but feel it. Her gaze shot to his face.

"Don't," he said. "There are photos in that stack you don't need to see."

She frowned. Then, belatedly, she realized what he meant.

"Crime scene photos," she whispered. He nodded, and a different kind of shudder went through her.

"You saw the reality," he said, his voice so gentle it made her throat tight. "It's hard enough to get that out of your mind without reliving it in pictures."

"It's impossible," she whispered.

"I know."

Something about the softness of his tone, the sense that he really did know, blasted away her last barrier. If he'd been brisk, businesslike as he had been before, she could have withstood it, but this gentle understanding was too much. She shuddered again, tried to pull back. But then he was pulling her toward him, and she could not find the strength—or desire—to resist.

She was leaning against him, his arms coming around her to hold her against his chest, when the storm broke. She couldn't hold it back, not even with thoughts of how much she didn't want to do this in front of him, let alone in his arms. It had been a while since she'd had a meltdown, and she'd dared to hope she was over the worst of it. But this was as powerful, as overwhelming, as soul-killing as that first day of realization, and she wondered at that even as it reduced her to a sobbing mass of pain.

"I miss her so much," she gulped out.

"I know." He hugged her tighter.

For a long time he just held her, and his warmth, his steadiness, his strength helped her recover more easily than she'd expected. Her eyes burning, her cheeks wet with tears, she drew in a deep breath, enough to say, "I thought I was past this."

"Grief isn't linear, Katie. It's more like a cloverleaf you can get stuck on, going in circles and then back the way you came, and then around all over again."

She turned the analogy over in her mind, and it made perfect sense to her. That was exactly how she felt. She didn't question how he knew, but asked, "Does it ever end?"

He went still. She looked up at him, not even caring what her tearstained face must look like; this was too important. He closed his eyes for a moment, then opened them and met her gaze.

"No," he said simply.

She'd known that, deep down. She acknowledged his honesty, even when it would have been easier to lie, to give her some banal reassurance that of course she'd get over it, that this horrid pain would someday end.

"There will always be more of those cloverleafs," he

said, still holding her close, "and they'll be just as intense, but they'll be smaller, easier to get out of and come less often."

It rang true to her, just as the rest had. "You're very wise, Mr. de Marco."

He let out a breath, his mouth quirking upward at one corner. "I've just been taught well."

For the first time she thought, really thought about what he must have seen and heard in that stellar career. "You've seen the ugliest things, haven't you?"

"I've seen people at their worst, and best. Not enough of the latter to erase the former, unfortunately."

"Is that why you quit?"

"Partly."

"And the rest?"

"Is for another day," he said. "Are you all right?"

She realized abruptly that she was clinging to him, and draped over him in a rather suggestive manner. And that he probably wanted her off of him, but was too well mannered to say so to a clearly distraught woman. Still, it was a struggle to sit up, to pull away from the comforting heat and strength. She spent a moment wiping her cheeks and trying not to think what her mascara must look like, and not really caring anyway. Not now.

"I suppose you've been confronted with more than one weeping woman in your work," she finally said, pleased her voice sounded almost normal.

"A few."

"Practice makes perfect, even in offering comfort, I guess," she said, lowering her eyes and wincing inwardly at the inanity of it.

"I wouldn't know. I've never offered it before. I left that to my assistants."

Her gaze shot back to his face. He looked slightly bemused. It was that expression that made her ask, "Why now?"

Bemusement vanished. His gaze locked on her. "I think," he said slowly, "the question is, why you?"

She couldn't look away. She wanted to, the full intensity of his gaze, of those smoky eyes, was too much. Moments ago she'd been gulping in air as she sobbed; now she could barely take a breath.

It was he who broke the contact that was almost physical. And it was a good thing, because she doubted she could have looked away. It wasn't that she'd felt trapped or pinned, just that her brain had locked on to the crazy idea that if she looked away from him even those shallow breaths would stop.

Cutter made a low, soft sound. Glad of the distraction, she reached to pet him. The action allowed her to regain a little control, and as always, stroking the dog calmed her. Odd knack he had.

And apparently Gavin had it, too, even if he hadn't used it before.

So why now, or as he'd asked, why her?

Maybe it was the setting. It was personal, here on the floor before a fire, in a place that was more like a home than an office. Or maybe it was simply Foxworth, and their philosophy, that had changed him. Maybe they had a "comfort where needed" clause or something. That would fit. It was Foxworth, and he was doing what he was supposed to do.

And she'd be a fool, worse than a fool, to read anything more into it than that.

Chapter 22

Gavin stood beside the fire, staring into the flames. Then he moved his head to glare down at Cutter. "So what's with you, dog? Isn't the comforting and soothing thing your shtick?"

The animal, who had been watching as Katie retreated to the bathroom—no doubt to be embarrassed to see her mascara had succumbed to the torrent of tears—lifted his head to give Gavin a look he could only describe as smug. To make it worse, the dog's shoulders twitched, almost like he was shrugging.

You didn't need me.

Gavin grimaced as the words formed in his mind, the verbal equivalent of what the dog's expression and action would mean in a human. He was beginning to understand why Quinn and Hayley and even Rafe had taken to anthropomorphizing this animal.

He supposed he was getting used to the presence of his

self-appointed shadow. He even found himself conversing with the dog as if it were a two-way conversation. And sometimes he would swear it was; Cutter was a very expressive animal. He wondered, as he tried to refocus on the job at hand, how many people had pets because they felt awkward talking to themselves.

Then he wondered if he was focusing so much on the dog to avoid thinking about the woman in the other room, and his own question.

Why her?

He'd meant what he'd said. In all the years he'd been a practicing attorney, he had been confronted more than once with a weeping female. More than one weeping male, too, for that matter. He had always left it to his assistants to deal with, to do whatever it took to get the person, be it client or witness, back in hand so he could proceed with the job. It had been necessary then. If he'd gotten too emotionally invested in a case, it might affect his judgment, cloud his thinking when it was crucial that it be clear and sharp.

But Foxworth existed for entirely different reasons, and his function with them was entirely different, as well. But until now, it hadn't run to this.

He supposed it was in part because of the jolt of fear he'd felt when he'd first realized who his late night visitor was. He'd just been going over his conversation with Detective Davidson, and in fact had been somewhat stuck on that one part, about the possibility Laurel hadn't been the target at all.

Unlikely didn't mean impossible. He couldn't be one hundred percent certain that Katie hadn't been the target, or that she might not be now. What if this had been some vendetta against Laurel that could yet spread to Katie?

He'd seen too many crazy cases to pretend it didn't happen. He was mulling those over when Katie had unexpectedly arrived, so the first reason that shot into his mind for her to come here was that something had happened. And in that mindset his imagination had made the leap to her being hurt.

Cutter's head came up, and a moment later the bathroom door opened and Katie came out. She'd cleaned up the streaks of mascara, and looked fairly composed as she came back.

"Sorry for the meltdown," she said calmly.

"Don't apologize for caring. She was your friend."

"I wasn't," Katie said. "Just sorry you had to deal with it." She looked at him steadily. "But thank you for doing so."

Gavin almost brushed it off with something light. *Just part of the Foxworth service.* But looking at her, at those blue eyes of hers, slightly reddened from tears, he couldn't bring himself to do it.

In the end, all he said was, "You're welcome." Because *my pleasure* would send him down a mental path he didn't dare to tread just now. This woman did crazy things to him, and he didn't know what to do about it. And Gavin de Marco didn't like not knowing what to do.

She sat in her old spot, gave Cutter a quick pat and turned her attention back to the papers. He'd thought she might leave after that emotional episode, but she again proved herself tougher than that. Katie Moore would do what had to be done, whatever it might be.

He sat back down himself, and they went over the rest of his discussion with Davidson. She seemed worried that the detective had said they did have a motive, but heartened by his assessment that he wasn't completely sold on her father's guilt.

"I think he's a good cop," Gavin said. "He's not convinced yet, so he'll keep going after the truth."

"Good," she said. "If he does that, then he'll see my father is innocent."

He wanted to warn her not to be so certain, but given she'd already been through enough distress tonight, he held it back. Besides, that outlook was his, not hers. It wasn't her fault that he could count on two hands the number of people he totally trusted.

He settled for saying, "It's going to take more than his uncertainty to get him completely off your father."

She nodded. "I know. And I don't just want the police not suspecting him any longer. I want him proven innocent."

He knew she passionately believed finding the truth would do that, and he hoped, so fervently it surprised him, that she was right.

He also knew he'd better keep his mind on the task at hand, because after holding her in his arms, the thought that she was passionate about anything stirred feelings he didn't want to deal with right now.

Or maybe ever.

She was looking at the page he'd labeled "Possibilities," where he listed some of the most frequent reasons for murder under these circumstances. He watched as her eyes widened, and guessed she would never have thought some of them viable reasons to kill someone. Her gaze then skipped to the next page, which he'd labeled "Probabilities." Those he'd culled from the possibilities list as most likely to apply here.

Then she moved to the one labeled "Suspects," with a column for "Motive." Ross Carr was at the top, with the obvious motives listed, but next to that in caps he'd written "Solid alibi." Under that was "Other Acquaintances." As she scanned the names, her expressive face shifted from grimace to frown. She lingered the longest over the last name, her father's, next to which he'd written "Jealousy of time spent with K? Disapproval? She saw something? He saw something?" And next to that speculation, he'd written in caps, "Weak," for that's what he felt those motives were.

Underneath that was the most problematic of all, for there was nowhere to even begin: "Random."

When at last she looked back at his face, her expression troubled, he felt a pang of regret that he was going to have to make her go through it all again.

"What is it you're looking for, beyond the obvious?" she asked.

He shrugged. "Connections. Patterns. It helps me if I run the data through my brain first."

"By reading, distilling, then writing it," she said with a nod of understanding. "It's a different process than just reading it alone."

"Exactly." He wasn't surprised she understood. "I'll need to talk to you again, in detail, but it can wait until—"

"Now."

He stopped, studied her for a moment. "It's already late."

"I know you're probably still jet-lagged, and you've been working hard on this, so if you need to get some sleep I'll go. But if you're going to be awake anyway, let's get it over with."

"What about your sleep? Don't you have a big deal to prep for, tomorrow night?"

Her gaze flicked from him to Cutter, then back. "Appointing yourself my keeper?"

He couldn't stop his smile then. "Touché."

And so they began again. To her credit, she gave him no protest when he queried her on the smallest things, just marveled at the depth of Ty's work.

"I'd completely forgotten about that meter reader," she said, indicating the name of the man Laurel had filed a complaint with the city about when she caught him peering in her bedroom window at her as she dressed.

"He's unlikely. He apparently pulled that on several women, and they're all fine, plus it appears he's left the area."

"And the woman from that chain reaction traffic accident? That was years ago, and Laurel was just in the middle of the string of cars."

"But Laurel was the one who said she'd seen the woman at the stoplight moments before, on her phone."

"True," she admitted. "But a woman? Really?"

"'Deadlier than the male,' I believe is how the old phrase goes." He saw a slight shiver go through her and added, "I agree it's unlikely, but it's a base that needs to be covered."

She looked up from the page she was holding. "Is this how you did it? Before, I mean?"

"Same general approach, yes."

"Fascinating," she said, and from her expression as she looked back at the various stacks, he thought she meant it.

"Anything to add?" he asked when they'd finished discussing the list he'd made.

She looked doubtful but said, "Now that you have me thinking that way, there was a delivery driver that used to flirt with her all the time, asking her out, and she always said no. I always thought it was just sort of a game with them, but maybe he wasn't as accepting of her rejection as he seemed."

"Good," he said, adding to the list the name of the company she gave him. "Anyone else?"

Slowly, she shook her head. "I couldn't tell you the number of guys who asked me about her, if she was married or seeing anyone. And a couple of women who asked me if she was straight. No one stands out, though."

"Why did they all ask you?"

Katie shrugged. "I guess I was easier to approach. Laurel had that glam thing going on."

"And you?" he asked softly, even though it had nothing to do with the case.

"Me? I was just the sidekick. The bestie. Or in their case, information central."

She smiled, and it wasn't the least bit wry or rueful. She'd apparently been content to be just that for her flashier friend. He, on the other hand, had had enough flash and glamour—female and male—to last him a lifetime. And now he found it hard to even hold a conversation with one of those kinds of people if there were still waters like Katie Moore in the room.

He shook off the realization and pressed on, making her dig deep. It was an awful exercise, going through everyone you'd ever had contact with, searching for a possible murderer, but it had to be done and no one could have quite the perspective and range of knowledge as the victim's best friend. He knew that women shared things a guy would never even think to talk about, even to his best friend. He wanted it all, because you never knew which small piece might solve the puzzle.

A detailed picture began to emerge in his mind, of a vivacious, lively, and slightly "short of good judgment" woman, and the quieter, more solemn, levelheaded—and probably smarter—best friend.

Yes, these days it was the calm, the quiet—and the brain—that drew him.

Like Katie Moore did.

Damn. You're losing—

Her quiet gasp cut off his thoughts and he looked at her. Her eyes widened, and she was staring at him in shock. Had she remembered something, thought of someone, some possible suspect who could shift the whole case?

"You…" she began, then faltered.

"What?"

"Tell me you don't think I should be on that list? That I was jealous of her, tired of being her…what do they call it, her wingman?"

She was shivering again, her expression horrified. He reached out, grasped her shoulders.

"Katie, no. That never, ever occurred to me. You couldn't. You wouldn't."

He meant it, more than he'd meant anything in recent memory, except his gratitude for working at Foxworth. And that alone told him volumes.

She leaned into his arms again, and he felt the shivering ease, then stop. He was seized with the crazy urge to stay like this forever, make sure she was never hurt or scared or distressed again.

She looked up at him then, those wide, clear blue eyes still slightly reddened. He wanted her never to cry again, either. He could think of a lot worse things to spend his time on than seeing that never happened.

And then he did the only thing he could think of to do next.

He kissed her.

Chapter 23

For an instant, the barest split second, Katie thought she was imagining it. Her overactive subconscious had merely fed on emotions she'd been fighting and had somehow manufactured this moment.

But the feel of his mouth on hers was fiery, breath-stealing and very, very real.

Sensation rocketed through her in a way she'd never experienced. She had, on occasion, pondered the strange way that a pinch here could make you feel a twinge somewhere else. But she'd never understood how thoroughly some things were connected in the body. Never understood how a touch of lips could ignite fire in so many places at once.

Until now.

Hungry to understand more, she parted her lips, wanting to taste, to explore. And when suddenly the kiss was over, when the taste of him was suddenly out of reach, she felt bereft.

Through the echoing waves of surging heat she fought the urge to follow him in his retreat, to stay close. She wasn't even sure why she was resisting. She wanted more, didn't she?

A chill swept her as the obvious answer hit her.

She wanted more, but clearly he didn't.

The fog cleared, just in time for her to hear him speak.

"My apologies. That was…inappropriate."

Katie fought to find words. Thought of the papers that were now scattered around them. Lists. "I could give you a long list of things that kiss was. *Inappropriate* wouldn't be on it."

He stared at her as her mind raced. Did he want more of the luscious heat and sensation, after all? How could he not? Unless…it wasn't like that for him.

A new emotion began to well up inside her as she remembered exactly who she was looking at. Gavin freaking de Marco. Why would he be interested in a small-town girl with a quiet life and a quieter job?

It was much more likely that he'd tried to comfort, or distract, and she'd misread his intentions.

"Katie," he finally said, and the regret in his tone seemed to confirm her guess.

"Sorry," she said. "I think I misinterpreted that."

She saw something flash in those dark eyes, something bright and hungry. It was gone in an instant, but it had been there and real. And it blasted all her rationalizations to bits. She couldn't help the relief that flooded her; it hadn't been one-way. That glorious, surging tide hadn't been only in her.

"Attorney. Client." His voice sounded tight, as if he were finding it hard to speak.

Katie's brow furrowed. "Are you saying you meant…ethically inappropriate? I'm not your client, not like that."

"Fine line."

"But a line, nevertheless."

She saw him take a breath, and when he spoke his voice was steadier, and that look in his eyes had faded. "Mixing business and personal when it comes to legal matters—especially involving murder—is never wise."

Katie gave herself an inward shake. However dreary her social life had been lately, she hadn't yet been reduced to trying to talk someone into wanting her. And if he really did have professional scruples about it, she had no right to try and talk him out of them.

"Fine," she said briskly. "Let's get back to those legal matters, then."

When she picked up another of the pages, she heard a low, sour-sounding huff from Cutter and looked over at him.

The dog was looking at Gavin, and something about the angle of his head and the lowering of one brow made his expression seem like one of pure disgust.

It almost made her laugh, but she stopped herself.

Because it would be inappropriate.

Gavin first drove by the library early the next evening. Her car was there, and he knew she would be there for the duration. The library would close at its normal time, she'd told him, but reopen an hour later fully decked out and ready for the children's Halloween party. Since it was a school night, the event needed to start early so it would finish in time for a reasonable bedtime, she'd told him.

He'd had the idle thought that she'd make a good mom. Which was not the kind of thought he usually had about an attractive woman, and another warning jolt went through him.

It was simply, he told himself, that he'd spent too many years among women the term *good mom* would never apply to. Katie was such a stark contrast, that was all.

He kept driving until he could make the turn at the end of the block and head over to the state highway. Here and there he spotted costumes, on both kids and adults, as the evening's festivities began, apparently undaunted by the light but steady rain. He drove past what appeared to have once been some kind of buoy next to someone's mailbox, large and round, and now wearing a rather startling jack-o'-lantern face. Clever, he thought, but it was forgotten as he made the last turn and slowed in front of Steven Moore's house.

Gavin pulled into the driveway, effectively blocking the carport. He didn't really think it would be necessary, but he did it anyway. He wanted to talk to the man without Katie present; even when not in the room the presence of a loved one could affect what was said. He wanted to be sure Moore wasn't putting up a front. He couldn't quite bury the feeling that the man was hiding something. At the same time, he couldn't make himself believe Moore was a brutal murderer.

And deep down his gut was churning, afraid he was denying the obvious because of Katie. Because of how he was beginning to feel about her.

How you already feel about her, idiot.

He got out of the car, barely managing not to slam the door in his self-directed irritation. Cutter would probably yap at him if he did. Moore answered the door promptly, a bowl of candy in his hand, clearly expecting a trick-or-treater.

"Mr. de Marco," he said, startled.

"Happy Halloween," Gavin said, eyeing the bowl of treats. "Been busy?"

"Not yet, not like it usually is. Must be the weather."

Interesting, Gavin thought. Unless he was bluffing, it hadn't occurred to the man that the lack of kids coming to his house might be because word was out he was a murder suspect. He couldn't possibly be that naive, could he?

Then again, he'd raised Katie pretty much by himself, and she had that same sort of innocence, the kind that was appalled by evil and the last to see it or believe it when it arrived.

"I need to talk to you again."

He kept his gaze on the man's face, but saw no trace of hesitation or worry. "Of course. Come in. I have coffee on."

Gavin followed him into the kitchen in the back of the house. He waited purposely until Moore was pouring coffee into two mugs before saying, "Tell me about your wife."

The stream of coffee didn't waver, but there was surprise in Moore's voice when he said, "Kathryn? She was the love of my live. She made me a better man. Not a day goes by that I don't think about her." He turned and handed Gavin a mug. "Kind of hard not to, since Katie's the image of her mother."

"Is she?"

Moore didn't answer, but walked over to a desk in the corner, pulled something out and brought it back. "Back in the days before digital, when Katie was small."

It was a photo album. Gavin found himself strangely reluctant to open it, though he couldn't explain exactly why. He'd dealt with families struck by tragedy countless times. This should be no different.

Except it was.

He made himself open the leather cover. Moore hadn't exaggerated. The woman in the pictures was indeed the spitting image of Katie. Or vice versa, he supposed. It tugged at him in a way he didn't understand, the image of this woman dead and gone for years now. It wasn't just the resemblance, it was the pure happiness in her eyes, those eyes so like Katie's.

A bit belatedly he realized the little girl she was hugging so tightly was Katie herself. A sunny, bright-eyed child with blond pigtails that reminded him of the jaunty ponytail she wore much of the time now. Both of them were looking at the holder of the camera with such love it made it hard to breathe for a moment.

He glanced up at Katie's father and caught the shadow in his expression. It wasn't the powerfulness of recent grief, but the sadness of long-ago loss and a life never put quite right again. Gavin was certain that whoever and whatever Steven Moore was now, he had once loved Katie's mother completely. And they had loved him in the same way.

Could a man who had inspired such love truly have turned into a vicious, cold-blooded killer? Had the loss of that love triggered something that had lain dormant in him, something dark and evil?

But he'd still had Katie, and had by all appearances raised her to be a caring, loving young woman. Was that it? Was Gavin refusing to see the truth because of Katie? Was his judgment once more impaired because of his attachment to someone?

It was all he could do to focus on what he'd come here for. He spent the next two hours trying every tactic he knew to shake the man's story. He got him talking about random things and then zeroed in with a question that arrowed to the heart of the case. He acted as if he had total belief in Moore's innocence, but then turned on him as a prosecutor would, slamming him with ruthless questions.

When he was done, he was left in much the same place

he'd been before. He had no more indication the man was a killer, but he also was more certain than ever that he was hiding something.

Chapter 24

Katie was glad of the chaos of wrangling nearly three dozen children. It kept her from thinking about last night.

"That's not a real hatchet." A boy dressed as a zombie spoke to a smaller boy dressed as a lumberjack.

"Spider-Man's better than Iron Man!" Obvious who the combatants were there.

"Well, if Spider-Man was honest, that string would be coming out of his butt!"

Score one for Iron Man, Katie thought as she shepherded her flock of characters into the meeting room. She was gratified when all chatter stopped as they looked around the room. She, Heather and Roger, the maintenance man whose son was coming, had put on the finishing touches barely ten minutes ago. Gauzy, webby-looking drapes had been set in motion by a hidden fan. Spooky lighting, more ghosts, jack-o'-lanterns and a raven or two decorated the room, while haunting sounds played softly over the PA. The best part was Heather's brilliant contribution—slipcovers that made the plastic library seats look like old, crumbling tombstones. The kids were awed.

She glanced at Heather attired in Wonder Woman's very recognizable costume. She had been so sweet, coming to her with the idea, but very hesitantly.

"I don't want to do anything that would upset you," she'd said earnestly.

Katie had given her a heartfelt hug. "I love you for asking, Heather, but I don't expect the rest of the world to tiptoe around me. And it's too clever an idea not to use. The kids will love it, and now I'm prepared for it so I'll be fine."

Heather came over to her now, grabbed her arm and drew her off into a corner as the kids inspected the room and pronounced it a sufficiently spooky place to spend their Halloween night.

"Gavin de Marco?" Heather stage-whispered. "Your lawyer, the hunk that was here, is Gavin de Marco? And you didn't tell me?" When Katie's eyebrows rose, Heather rolled her eyes. "Please. It's all over the place. Half the posts in my feed last night were about him. With photos from the Coffee Hut."

Katie sighed. While the kids picked out their tombstones, she told the story of how Gavin de Marco had dropped into her life, all because Cutter had run off with her cell phone.

Heather was surprisingly accepting of the idea that the dog had planned it all. "I've seen some pretty darn smart dogs. I mean, just watch those dogs that herd sheep and cows. Those guys are amazing. Can't be that far from herding sheep to herding people. We're just more stubborn."

Katie laughed, inwardly relieved she'd successfully gotten Heather off the subject of Gavin. She wondered what her friend would say if she casually mentioned he had kissed her.

Would she even believe her? Katie barely believed it herself.

"You make a great Elsa, by the way," Heather said, tugging playfully at her braid.

Katie smiled. "And you're truly our Wonder Woman."

Once the children appeared to be settling, she headed up front to where one of her own dining room chairs had been placed, padded and draped to look like a throne. She swirled the long skirt of her light blue costume dress theatrically, and put on her best royal voice to welcome them all. She wasn't a performer by nature, but she did enjoy this. She watched the kids gradually lose their feigned boredom and sophistication and get caught up in the story she began to tell them.

By the time she finished the second story, a classic Edgar Allen Poe, they were rapt. She handed off to Heather, who would be giving them a more modern touch with a zombie story, suitably expunged for the audience, of course. And finally Katie came back with a reading of a section from one of the boy wizard stories known around the world. Then she handed out the appropriately decorated cupcakes and put on one of the films made from that series.

By the time they were done they'd kept thirty-three kids safely engaged for nearly four hours, and counted it a job well-done. And when Heather opened the door and regular light flooded in from the hallway, Katie was surprised to see several parents already there to pick up their kids, but who had quietly stayed in the back and watched the end of the movie themselves.

The children chattered happily as they headed out. Next year, if word got around, they might draw even more kids. They could—

"I like the costume."

She whirled around, smothering a gasp. Gavin stepped

out of the darkest corner of the back of the room. He was looking her up and down with an expression that made her very aware of how the light blue gown bared her throat and nipped in at her waist before it flowed down to her feet in a waterfall of sparkly fabric.

"What are you doing here?" she finally managed to get out.

"I believe you invited me."

"Oh. Yes."

But she had never, ever expected him to actually show up. She hoped she didn't sound as flustered as she felt. And she was very, very glad she hadn't known he was there. She had the feeling it would have turned her into a bumbling fool. Kind of like she was feeling now.

I'm such a pitiful sucker for brains and dark eyes. And thick, shiny hair that has a mind of its own in that charming way. And that way of moving that speaks of grace and power. And why don't I just drool on him and get it over with?

Only then did she realize Cutter was with him. Once she did, as if he'd been waiting his turn, the dog stepped forward and politely nuzzled her hand. She scratched that spot behind his right ear she'd learned he liked. And immediately she felt calmer, or at least not so flustered.

"Roger said it was okay to bring him in because it's a public meeting room, not the library."

"Yes. Yes, it's fine. He was so quiet I didn't even know he was here." *Or you.*

"Well, well," Heather said as she came back into the room, the last of the children safely stowed with their respective adults. "Look who's here."

Gavin looked at her and smiled. "Wonder Woman lives."

"You'd better believe it," Heather said. "I may be small, but I'm tough."

"'Though she be but little, she is fierce,'" Gavin said.

Heather looked at Katie then. "A man who looks like that and quotes Shakespeare. How could any woman resist?" Thankfully, since Katie couldn't think of a thing to say to that, Heather turned back to Gavin, who looked a bit discomfited himself. "Although, strictly speaking, you should be in costume."

"I'm a lawyer," Gavin said drily. "Many would find that frightening enough."

Heather burst into laughter. "And a sense of humor, too! Snatch him up, Katie, before someone else does."

"I'm sure Mr. de Marco could do much better than a small-town librarian," she said primly. "Good night, Heather," she added.

"He'd be a lucky man," her assistant said firmly, but she took the hint and left.

"She was right."

Katie tried not to look at him. "Right?"

"I'd be a lucky man."

Katie's heart leaped, missing a beat, then hurrying to catch up. "She's just soft for a man who can quote Shakespeare."

His voice dropped to a whisper. "What poet do I have to quote to make you soft for me, Katie?"

Katie's mind tumbled into chaos.

"Inappropriate again." His voice had changed to something tight, irritated. And somehow that gave her back the power to speak.

"Didn't Quinn and Hayley meet on a case?" Hayley had told her that at some point, but right now she couldn't exactly remember when.

He didn't pretend to miss her point. "Yes."

"So *inappropriate* is your decision, not Foxworth's."

"Attorney," he reminded her.

"Not the client," she retorted.

"No, you're a queen. It suits you." He glanced down at her costume and looked her up and down again before adding softly, "Although the ice does not."

She was surprised again, this time that he recognized the animated movie character so loved by young girls. Then again, the image was hard to avoid; the story of the icy queen and her steadfast, loyal sister had quickly become a classic.

"We had a client with a little girl last year," he said, reading her expression. "She was…enamored. I heard the whole story."

The image that formed in her mind then, of the famous attorney listening to a child's version of the tale, made her chest tighten almost unbearably.

"I'd better close up," she said rather hastily.

"Then I'll walk you to your car," he said, clearly not intending to leave her there alone this late. She appreciated that, even though it seemed unnecessary in this quiet, generally peaceful place. "I spoke to your father again this evening."

"I know. He texted me. Said he'd hate to be an opposing attorney."

"I was fairly tough on him."

She considered that for a moment. "But no tougher than a prosecuting attorney would be, if it heaven forbid came to that?"

"Exactly."

She could see that it was necessary, although she hated the very idea that her father could be subjected to such a thing for real. But she wasn't sure the cloud of suspicion wasn't worse. He needed to be proven innocent, and there was nobody who could do that better than Gavin. So she couldn't be anything other than glad he was there.

Even though *quiet* and *peaceful* were not words she could apply to herself when he was around. She thought the sound of his voice when he'd asked what would make her soft for him would be with her forever.

And she feared she already was.

He'd walked her to her car and was nearly back to his rental, pondering if he should follow her home to make sure she got into her house safely, when Cutter growled. He glanced at the animal, saw the dog staring into the shadows of the community center. The parking lot itself was brighter with the faintly yellowish glow from the tall streetlights. He wondered what Halloween character was hiding in the shadows. Then he recalled the dog had taken some pretty chilling costumes in stride tonight, without reacting like this.

He turned, looking where the dog was focused. Saw a slight movement. Animal? Person? Something glinted, catching what light there was. Metal.

A knife.

A big knife. One that looked as if its job was carving up animal carcasses.

Or people.

He was still trying to convince himself it was only a prankster in a Halloween costume when the figure exploded out of the darkness. He got the barest glimpse of a black ski mask pulled down over a face. Red trim around the eyes and mouth. Male. Nearly his own height. That was all he had time to notice before the dark-clad figure lunged at him. In the same instant Cutter launched himself at the figure.

The dog caught the attacker's free arm and the man screamed, waving the knife wildly. Gavin dived at the man, hoping he could take him down while he was preoccupied with the animal who had a death grip on his left wrist.

They careened back, the three of them falling into the shrubs where he'd been hiding. Gavin felt the scrape of a branch or thorn on his shoulder as they hit earth that smelled of damp mulch. Cutter snarled, a chilling sound. The man kicked out and connected with Gavin's left knee. He ignored the sharp pain, then an echoing pain, sharper yet, from his left shoulder.

He could hear Cutter, that snarl rumbling from deep in his throat. The man twisted, trying to pull free from the dog's grip. Gavin heard the rip of fabric, then a grunt. A curse, low and harsh. If he could just get some leverage he could pin the guy, but the dirt there was too soft. And that damned knife...

Somehow the man twisted free and got his feet under him. Cutter went for an ankle as Gavin tried to grab the man. Pain shot through his shoulder again, and he couldn't quite reach. A split second later the attacker was running, Cutter after him. Gavin tried to call him back, but the dog wasn't having any of it. He got to his feet and started after them.

"Gavin!"

He stopped dead. When he turned, he saw Katie running toward him, her costume gown sweeping after her. He didn't understand. She should have been gone. He'd seen her safely to her car. He glanced in the direction Cutter had gone. There was no question, he couldn't leave Katie there alone when there was some crazy with a knife running around. Cutter was on his own, at least until he could get Katie safely back inside.

And then she was there, her eyes wide with concern. "What happened?"

"Not sure. Guy with a knife and a ski mask." He peered

into the darkness, but could see nothing beyond the circle of light from the streetlamp. The park below the building was dark and quiet.

"My God," she exclaimed. "Are you all right?"

"Fine. Except Cutter went after him." He made a decision, the only one he could make. "Get back inside the building. Relock the door. Then I can go find Cutter." *I hope.*

"As long as you don't find the guy with the knife, too," she said, and he found himself liking the note of worry in her voice.

"I just don't want to explain to Hayley why I let her beloved dog get sliced up with a hunting knife," he said as they ran back toward the building. He shook his left hand; apparently that flower bed had been muddier than he'd thought, since it was dripping off him.

"We should call the sheriff," she said as she unlocked the library door.

"You can do that inside." She stepped in, reached for a light switch. He stopped her with a hand on hers. "Don't turn that on until I leave. I need my night vision. Now lock the door behind me."

She didn't answer. She was staring at his hand. He pulled it back, thinking this was a hell of a time for her to get prickly about being touched. She spun around to face him, and he had the crazy feeling he was about to get chewed out.

"You're hurt!"

He blinked. His brow furrowed. Sure, they'd hit the ground hard but the ground itself had been soft. And whatever branch or thorn had snagged him must have scratched deeper than he'd first thought because his shoulder was hurting.

Katie grabbed his hand. "To heck with your night vision," she said and flipped the switch. Light flooded the entryway.

He stared at her red-stained hand and realized the wetness he felt wasn't mud.

It was his own blood.

Chapter 25

Gavin tried not to wince as the EMT wrapped the bandage around his shoulder tighter. Cutter, who had thankfully come trotting back from his pursuit looking none the worse for wear yet mightily displeased, gave a slight whine. The EMT repeated her recommendation that he get himself to the emergency room for a couple of stitches; he'd already declined their transport. Gavin nodded again, although he had no intention of doing so. He'd have Quinn do it before he'd subject himself to what an ER visit would bring down on him.

He would have avoided the medical response, too, if it had been up to him, but Katie had called them before he realized what she was doing, once they'd discovered it hadn't been a branch or thorn but the assailant's blade that had gotten his shoulder. When he had protested, she'd given him a look befitting the ice queen of her costume.

And that had, unexpectedly, warmed him rather than

irritated or amused him. As did the way she was hovering now, watching. If the sight of his wound disturbed her, it didn't show.

Or she's more worried about you than disturbed by all the blood.

Again red flags snapped in his mind as if ripped by a gusty wind. *Do not go there. Don't even visit that territory.*

He was surprised, but almost grateful for the distraction when a man in a dark suit and white shirt, sans tie, arrived in a unmarked vehicle that still screamed cop. A uniformed deputy had taken the basics, what little Gavin could provide, and he hadn't expected any more than that.

"Heard it was you," the tall, lean man said as Cutter greeted him effusively.

"Brett," Gavin said as he shook hands with the detective he had come to like and admire in the days after he practically single-handedly toppled a sitting governor. "Didn't expect you."

"I was out and about anyway," Brett Dunbar said. "Busy night for us, Halloween and all."

"How's Sloan?"

"Still the best thing that ever happened to me."

"You're a lucky man."

As soon as the words were out of his mouth he was remembering what Katie's coworker had said that day. And his own agreement. *I'd be a lucky man.*

"Who's the princess?" Dunbar asked, glancing over to where Katie was talking to the EMT. No doubt she was asking if there was a way to force him to go to the ER.

"Queen," he corrected. "That, my friend, is the librarian."

Dunbar blinked. Gavin thought of all the stereotypical jokes, but if the detective thought of any of them he had the grace not to voice them.

"Suits her" was all he said.

Indeed it does. "She had a party here tonight for kids, scary stories and a movie. It was a big hit, once she separated Spider-Man and Iron Man."

Dunbar chuckled. "Impressive, given what she's going through personally."

She's impressive, period. But he only nodded.

Dunbar turned back to face him. "Want to run through it again for me?"

In truth, he didn't, but the detective had come all the way out here, and Gavin knew it was only because of him. An unsuccessful mugging was hardly worth his attention.

"I don't have much," he admitted ruefully. "Guy came out of the dark, wearing a full ski mask and waving that damned knife. Cutter went for one side, I went for the other. He nicked me as we went down."

"Then he took off?"

Gavin nodded. "With Cutter after him. I would have followed, but…" He glanced over toward Katie. The thought that this had happened so close to her made him a bit queasy.

"Of course," Dunbar agreed. "You couldn't leave her alone out here. Too tempting a target."

Tempting. Oh, yeah… Especially in that outfit that seems to highlight every luscious curve.

"—description?"

Belatedly he tuned in to Dunbar's question. "Not much," he admitted. "Just under six foot, I think. Medium build, jeans, light-color shoes, and a dark hoodie with a logo on it. The ski mask was black, with red trim. Fairly strong, but he didn't handle the knife like a pro. More the slasher type. Sorry, but that's about it."

"That's more than a lot of people get," Dunbar said. "Any idea on the logo?"

"Long, horizontal, looked like the head of…something. With a point."

"Seahawks logo, I'd guess," Katie said as she came up to them. "They're practically ubiquitous around here these days. I think half the population has one. Dad and I bought them for each other last Christmas."

"Win a Super Bowl and people who never used to care start caring," Dunbar said, smiling at her.

"Katie Moore, Brett Dunbar," Gavin said by way of introduction.

"Really?" Katie sounded as surprised as he had been at the man's presence. "Thank you for your help, Detective Dunbar. With this, and my father's case."

"Haven't done much, but you're welcome."

"Do you think you could talk him—" she nodded at Gavin "—into being sensible and going to get stitches?"

Dunbar grinned. "I could try, but given that he knows my aversion to hospitals, he might doubt my sincerity."

Katie threw up her hands. "Okay, I give up. But I reserve the right to say 'I told you so' if it gets infected or doesn't heal right."

"Duly noted," Gavin said.

Cutter nudged her hand, and she stroked his head. "You've got more sense than the both of them, don't you?" she asked the dog.

"He came back on his own?" Dunbar asked.

Gavin nodded. "Maybe the guy had a car down the hill."

Dunbar looked thoughtful. "If he took off on the highway, cameras might have picked him up. Might not get much in the dark, but it's worth a look."

"I can put Ty on it and save your guys the time."

"And get it faster," Dunbar said, his mouth quirking. Then, seriously, he asked, "Connected?"

Gavin had been pondering that since it had happened. "Maybe."

"Wait," Katie said suddenly, obviously following their cryptic conversation. "I thought the guy just waited for somebody alone. Are you saying this attack wasn't random? That he was after Gavin because of the case?"

Gavin shrugged. "At the risk of committing a logical fallacy, it has a tendency to be true."

She stared at him. "Never mind the 'post hoc, ergo' stuff. This has happened to you before?"

"My presence does have a tendency to provoke things," he said carefully.

"I'd guess," Dunbar said, "it's that annoying other tendency, that around you the truth seems to come out. I'm also guessing you don't threaten easily."

"I'm stubborn that way," Gavin said with a grin.

"*That* way?" Katie said rather sourly. "I'm going to go lock up. Again."

"All right," Gavin said as she turned to go, not reacting to her tone. "Cutter?"

The dog instantly understood and was on his feet. He stuck close to Katie's side as she walked back toward the library doors.

Dunbar looked at Gavin's arm, his blood-soaked sleeve. Then he glanced at Katie, then back to Gavin.

"I assume you didn't miss that bit of information she dropped," Dunbar said.

"You mean that her father has a hoodie like that? No, I didn't. And from what I've seen of him, he's pretty fit and could still move that fast."

Dunbar nodded slowly. "I'd hate for it to be true. She seems nice."

"She is."

"And smart."

"She is."

"And worried about you."

That one stopped him for a moment before he said, "That goes back to her being nice."

"Hmm."

Gavin had noticed before that Brett Dunbar could say a great deal without speaking a word. He saw the man's eyes flick toward the building, toward Katie and Cutter. Then back to him. And he didn't like the speculation he saw in his expression. Not from a man who had experienced Cutter's machinations firsthand.

And who had ended up with the woman who was indeed the best thing that had ever happened to him.

Don't go there. Don't even think about going there.

As he watched Katie secure her domain and turn with Cutter to come back, he had the crazy thought he should be saying that to the dog instead of constantly repeating it to himself.

Chapter 26

Katie was beyond frustrated. By the time all the details had been handled it had been a very long day. She was tired, yet she couldn't fall asleep. Even the sound of the rain, which had begun again just as she arrived home, didn't help lull her.

She finally gave up for now, pulled on a pair of lounge pants and a long-sleeved T-shirt, and shoved her feet into her favorite shearling winter slippers. After what had happened at the library following the party she should be nothing but glad it was over, and that no one had been seriously hurt. That is, if you didn't count a wicked gash and copious bleeding as seriously hurt, as Gavin obviously didn't.

She kept replaying the moment when she'd realized the wetness she'd felt when he'd touched her hand was blood. Remembering the bright, unmistakable redness of it when she'd flipped on the light. Reliving her horror as it dripped from his hand to splat on the floor.

That moment should have warned her, but she'd been too swamped by the images in her head to think clearly. But now she had to admit the truth. No matter how ridiculous it was, no matter how foolish, she was getting herself in a tangle over this man.

She supposed it was only natural. How did someone who'd lived, for the most part, such a quiet, unobtrusive life, come in contact with someone like him and not get sucked into the vortex? Gavin de Marco was a force of nature, one to be reckoned with, and she obviously wasn't immune.

On the thought, her cell phone signaled an incoming text. She'd forgotten to even get it out of her purse, and if she hadn't already been awake and pacing, she probably wouldn't have heard it. She frowned, wondering who'd be texting her after midnight. As she walked to the dresser, where she'd left the purse, she tried to rein in her thoughts that it had to be more bad news.

She pulled the phone out and read the text.

From Gavin.

Hope you don't get this because you're asleep.

She let out a sigh, then tapped the screen to bring up the keyboard. I wish.

Are you all right?

She blinked. Read it again. He was asking her? I'm not the one who got carved up with a hunting knife.

It was barely a slice.

That should have had stitches right away.

Not enough to put up with what a trip to the ER would
have caused.

She stared at that one for a moment. It had not occurred
to her what kind of commotion Gavin de Marco showing
up in an emergency room after a knife attack would create.

Never thought of that.

No reason you should. Quinn came by. He stitched it up.

She blinked. Then she remembered Quinn Foxworth's
military background and realized he was probably quite
capable. His work might lack a bit of finesse, though.

Ouch.

She got back a smile. A bit. Sorry it was messy. Try not
to let it remind you.

She stared at the screen. It was true, she hadn't seen
dripping blood even on a small scale since that awful night,
so she couldn't say the memories hadn't slammed into her
mind. But practical concerns, especially in those moments
before she knew he wasn't horribly injured, had pushed
them out again.

She tapped at the keyboard again.

Too late.

The moment she hit Send she wished she hadn't. The
last thing she wanted to do was whine to him, of all people.
He was the one physically hurting. She was just dealing
with memories. She—

Answer the door.

What? She stared at the phone. A split second later a quiet knock came on her front door.

For an instant she thought of not answering. But she could hardly pretend she wasn't here or hadn't heard it when she'd just been texting him.

She sucked in a deep breath and walked to the door. She spared a brief thought for her no doubt tousled appearance, then decided after tonight she didn't care.

He, on the other hand, looked none the worse for wear. He'd changed, thankfully discarding the blood-soaked shirt. He wore a heavy, cable-knit sweater that looked too damned sexy on him. He certainly didn't look like he'd nearly had his throat slashed mere hours ago.

Life was damned unfair sometimes.

"You're not all right," he said without preamble.

"I'll be fine." Cutter was with him, she noticed. The dog stepped forward and automatically she patted his head.

"You should be sleeping," Gavin said.

She couldn't hold back her wry laugh. "Not likely."

"That's why I'm here. To go over what happened tonight. Get you past it."

"Again? To get past it, you want me to hash it out all over again?"

"Yes. Ignoring it doesn't work."

She couldn't deny the truth of that. She'd tried too often to ignore the emotions that those memories, those awful images, brought on. She'd only succeeded in delaying them, which in turn only seemed to intensify them when they finally broke loose.

Cutter gave a soft woof. She realized belatedly she was still standing holding her front door, and they were still out on the porch. They were under cover from the rain, but it still seemed beyond rude to keep them standing out there. Especially since Gavin clearly wasn't going to be easily persuaded that he was the one who should be resting.

With an inward sigh she stepped back and gestured them inside. If Gavin had noticed her reluctance it didn't show, but she imagined his poker face was pretty good. It had to have been, given his reputation for startling juries with unexpected turns in cases.

"Ty's pulling the video from the traffic cam near the library," he said as he stepped inside, bringing with him the scent of rain and the outdoors.

"You really think it's connected?"

"Doesn't matter. When somebody comes after me like that, I like to know why."

"You say that like it happens a lot."

"Not so much anymore," he said.

She saw him look around the living room. It wasn't perfectly tidy. The latest *Library Journal* was on the coffee table next to her tablet, and the heated throw she used when curled up in her favorite chair to read was sliding onto the floor, but she didn't care. It had taken her time to get this room just how she wanted it, and she'd been grateful for the distraction of doing so when she'd first moved in. She'd relocated to get away from the scene of tragedy, but at first the new surroundings only reminded her of why she was no longer where she'd been.

But now it was her own place, her own quiet refuge in the woods, and she loved it. She loved the blue and green tones of the outdoors brought inside, loved the textures of the furniture and the patterned rug, and the way the bright, vivid colors of the painting she'd bought at the local arts fair and hung over the couch contrasted with the cool colors of the rest.

Cutter, tail wagging gently, began to inspect the room

less surreptitiously than Gavin had. She didn't think there was anything he could get into that would hurt him, so she let him go and turned back to her human guest.

"This is nice," he said. "Comfortable."

"If that's your way of saying it's not fancy, agreed."

His gaze shifted to her face. "Something wrong with that?"

"Not for me. I would have figured you for more of a chrome-and-glass kind of guy." In fact, she knew it, having seen in her research photographs of the office he'd had at the peak of his renown.

"I had it, once," he admitted. "Doesn't mean I liked it. It was part of the image. This, I genuinely like."

She couldn't even imagine what it would be like to live like he had. But the tone of his compliment had seemed sincere, so she decided to take it at face value.

"Thank you. I'm afraid there's no coffee," she said, "but I have cocoa."

He shook his head as he sat down at one end of her small couch. "I didn't come here to make you work. At least, not at that. Besides, the last thing you need is caffeine keeping you awake."

"No caffeine seems to be required," she said wryly, walking toward her chair. At least sitting there, safely apart, had been her intention, but somehow Cutter got in the way. And he kept getting in the way, until she had little choice but to sit down on the couch, as well. Strangely, the thing had never seemed so small as when Gavin was barely two feet away.

She looked at him and noticed him glaring at the dog rather balefully. As if the animal had done this intentionally.

Or as if her sitting so close was annoying.

Tough, Mr. Famous Lawyer. It's my house, I'll sit where I want.

Of course, she hadn't intended to sit there. The dog made her. Still…

She shifted in her seat till she faced him. Mr. Famous Lawyer.

"If I asked you something," she said slowly, "would you give me the truth?"

He raised an eyebrow at her. "I don't lie."

She gave him a sideways look.

"I don't," he repeated. "Ever."

"And what about those lies of omission?"

"If I can't or won't tell you something, I'll say so."

"What's the difference?"

"The difference is honesty, admitting there is something you're not saying. Like there's a difference between something honestly slipping your mind, and withholding something the other person needs to know or should know."

Her tone was a bit frosty when she said, "And have you decided which you think I did, about my father's past career?"

He studied her for a moment. "I think," he said slowly, "that you're just not used to thinking the way I have to."

That simply he disarmed her, melting the frost and making her feel a bit of an ache for him, for she couldn't imagine living a life where you had to think that way all the time.

"How do you ever trust anyone?" she asked, more rhetorically than anything.

"Very carefully," he said. "But I don't think that was the question you wanted to ask."

He waited, silently, giving her room to ask or not. Either choice would tell him…something, she supposed. She hesitated, then admitted she wanted to know badly enough to betray…whatever this would betray to him. And she asked her question.

"Why did you really walk away?"

Yvonne Harris

... sa das das das ...

Chapter 27

Gavin was startled; he hadn't expected that from her now. He thought he'd headed her off when she'd asked earlier.

He'd been asked for the real reason before. Often. By acquaintances who were genuinely curious, more often by reporters who were rabid for a juicy story. For the most part they all got the same bland, noninformative, packaged response. Not that it mattered. What saw publication was all the usual speculation. He was rich enough to never have to work again—that much was true. He had nothing left to prove—he supposed that one was true, too, but still not the reason. He wanted to run for office soon—so far from truth he'd burst out laughing the first time he'd seen that one.

His true reasons were his own business, and not something he wanted to share with a gossip-hungry world.

And yet now, sitting here in this cozy room, too close to the woman who threatened to convince him there were people you could trust on sight, he felt an urge he couldn't resist. And to his own surprise, he abandoned the usual practiced response.

He had to think for a moment. He'd almost never told the whole thing except to Charlie, who asked, and Quinn, who had never asked, but Gavin had felt he deserved it before he hired him. He took a deep breath, and started.

"When I was in college my best friend, Ben Olsen, was arrested for murder. I knew there was no way he could have done it, and he swore to me he didn't. But he was convicted and sent to prison. Consensus was it was because of an incompetent, inexperienced attorney."

"I'm guessing that was your inspiration? To become a defense lawyer?"

"Yes." Nearly two decades later it still left a bitter taste in his mouth, even knowing how it had turned out in the end. "While I was in school, I spent every free hour searching for new evidence to get the case reopened. I visited Ben in prison regularly, made him go through it time and again, trying to find something, some new angle, anything that would convince a judge to take another look. And every time I worried more as Ben got worse. Being locked up was pushing him to the edge. By the time I passed the bar, I wasn't sure how long he could hold on."

"I can't imagine," she said softly.

"It went on while I was getting established. I built that reputation as much in the hope it would help Ben as anything else. I wanted the fact that I knew he was innocent to be worth something."

He stopped, swallowing against the lump forming in his throat. She was watching him intently, and something in her eyes made him able to go on.

"And then… Ben got cancer. And it became imperative to find something, fast. So I put everything else on hold. It was all I did for six months, 24/7. I was…driven."

"Understandable."

His mouth tightened. "Yeah. Until Ben took a turn for the worse. Or worst."

"He died? In prison?"

He nodded, becoming aware of how hard this next part was going to be. But he was in it now, and he was going to finish it.

"Gavin, I'm so sorry—"

He held up a hand to stop her. "Don't be." His voice had become a cold, harsh thing. "On his death bed, Ben confessed."

She drew back sharply. "What?"

"He confessed he'd done it, told them where he'd buried the body. They found it right where he said. All the forensics matched his story. He'd done it."

"He lied to you? All those years he let you go through that?"

"I was so convinced he was innocent I built my career, my entire life around saving him, and others like him. And then he destroyed it all."

"My God. No wonder you have no tolerance for liars. And that's why you walked away?"

"I walked away because I no longer had any faith in my own judgment."

Her brow furrowed. "But you were right, all those other times."

"Was I? How do I know somebody I got off, who's out walking around, wasn't another case where I was wrong? How do I know I didn't get off a vicious child molester, or worse, just because I took his case and the state pled out to a lesser charge? And that's not even counting the times when I had to withdraw for an unrelated reason and the buzz was that client must be guilty, when I knew he wasn't. My reputation was a double-edged sword, and I'd lost control of it. I didn't wield it anymore, everyone else did. Judges started refusing to let me withdraw for anything short of a blatant conflict of interest because it would prejudice the case."

For a long moment she was silent. And he felt scoured out, with nothing left to say. He felt like he was teetering on the edge. When she finally spoke, her voice was so gentle it brought him even closer to that edge.

"You must have felt like your entire life was based on a lie."

"It was." His voice sounded as bleak as he felt. "And I was so damned tired of being a step back. Dispassionate, detached. I'd started not to feel anything at all anymore. If I hadn't met Quinn when I did, I'd be digging ditches somewhere, and glad of it."

And then Katie changed course completely, and caught him by surprise.

"I did my homework on you, you know."

"I would expect no less." She was a librarian, after all.

"And nowhere," she went on, "did I see even a hint at what you told me, about why you quit."

"Not something I advertise," he said drily.

"Who else knows?"

"Charlie. Quinn."

"Your family?"

"My mother did. I suspect she told my father. Moot point. They're both gone now."

"I'm sorry." Her words resonated. From her it wasn't some routine, meaningless expression of sympathy. She'd lived it; she knew. But thankfully she left it at that. Perhaps also from experience. "Who else knows?" she asked.

He shrugged. "No one. Not from me, anyway."

"Why did you tell me?"

And there it was, the question he couldn't answer because he wasn't sure himself. And that was because the only answer he could think of would be foolish beyond belief.

Something must have shown in his face, because the next thing he heard, in that low, gentle voice that felt like brushing his skin with soft velvet, was, "When you figure that out, come tell me."

"You say that like you already know the answer."

"I do."

He went still. He couldn't deny he wanted her. And she had to know it, after he'd slipped and kissed her, an action he still didn't quite understand. He shoved that aside to confront the matter at hand. Did she think this…oversharing was part of that? That he was the kind of man who would bare his soul, as it were, just to get her into bed with him?

He'd never put it in so many words before, not even in his head. And now that he had, his imagination fired up as if it had only been waiting for that. Images poured through his mind. Katie coming to him, naked and wanting. What her skin would feel like in the soft, hidden places. What her eyes would look like hot with desire, and aimed at him…

"Gavin? Are you all right?"

Hell, no. "Just what is it," he said with an effort, "that you think you know?"

She gave a light, simple shrug that was completely at odds with where his mind had just gone. "You're starting to trust me."

He stared at her. After that flood of racy, lascivious visions he was having a little trouble with her take on it.

"I know you thought I purposely didn't tell you about my father's past work, but I think you see now I didn't really lie. I just didn't see the connection you were making, because, as you said, I'm not used to thinking the way you do. The way you have to think to do what you do."

"I see." It was all he could manage.

"And as I said, it's no wonder you can't tolerate liars. Why that above all things is what you can't forgive. But I don't lie, any more than you do, and I think you see that now."

"Got me all figured out, do you?" He hadn't meant to sound mocking, but it came out that way anyway. On some level he knew he was flailing out because Katie Moore was digging into places he ever and always kept hidden.

And who opened the door for her?

"I would never presume to think I had you all figured out," she said. "That would be a lifelong challenge."

Lifelong.

Gavin sucked in a breath, wondering why it was suddenly so hard to get enough air. Maybe that was it. His brain was starved for air—that's why he'd told her that pitiful tale. Hypoxia might explain it.

Even as he thought it he nearly laughed. He could almost feel his mind squirming, looking for a way out of the simple truth of what she'd said. He was beginning to trust her. In fact, he'd gone well beyond just beginning. But it wasn't his usual conscious, carefully considered process. It had happened on some level he hadn't even been aware of. Some level he hadn't even realized existed before.

A level that heard the word *lifelong* and yearned instead of recoiling.

Chapter 28

Katie didn't know what she'd said that hit him so hard, but she hadn't been giving it her full attention. She was still too thankful that this was likely the source of his doubts about her father, why he suspected everyone of lying at some point.

She didn't care for the "guilty until proven innocent" aspect of this trait of his, but now she understood it. Given his history, it would be amazing if he didn't feel that way. For her, it would be like finding out her father was in fact guilty; it would shatter the very foundation of her life, her entire concept of who she was.

But now she was staring at him, and the way he was looking back was sending shivers through her. And making her think of that kiss. That inappropriate, heart-stealing, pulse-pounding kiss. That kiss that had been so quick, over so fast, that there was no way the memory of it should be able to do this to her.

And yet here she was, her heartbeat quickening, her skin flushing, long-dormant parts of her awakening. And no amount of telling herself she was a fool seemed to help her get herself back in control.

Not when he was looking at her like that, as if he was thinking the same thing.

"I'd better get out of here." He said it sharply, almost harshly.

"I didn't mean to make you angry." She still wondered what had set him off.

His eyebrows rose. "Angry? When you were looking at me as if—"

He cut off his own words, and she couldn't help herself, she couldn't just let it go. "As if what?"

The answer came in a low tone that practically vibrated up her spine. "As if you wanted me to kiss you again."

Her breath caught. One part of her, the part that he brought voraciously to life just by looking at her like that, wanted to say simply, "Yes."

"There are so many reasons that would be a mistake," he said, his voice even lower, rougher.

"And only one reason it wouldn't?"

"I can think of several, but they're all just different words for the same thing."

She could think of several, too. *Want. Need. Desire. Crave. Yearn.* She'd never felt anything quite like this. The intensity of it was nearly overwhelming.

He turned to go, clearly determined not to make that mistake, as he called it. She stiffened her spine, reeled in her uncooperative senses.

Fine. I'm certainly not going to beg the man to kiss me. She thought it with solid determination. At least, she thought it was solid until her sneaky mind added in almost a whimper, *Even if that's what I feel like doing.*

She hadn't made that whimpering sound. She knew she hadn't. And yet Gavin turned back suddenly. Crossed the three feet between them in one stride. She felt his hands cup her face in the moment before he lowered his mouth to hers. The unexpectedness of it didn't lessen the jolt, or slow the fire that leaped to life in her anew, as if it had only been banked, not extinguished. The feel of his mouth on hers rekindled it thoroughly, sending heat and sensation racing along every nerve. She forgot to breathe, and when he finally pulled back she sucked in air in a gasp.

She stared at him, seeing an echoing heat in his eyes, but unable to tell if he was glad or regretted that his determination had crumbled.

And then he was gone, without another word, leaving her with senses clamoring for more, need caroming around inside her, and a wry—and tardy—common sense telling her she should be thankful he hadn't pushed for what she would have apparently given him without another thought.

She should be thankful.

But she wasn't.

Gavin didn't make a habit of calling himself names, but he was still rattling them off the next morning. Especially when he looked in the mirror to shave, after a night of restless sleep that had him thinking he'd have been better off if he'd just stayed awake all night. As it was, he had a dull, thudding headache and his eyes looked as if he'd been on a three-day bender. Even Cutter had stayed clear, as if sensing not even his calming presence was going to help.

But at least he had a plan. A plan that would keep him safely out of Katie's orbit for a couple of days, at least. Which wasn't the goal, he assured himself. He'd just moved something up on his mental schedule, something he'd planned to do in the next few days anyway.

He had the names and details on the witnesses who had backed up Laurel's ex-boyfriend's story, had copies of their sworn statements, but for him nothing took the place of an in-person interview. That after this much time they might be less certain of their stories could be both a curse, in that the details might be fuzzy, and a blessing, in that they might not feel the same urgency to stick to the narrative.

If there was one, he thought as he got dressed. The police had been satisfied the dozen or so witnesses from the party Ross had been at during the time of the murder had been truthful. And given some of the rather embarrassing details of that night they had confessed to, he tended to agree. It had taken a promise from the police not to pursue the details of some of the more illicit party favors to get anything at all out of a couple of them.

"You look like you've been rode hard and put away wet, as my gramps used to say."

Gavin whirled to face the man who had seemingly appeared out of thin air in the doorway of the bedroom. Rafe Crawford looked at him steadily over a mug of coffee Gavin could smell and suddenly craved.

He fought down the images the old saying had blasted into his mind, images that had nothing to do with horses and everything to do with a naked Katie Moore riding him. Hard.

He swore under his breath, glared at the dog beside Rafe for the lack of warning, and headed for the kitchen, thinking if the man hadn't left enough coffee for another mug, he was going to take his head off. Then he remembered who exactly he was dealing with and realized taking on one of the best snipers in the world was hardly within his skill set.

"And they call me grouchy before my coffee," Rafe observed, his tone almost amused as he watched Gavin fill a mug and get to the caffeine infusion. "But then, you sleep even less than I do."

Gavin grimaced. "You here for the day?"

Rafe nodded. "Generator wobbled a little on the last exercise cycle, and the chopper needs service."

Gavin nodded. Idleness did not suit the man. In that they were alike.

"I'm going down to Tacoma," he said. "Witness interviews."

Rafe lifted an eyebrow at him. "Any reason you're telling me, not Quinn?"

"Quinn knows. But I'm leaving him here," he said, gesturing at Cutter. "Might take a couple of days for me to track down everyone I want to talk to, so I'll probably be staying over. If you're going to be here, saves me dropping him off at their place."

"Fine with me," Rafe said with a shrug. "He can supervise." He gave Gavin a considering look before adding, "Does he know you're leaving him behind?"

"Quinn?"

"Cutter."

Gavin blinked. Then his mouth quirked. "I haven't discussed it with him, no."

"Better. Or you'll find him in your car and not so easy to get out."

Gavin had the sudden feeling that he was far from knowing all the ins and outs of dealing with this dog. "And just how do I do that?"

Rafe shrugged. "Just tell him 'Not this time.' Now, that doesn't mean he'll accept it. He may have his own reasons for insisting he go along, in which case you might as well give in and save the energy."

"I'm beginning to see who really runs this place," he said drily.

"Hard to argue with his track record," Rafe said blandly.

Gavin wondered exactly which track record he was talking about, but didn't ask because he was afraid he knew. Which brought him right back to the subject he'd been trying to avoid. Katie.

He gave himself an inward shake. Wondered if there was something about the surroundings or the atmosphere here that screwed up his focus. He looked at Cutter and said firmly, "Not this time."

The dog angled his head as if thoughtfully considering. And then he walked over and sat at Rafe's side.

"Looks like you got permission," Rafe said, with a grin Gavin had never seen from the man before. That dog was a miracle worker in more than one way.

Gavin sat in the all-night diner, tapping his pen on the pad with his notes. The remains of his meal—a burger that he'd figured was the safest choice but had actually turned out to be pretty good—was pushed to one side but the coffee cup, due for another topping off, stayed close. There weren't a lot of other customers at this hour somewhere between late night and early morning, so he didn't feel pressured to leave. And the waiter was a good one who, when he saw Gavin was working intently, just refilled his coffee without saying a word and otherwise left him alone.

The first night here he'd tried working in his hotel room, but the bed seemed to mock him. He was seriously tired, but his brain was in overdrive, and he knew if he lay down he would be wide-awake the moment his head hit the pillow. And if he let his guard down enough to try and sleep, he knew where his unruly mind would go. So tonight he didn't even make the effort.

He stared down at his notes. Considering the months that had passed, the stories from the witnesses had stayed quite consistent. He reread the statements of four men he'd spoken to the last couple of days, one of them Carr's admitted best friend. The man had begun by reaffirming the alibi and, after a drink or two provided by Gavin, ended up cheerfully recounting some of the raunchier details of the party.

One of those details led Gavin to add a name to his list of people to talk to—the girl Ross had hooked up with at said party. The men had confided they'd thought it just a one-time thing, that Ross *might* have gotten her a little drunk, or otherwise convinced her not to fight it. Gavin had wondered if they were suggesting he'd used something stronger than alcohol, but he wanted the rest of the story more than he wanted to pursue that. Anyway, according to the witnesses, Ross and the woman had taken over the back room set aside for just such encounters.

It must have been good, one of them had joked, *because Ross is still hanging with her.*

When Gavin had tracked her down, the girl had looked to him to be not even old enough to drink, which he supposed said more about his jaded state than anything. She'd been shy about sharing details, but finally admitted she'd been too drunk to remember much, but was grateful Ross had made sure she got home after the party ended in the wee hours. And that was why she'd agreed to see him again the next day and then the day after that, until, she said with a genuine blush, they were apparently a thing.

He believed them. All of them. Believed they were telling the truth. At least as far as they knew. Which didn't bode well for Steven Moore. And just how would Katie feel if he ended up proving her father guilty instead of innocent?

He was in no way ready to face that possibility yet. He could have headed back to Foxworth tonight—well, yesterday, really since it was after midnight now—but he had opted to stay, telling himself he wanted to go over everything once more. It had nothing to do with staying away from Katie one more night. And asking Quinn, when he'd spoken to him this afternoon, to pass along that the alibis indeed seemed solid had nothing to do with him not wanting to talk to her.

Nothing at all.

He downed the last of his coffee in a gulp, then stood. He picked up the bill, glanced at the total, doubled it for the tip and dropped cash on the table. He paused long enough to thank the observant and efficient waiter, then headed out into the chilly night air. After the warmth of the diner it felt like a slap in the face.

Just what he needed.

Chapter 29

Katie took a last look at the public meeting room on Friday to be sure they'd gotten all the Halloween decorations. They hadn't gotten to it until this morning, but nobody had seemed to mind the decorations lingering for a couple of days. But there was a community meeting scheduled here tonight, so she made sure every last ghost had been vanquished.

Except for that one floating around in your head. The one named Gavin.

She shook her head sharply. She saw Heather approaching, and felt a twinge at what probably was showing in her face. To head off any questions from her too observant friend, she spoke first.

"Why don't you take off? I can finish up here, and you can go get your kids."

"Last patron just left, so thank you, I will." But undeterred, she added, "I was hoping you'd have a hot date to-night. Where is that gorgeous man, anyway?"

Gone. A couple of kisses and he ran like hell.

"Never mind," Heather said, her eyes lighting up as she looked past Katie toward the glass doors. "He's here."

Katie sucked in a breath she was sure was audible, and barely stopped herself from spinning around to look.

"You have fun," her friend said archly. "Lord knows I would, with that man. As much and as fast as I could get it."

And then she was gone. Katie heard her say something, no doubt to him, because it was in that light, flirty voice she could turn on like a spigot. Katie still hadn't turned to look. Instead she made a last, unnecessary circuit of the meeting room, then carefully—very, very carefully—closed the door and locked it. And then, the keys clutched so tightly in her hand her knuckles were white, she turned around.

He looked like hell. At least, as much as he could. His hair looked windblown, as if he'd driven all the way back from Tacoma with the window down. He was clean shaven, but she noticed a nick on his left jawline, as if he'd gotten too rushed or heavy-handed with the razor. His eyes were a bit bloodshot, and he looked beyond weary. As if he hadn't slept the entire time he'd been gone.

She'd intended to not say anything, to make him say the first words, because she had no idea where things stood between them. But when he just stared at her, she finally broke, with a wry acknowledgment that she'd been fool-ish to think she could outmaneuver the man who'd tricked serial killers into confessions. But the only words that she could manage were the ones she'd already thought.

"You look like hell."

His expression didn't change. "And you look incredible. As always." Only then did his mouth quirk upward at one corner, in that way he had. "Even if you do look like you want to throw those keys at me."

Since there were several keys on the ring run through a large wooden carving of an evergreen, that would definitely hurt.

"Hadn't occurred to me, but thanks for the suggestion."

Something in his gaze shifted then. "No, it wouldn't, would it." It wasn't a question. "You don't live in that kind of world."

"I don't have that kind of nature," she corrected. "And aren't you out of that kind of world now?"

"I am," he said quietly. "But sometimes I forget. Both that that's not my world anymore, and that there are people who really are what they seem. People who are good and honest and true, as Hayley says."

"Hayley is wise."

"Yes. And I—as she told me in no uncertain terms this afternoon—am an idiot."

Katie's eyebrows rose. She would have liked to have seen that exchange. "And what brought on that assessment?"

He drew in a deep breath and then let it out as he gave a rueful grimace. "You."

Katie blinked. She hadn't expected that.

"And Cutter," he added, confusing her even more. "It seems I'm trying to avoid the inevitable."

"Which is?"

"You," he repeated.

She'd been called a thing or two in her life, but never inevitable. She wasn't sure how to take that.

"He's outside, by the way. He let me go to Tacoma on my own, but apparently that's as far as my leash goes."

She couldn't help but smile at that.

"It's probably cold out there," he said. "And about to rain."

"He's got a lot of fur."

His mouth quirked again. "You're not going to make this easy, are you?"

"I'm not even sure what 'this' is."

He sucked in another breath. "This," he said, "is me apologizing."

"Wow. You need some practice."

He let out the breath audibly. "Yeah."

"Apologizing for what?"

"Kissing and running."

She hadn't expected him to admit that. "So why did you?"

"I had to...wrestle with something." He held her gaze now. "Like how you would feel if it ends up I help to prove your father guilty instead of innocent."

The words rocked her, made her wonder if he'd learned something down south that he hadn't mentioned. Something she wasn't going to like. Perhaps he'd met with the police there, and was now convinced they were on the right track.

She steadied herself before asking, "Are you speaking theoretically or specifically?"

"Theoretically." He seemed to realize where her mind had gone. "I have nothing new or more than the police do. Which is only theory."

She breathed again. And then she realized the full import of what he'd said. He'd kissed her. Twice. Had clearly wanted more. But instead he had vanished because he was worried about how she'd feel if he ended up being the one who proved the police right.

From the safety of her certainty of her father's innocence, she was thoroughly touched. She wondered if he even realized what his actions revealed.

She did realize what her reaction revealed. She'd turned

to mush inside so fast it was impossible to deny. And even knowing she was setting herself up for heartbreak—because he would leave, she knew that—she couldn't walk away from this.

She spoke words she'd never expected to say to him. "Come home with me."

The breath he sucked in was audible. She saw in his eyes, his face, that he knew exactly what she was saying.

She might regret this. Probably would.

But she would regret not doing it even more.

He still liked her place.

He followed her in, looked around once more. It felt more like a home than any place he'd ever lived, including his loft now. That was just the place he went when he wasn't working. This was a place he could see spending time not doing anything in particular. A place he could see just relaxing. Or working through a list of things to keep it in shape.

Or sleeping in, wrapped around Katie?

Oh, yeah. He could see that.

He ordered his body to calm down as he shrugged off his jacket. Now that it seemed he was going to get what he'd wanted from the moment he'd opened Quinn's door to her, it was a lot more difficult.

Besides, she could still change her mind. She'd seemed eager enough when she'd suggested her place. It was closer, she'd said, and there was a drugstore on the way for…a certain purchase. The mere mention of protection had her blushing and him fighting down a wave of renewed heat.

He wouldn't blame her if she was just avoiding Foxworth; for all the homey atmosphere it was still a workplace and only temporarily his place.

His train of thought derailed as something else hit him.

She'd chosen to let him into her home, her sanctuary, where she'd come to rebuild a life shattered by a tragedy no one should have to endure. He'd never had the feelings some people had for the place they lived, but he'd dealt with people who had, and understood it. And suddenly it seemed imperative that he let her know.

"Katie."

She turned, tossing her own jacket beside his on the back of the chair closest to the door. Somehow even that little act seemed significant.

She busied herself with Cutter for a moment, asking, with apparent seriousness, if he would prefer the couch or a blanket on the floor. His answer was to hop on the couch and curl up as if settling in.

Finally, she turned back to Gavin. As she stood there looking up at him, those blue eyes wide, her expression a combination of anticipation and nerves with a touch of wariness, he felt a jab of nerves himself.

"Are you sure about this?" he asked.

She laughed, and the nerves were in the sound of it. "Are you sure you should be giving me a chance for second thoughts?"

"I'm sure I would be sorrier if you end up regretting this."

She smiled then. It was steadier, the tension retreating. "I thought about that. I know you'll be gone soon. But I decided because I would regret passing this up even more. This…kind of feeling doesn't come along every day."

"No," he said fervently, "it doesn't."

He was past worrying about what that implied. And his body had had enough of being patient.

Tough. You're going to go slow and easy. This is Katie, and she deserves that.

"I'm a little rusty at this," he said, afraid he wouldn't be able to keep that vow.

She looked him up and down, and there was such pure appreciation in her expression he felt humbled. "Not," she said, reaching out to trace his jawline with one finger, "from lack of opportunity, I'm sure."

It was true. But he was honest enough with himself to understand why, that many of those opportunities stemmed from his reputation, status or just his looks, and were shallow, momentary things.

Katie Moore was anything but shallow.

"Lack of interest," he said.

She smiled. For a long moment he just stood there, staring at her, his blood pulsing so hard and fast he could hear it in his ears. Then he heard a rustle of movement as Cutter vacated the couch. In the next instant he felt a not insignificant shove at the back of his knees as the dog leaned into him. He had to take a step to keep his balance.

And just that easily he and Katie were pushed together. For a split second all the stories he'd heard of the dog's matchmaking shot through his mind, but then Katie was in his arms and it was gone. Everything was gone except the feel of her, the warmth of her, and this damned aching need that he realized now had been growing every moment since he'd met her.

He'd meant to kiss her softly, gently, as he'd vowed. But the moment his lips touched hers, that went out the window. She was too sweet, too hot, too entrancing to go slowly. And she was kissing him back. Hotly, fiercely, destroying the last remnant of his determination. What had come before was nothing, a mere spark: this was a conflagration.

He ran his hands down her back, pressed her closer, needing as much contact between them as he could get. She arched against him, and he felt her hands against his chest, not pushing away but stroking, as if she were tracing him. When he finally broke the kiss, only because he needed to breathe, they were in the hallway off the living room. He hadn't even been aware of moving. Which told him how far gone he was.

"Katie," he began, but stopped, with no idea left in his head of what he wanted to say beyond her name.

"Gavin," she said back at him, as if she felt the same. And he realized that it was all that mattered, that nothing more was needed but that heartfelt calling to each other.

It was the last coherent thought he had because she took his hand and led him to her bedroom. He barely noticed the room he'd never been in, because she began to unbutton the silky blouse she wore, one of those that managed to look businesslike yet incredibly sexy.

The moment the blue material separated over her breasts, revealing them nestled in a matching bra trimmed with delicate lace, he was lost. He could think of nothing but the fire inside him that had erupted into an inferno, hot, wild, demanding. And he was kissing her again, urgently, and when her lips parted beneath his he swiped over them with his tongue, amazed that a kiss could be so sweet.

He probed deeper, and the sweetness became a honeyed fire that threatened to consume him. He caressed her breasts through the bra, but it wasn't enough and he clawed at the straps to pull the lace out of his way. Then he cupped that soft flesh and it rounded into his hands as if made for them. She moaned softly, and it fired his blood even more. He was mad, mindless, and it was a place he'd never been before.

He didn't realize how mindless until his gasp for breath broke the kiss and he saw that not only was she naked to the waist, but his own shirt was unbuttoned and half off. And then he felt her hands moving down from his chest

over his abdomen, stroking, her fingers leaving little trails
of heat and fiery sensation everywhere they moved.

It was more than he could bear. He moved suddenly,
picking her up and going down to the bed with her. He
pulled off the rest of her clothes, felt her tugging on his and
did everything he could to help, short of letting go of her. Finally they were pressed together knees to lips, skin against
skin. He couldn't touch her enough, stroke her enough. He
wanted to learn every precious inch of this woman who had
reached him so quickly, in ways no other ever had.

When she began to caress him in turn, he nearly forgot
to breathe. Every touch stoked the fire that was already beyond bearing. He rolled her beneath him, groaning aloud
at the feel of her, and again at the way she seemed to welcome his weight. And when her hands slipped down to
cup his backside, her name and an oath broke from him
in one breath.

When he could take no more he lifted up slightly, looking into her eyes. She arched upward, pressing herself
against him, and he could feel the taut points of her nip-
ples against his chest. He couldn't ignore that readiness,
could he? He bent his head and caught one with his lips,
flicked it with his tongue, then suckled deeply. She cried
out, her body fairly rippling in response.

He was too close, he had to pull back. But when he did,
her hand slid down his body, then hesitated, almost shyly.
He couldn't resist and took her hand to move it that last
critical distance. Her fingers curled around his erection,
stroked. His breath came out in a hiss, and her name broke
from him just at her touch.

He was hanging on to his last bit of control by a thread.
For a man used to ever and always being in control, this
was uncharted territory, a place he never thought he would
find. He fumbled for a moment, but her hand was still on

him and she guided him. And then he was sliding into her body, his way eased by her own readiness, and that alone roused him even further. When he was sheathed in her, her body hot and tight around him, he shuddered at the feel of it. And then she moved, as if wanting him deeper, and that thread snapped.

He became something he didn't even recognize, voracious, starving, and she was the only thing that could slake his hunger. The man known for orchestrating a trial, for coaxing a jury with elegance and finesse, for having a mind that never lost track or focus, was beyond thinking of anything other than the woman in his arms. It wasn't simply that she fired every sense, inflamed every nerve. It was more, deeper, and if he hadn't been so consumed by the sensations she was triggering he might have been alarmed at the intensity of it.

In the end he could not think at all but only feel. When he felt her body clench around him, heard her cry out his name in a voice unlike anything he'd ever heard, he gave up trying to hold back. He groaned her name in turn and poured himself into her.

He had never believed in this kind of fierceness but now he had no choice but to believe. Because Katie Moore had not only reached places in him that had never been touched, but she had reached places he hadn't even known existed.

Chapter 30

Gavin had always figured it would be Katie who had second thoughts. That was, during those moments when he'd allowed himself to even consider giving in to the need she inspired in him.

Of course, he'd been incredibly, impossibly, a million times wrong about what that would be like, too. Heat rocketed through him at the memory of all the times they'd come together last night, making the cold outside the car now and the rain splattering on his windshield meaningless. He felt his body clench involuntarily when he thought of the last time, in the early hours of the morning, when it had been Katie who had awakened him, wanting. And in those moments, nothing could have shaken his conviction that she was the most genuine, honest woman he'd ever met.

But now he was in a quandary. The logical, common sense side of him was declaring last night a mistake. An unwise, entangling, complicated mistake. But every other part of him, body, heart and soul, was reveling in the wonder of the purest, most consuming experience of his life, both physical and emotional. All the references he'd heard about mind-blowing sex applied, but there was so much more.

So much that last night he hadn't been able to even think coherently about those reasons it was a mistake.

But now, as he drove to Foxworth in response to Quinn's call, Katie driving behind him in her own car so she could get to the library in time for Saturday hours, all those reasons hammered at him. That he was, in essence, working for her was only the smallest of them.

The largest was a looming fear that what faith he had left in his judgment was going to be destroyed. He'd sensed all along that Steven Moore was hiding something. Yet he hadn't believed it was guilt for the murder of Laurel Brisbane. But by then he was already attracted to Katie, and now he couldn't stop wondering if he'd done it again, let his attachment to someone cloud his vision.

Although, what he felt for Katie was a lot more than just attachment. It was like nothing he'd ever felt before.

...a lifelong challenge.

He knew in his gut that the words she'd said would apply both ways. It would take a lifetime to learn all the qualities of this woman. And what an amazing exploration it would be, of the Katie who could discuss deep philosophies or quote poets, then turn around and dress up as an animated character to entertain a bunch of kids.

And me, too.

He couldn't deny that seeing her in that long, silky blue dress with her hair down in a braid had been…entertaining. At least, it had had him entertaining thoughts that had only propelled him further down this path he'd tried to avoid.

He should have tried harder, he thought as he made the turn the GPS indicated, only vaguely aware of where he was in relation to Foxworth. He should have tried harder because what if his instincts had betrayed him again? What if the more he was personally connected to a case, the more likely his gut would go haywire?

For the first time in his career, both in the limelight and out, Gavin considered options he never would have thought of before. Options like not digging too deep, for fear of what he might find. Like looking for innocent explanations instead of the truth.

Like lying.

He felt the thought as if it were a physical thing, a solid blow to the gut driving all the air out of his lungs.

He had actually thought that. Thought about lying, the thing he hated most, to protect Katie's feelings. Because learning her father was guilty wouldn't just break her heart, it would shatter it irreparably.

And there'd be nothing of it left for you.

He groaned inwardly at the knowledge that a week ago he hadn't even known she existed. And now...

Memories of last night again shot through his brain like a summer lightning storm, the brilliance of them blinding him to anything else. Wouldn't hanging on to what he'd found be worth any price? Wouldn't—

Cutter yelped, sounding alarmed. Gavin's attention snapped back to his surroundings. The oncoming car he'd only been aware of on that autopilot level veered sharply, suddenly, into his lane. He hit the brakes. Rafe had told him once that in hot situations time sometimes seemed to slow down. It was really your brain kicking into overdrive, but the effect was as if everything else was going in slow motion. He'd never experienced it before, but he did now.

His mind sorted the possibilities rapid fire. Swerve right? Fairly deep ditch on that side of the road. Crash could be ugly. Swerve left? The other driver would likely try to correct, and put them back on a head-on course. Unless he was hydroplaning and had no control.

Or unless it was intentional.

The oncoming car was barely fifteen feet away now. He had no choice.

"Hang on, dog," he muttered and yanked the wheel to the right.

A gasp broke from Katie as Gavin's car swerved ahead of her. She heard an impact, and a loud scrape of metal. Something hit the street, bounced toward her. In a split second she decided to go over it with the center of her vehicle, her brain telling her it was small enough and to keep her tires away from it. She caught only a glimpse of the other car, the one that had sideswiped Gavin's rental. It sped past, clearly not intending to stop.

And then she saw nothing but Gavin's car skidding sideways. Heard nothing but the screech of tires. And then came the heart-stopping, horrendous thud that she'd swear she felt as his car ended up on its side in the ditch, facing back the way they had come. Which meant the driver's side not only took the brunt of the impact, but ended up embedded in the rain-softened dirt.

She hit her emergency flashers as she braked, hard. She left her car half in the lane, thinking it would both draw attention and act as a barrier. If it got hit, so be it.

She grabbed her phone and dialed 9-1-1 as she hurried toward the edge of the road. She tried to speak coherently as she half ran, half slid down the embankment, heedless of the mud, focused only on getting to the vehicle that was lying ominously on its side. She barely heard the dispatcher's assurances before she stuffed the phone back in her pocket and kept going. A memory flashed through her mind, of him getting into the car in her driveway just minutes ago. Of how she had been wishing she didn't have to work today, so she could stay with him, so they could have a leisurely Saturday exploring this new, wonderful thing that had sprung to life between them.

Had she seen him fasten his seat belt, or not? She couldn't remember. But surely he had.

A rush of sensation flooded her as she remembered those luscious hours in his arms last night. And in these moments now, when she was terrified of what she might find, she faced the truth. However foolish, however fast it had been, she had fallen, hard and irrevocably, for Gavin de Marco.

She heard a bark, realized that somehow Cutter had gotten out of the car. He seemed unhurt, because he was digging madly in the mud, sending up a spray behind him. Trying, she realized, to get to Gavin.

She skidded the last couple of yards. Felt the rush of cold water on her feet as she reached the bottom. The car was indeed embedded; it had hit hard. There was no point in her even trying to get to him from that side.

Cutter looked up at her, whined. She clawed her way over to the passenger door, peered through the wet, mud-spattered window. Belatedly she realized the back side window was down and noted vaguely that that must be how the dog had gotten out. Why had Gavin been driving with it down and why hadn't she noticed, she wondered inanely. Then she realized she was thinking of unimportant things to avoid the most important.

"Gavin!" It broke from her, everything she was feeling echoing in her voice.

And then Gavin moved, lifting his head. He looked at her. She saw blood streaming down the left side of his face. She bit back a scream; hysteria was the last thing he needed right now.

She reached for the passenger door. It unlatched, but seemed impossibly heavy. She got it open to where she could get her shoulder against the inside, then pushed. Since she was trying to open it almost vertically, it took her a moment. She didn't know if the latch would hold once she got it open, but as long as it let her in she didn't care.

She clambered in, heedless of the mud she was spreading from her boots. She heard a scratching noise, realized Cutter had jumped back through the window he'd escaped out of, and into the back seat. She grabbed at anything she could reach to keep from just dropping on top of Gavin.

"Pinned," he said, and she heard the sound as he tried to pull his left leg clear of the crumpled door and dash.

She had to tear her gaze away from his bloody face and order herself to calm down. She had to bend and twist awkwardly, but she got to where she could reach his leg. Urgently she ran her fingers over it, probing, looking for injury or a reaction from him.

"It's not broken," he said, sounding steadier. "Just trapped."

She reached farther, down to just above where the driver's door had crumpled inward. "I think it's your jeans, mostly," she said. "There's a piece of bent metal and it's snagged them."

"I told you I shouldn't have gotten dressed this morning."

Her head snapped around and she stared at him. He gave her a rather lopsided, wry grimace, but then he smiled, as if he were remembering what had prompted those earlier words. That he could look at her like that, despite being bloodied and trapped, sent a thrill through her that was entirely unsuited to the moment. She dared to hope she wasn't alone in this madness he'd brought out in her.

"When I get out of here," he said, his voice sounding

a little strained, "I'd like to talk about whatever you just thought."

No, you wouldn't, she thought, but she said briskly, "Let's take care of getting you out of here first. Although perhaps we should wait for the fire department."

Cutter gave a sharp bark then, and if he was expressing an opinion about waiting, it came through loud and clear.

"Agreed," Gavin said. "I want the hell out of here."

"Right," she said. "You don't happen to have a knife in the car, do you? I can go get my escape tool—"

"Glove box."

She scrambled over and opened the compartment. It only took her a moment to find a tool similar to the one she carried on her key chain only larger. In this land of water and bridges, it only made sense to have something that could both break a window and slice through a seat belt. The blade, however, was in a protected notch of the tool, and not really designed for slicing through an awkward fold of denim. And one she was having trouble keeping a grip on while sawing at it.

When Cutter wiggled his way first into the front seat, then down onto the floorboards, Katie almost shooed him away; he was only lessening what space she had to maneuver. But as she opened her mouth to speak to the dog, he caught the hem of Gavin's jeans in his teeth and pulled.

The fabric was suddenly taut, and Katie had both hands free to maneuver the blade. In a matter of seconds she had cut through the fabric and his leg was free.

Immediately he started to move.

"Are you sure you shouldn't stay still?"

"Nothing's broken," he insisted. "I'll be stiff and sore later, and probably have a hell of a headache, but right now I can move."

Cutter apparently agreed, for he scrambled back out of

the car. Katie, too, eased her way back out. Once she was standing on the muddy ground again, she held the door, making sure it didn't slam on Gavin as he worked his way up out of the car.

As Cutter nosed at him Katie looked him over anxiously, afraid there might be some serious injury—as if his bloody head wasn't enough—they hadn't noticed.

"I'm fine," he assured her as he reached down to Cutter. She thought he was just going to pet the helpful dog, but when he began to run his hands over the animal she realized he was checking for any injury. Something she should have done, she thought with no little regret. But he seemed to find nothing of concern, and gave the dog a final pat.

"Thanks for the help, buddy." He straightened, shifted his gaze back to Katie.

"I'm still trying to figure out how he got out," she said, relieved a bit at how easily he'd bent over to inspect the dog.

"Knowing him, he probably opened the window. He could have gotten to the button."

Katie managed a smile. "I wouldn't put it past him."

Gavin shook his head. Or at least started to, then stopped, quickly enough that her concern spiked again. "I know he was probably just trying to pull me out," he said, "but funny how he ended up doing exactly what you needed."

"More like amazing," Katie said, still not quite able to accept that he had escaped serious injury. What if something turned up later? It happened that way sometimes. Especially if that cut on his head was something more. She didn't want to think about that, didn't want to think of him being seriously hurt, or worse. What would she do if she lost him, now that she'd just found him? It had been bad enough when he'd been attacked outside her library, but now, after last night, she couldn't even bear the thought.

"I'm fine," he repeated. "But keep looking at me like that."

Her gaze shot back to his face. Sometimes she forgot she was dealing with a man who'd become famous in part because he could read people like few could.

Cutter let out a loud, sharp bark. It snapped her out of her emotional morass.

"Can you get up the slope?" she asked briskly, not wanting to have this conversation here and now. "I've got a first aid kit in my car. We can clean up that cut on your head."

Gavin was once more looking at Cutter, who was staring toward the road. "Might as well leave it," he said. "I'm guessing the cavalry's approaching."

Even as he said it she heard the siren. Cutter's sharper canine ears had obviously picked up the sound much sooner. Katie relaxed slightly; the professionals were there now, and if there was any hidden injury, like a concussion, they'd find it.

That was, they would once the younger EMT quit gaping at him.

"You are Gavin de Marco, aren't you?" he asked.

"Afraid so," Gavin muttered.

"We heard about your incident with the guy with the knife."

"News travels fast."

"Small department." The older partner, a man in his midthirties who was apparently training the younger, stepped in and took over. His brisk tone was a mild rebuke to the trainee's loss of professionalism. "Sheriff's traffic unit is on the way. Guy never stopped?"

"No," Katie said. "He just kept going. I didn't see which way at the intersection, because…"

She let her voice trail off and gestured at Gavin. The man nodded; she guessed he understood the priorities here because they were his, as well. He checked Gavin over quickly, then checked more thoroughly while the younger partner cleaned and bandaged the cut on his temple. He used his flashlight to do a vision test, then had Gavin watch his fingers as he moved them. Finally he nodded.

"Doesn't look like there's a concussion," he said. "And your leg will probably bruise, but I don't think there's any serious damage."

"Lucky me," Gavin muttered, but added a sincere "Thank you" to the medic.

The older man studied him for a moment. "First a guy with a knife, now a hit and run? How long have you been a trouble magnet?"

Gavin grimaced. "Normally, I'm not anymore. That seems to have changed since I got here, though."

Katie stared at him. A shiver rippled through her. She hadn't yet made the connection between the two incidents. She'd been too focused on him, and worrying if he'd been seriously injured.

But now she had to consider the very ugly possibility that neither of these events was random or accidental.

The possibility that somebody was trying to take Gavin out of the equation.

Because they were afraid he would do what he was famous for doing.

He'd find out the truth.

Chapter 31

"What the hell happened to you?"

Now there's a question. The earth moved? My world changed? I changed? Take your pick.

Gavin could only imagine what he looked like to Quinn, with his head bandaged, a bloodstained shirt, and a chunk cut out of his jeans. He gave him the condensed version, facts only. Without mentioning Katie; he wasn't quite up to explaining that. He'd sent her on to work, made one call and accepted the traffic investigator's offer of a ride to Foxworth, since it was so close.

As he expected, Quinn reached his same conclusion quickly.

"I don't believe in that much coincidence," he said grimly. Cutter barked as if to add emphasis.

"At least he's okay," Gavin said, looking at the dog.

"He's learned to take care of himself," Quinn said, "since the first time."

Gavin knew the story, of the operation where Cutter had gone down during a hail of gunfire. The dog had made a complete recovery. Quinn on the other hand, had never been the same; he had met both Hayley and Cutter, and changed his life.

And now he had met Katie, and one way or another, his life would never be the same, either. He knew that, that even if he walked away, went back to St. Louis and never saw her again, he would never be the same.

Hayley came out of the kitchen and handed him a much-needed mug of coffee. He took a big swallow, going for the effect rather than taste just then.

Hayley let him finish before saying, "So how is she?"

He froze, the mug halfway back to his mouth. "What?"

"Katie, of course."

"I…" He flicked a glance at Quinn, who was studying his wife, his head tilted as he considered her words.

"Please," Hayley said, her tone dry. "You weren't here, you weren't at our place, and where this crash happened is directly in between here and her place. Not to mention the sparks that practically ignite every time you're together."

"Look," Gavin said, "I know you think that—"

Hayley cut him off, smiling. "Cutter didn't just attach himself to you because you needed him, he also must have sensed you were ready."

"Ready?" Gavin asked warily.

"Or he knows Katie's the one," she added.

Gavin looked at the dog, who now sat beside Hayley, looking…smug. That was the only word he could think of for the animal's expression.

"You adjust to that," Quinn said, still laughing, "while I go get Ty started on digging into your nonaccident."

Glad of the distraction, Gavin said, "No traffic cams along there."

"No, but there are up on the highway, which he may have taken to get away. I'll have him look for a silver car with driver's side damage."

"And a missing mirror," Gavin said. "Katie nearly ran over it in the road."

And he had just confirmed Hayley's guess. Or maybe it wasn't a guess. Maybe it really did show. After last night, he wouldn't be surprised.

"She was behind you?" Quinn asked.

He nodded. "She had to open up this morning." His mouth twisted. "She was late, thanks to this. Oh, I borrowed Rafe."

Quinn frowned. "I was about to call him to ride shotgun with you."

"I'd rather he watched Katie. Just in case. Besides, he's a bit above watching over a guy who should be able to take care of himself."

"He wouldn't mind," Hayley said. "He admires you."

Gavin blinked, startled. Glanced at Quinn, who shrugged. "He admires anyone who's the best at what he does."

Hayley added, "Probably because he's the best, and he knows what it takes to get there."

"That's why I want him looking out for Katie," Gavin said, surrendering any pretense of detachment when it came to her.

"Your call," Quinn said.

"I told him I didn't want her to know."

"Then she never will, unless he has to act." At Gavin's nod, Quinn continued. "Meanwhile, Ty found something interesting."

"What?"

"That seminar that Ross Carr was supposed to be attending in San Diego? It was canceled. Hotel had a sewage problem. They tried to find another hotel or venue, but last minute, no luck."

Gavin frowned. "When?"

"First day."

Gavin got there instantly. "The day before the knife attack."

Quinn nodded. "Exactly. Hayley called and chatted up the receptionist at his job. She said about half the attendees just came home, but the others opted to stay and spend the week basking in the sun."

"Let me guess. Including Carr."

Quinn nodded. "But of course no one's seen or heard from him."

"Who would expect to?"

"Exactly. Perfect cover for dropping off the radar for a week."

"I presume you have Ty checking to see if there's any sign Carr headed home instead?"

Quinn nodded. "Nothing yet, but he's just started."

If it was there, Ty would find it, Gavin thought. And now he was really itching to talk to Carr. He had wanted to anyway, but this first and only blip on the screen of a solid alibi made it imperative.

Gavin found himself watching the time incessantly, telling himself it was because he needed what Ty was searching for, but knowing that in truth he was counting down the hours until he could see Katie again.

And that thought made him more edgy than anything else.

That is until an alert tone drew their attention, and seconds later Ty appeared on the screen above the fireplace. Without preamble, he sent them the photo he'd isolated of a damaged vehicle heading southbound on the state highway. The time frame fit, and the camera where it first appeared fit with the location of the crash. And the damage fit, driver's side, rearview mirror missing.

He stared at the image, at the make and model, remembered the flash of silver he'd seen in the instant before the crash. His stomach churned.

"Can you get the plate?" Quinn asked; it was nothing but a blur in the enlarged shot.

"Working on it," Ty answered. Gavin knew if it was possible at all, Ty and the Foxworth enhancement program—much of which Ty himself had written—would do it.

Instead of signing off abruptly without comment as he usually did, Ty cleared his throat and looked to the right of his own screen. Where, Gavin realized, he himself was sitting.

"Glad you're okay, sir," Ty said, sounding awkward.

Gavin knew what a rarity this was, both the comment and the "sir," so he held the young man's virtual gaze for a moment, before saying, "Thanks, Ty."

As the screen went dark, Quinn leaned back on the couch. "Now, that's a pinnacle few reach."

Gavin smiled; he liked the young tech genius Quinn had snatched off an unsavory path. "At least he's not afraid of me anymore."

"So he can focus on being afraid of Charlie," Hayley quipped, and they all laughed.

And it was a full minute or two before Gavin found himself contemplating what a meeting between Charlie and Katie would be like.

And wondering when he'd begun relating damn near everything in his life to her.

Katie tapped her finger idly on the steering wheel as she sat at the red light. There were four cars in front of her, which pretty much constituted a traffic jam for this place.

She smiled inwardly at how her attitudes had changed since she'd moved here from the city. When she realized she was smiling outwardly, too, she laughed. Happily. She wondered if everyone around her could read her expression as easily as Heather had; her colleague had guessed immediately how last night had ended up. And she'd been delighted, hooting with pure feminine appreciation for her taste.

"That man is pure *hawt*!" she'd drawled out with glee. "Good for you. About time."

And that brought Katie back to her main topic of thought all day: Gavin. Saturdays were always busy, the library full of people who couldn't get there any other day, so she hadn't been able to talk to him, but she'd texted a couple of times, just to be sure there were no unexpected after-effects from the crash. He'd assured her he was fine, and that they were working both on a possible new lead and on the hit and run.

He'd texted nothing more personal, and she told herself she shouldn't be disappointed. He was working, after all. She had hoped he might say something about tonight, about seeing each other. She felt a sudden qualm that perhaps he was having second thoughts.

"Never mind second thoughts, quit second-guessing," she muttered as the light changed.

Yet she found herself shying away from going home, and told herself it wasn't because she didn't want to be back there without Gavin, back at the scene where she'd learned more about what glory was physically possible between two people than she'd ever imagined.

Since he was wrapped up in work that was at least in part for her, she shouldn't complain that he hadn't said anything more personal. Guys didn't think that way, she reminded herself.

She would stick to her routine, she thought. She would stop by her father's place, which she did at least once a weekend. No reason to change that now. Especially now, when her father needed her support. And she hadn't even talked to him for two days. Of course, she'd been a little busy...

She felt the heat rise in her cheeks. No wonder Heather had guessed right off what she'd been up to last night. She wondered if her father would notice, and what she'd say if he asked.

Yes, Dad, as a matter of fact, I did have wild, crazy, superhot sex with the most amazing man last night. And by the way, he happens to be your lawyer.

Her fingers tightened around the steering wheel as she fought not to let the next words form, even in her mind. She failed.

And I think I love him.

She knew it was crazy. Love didn't happen that fast. Infatuation, yes. But that didn't last. He'd be heading back home soon, anyway. And he'd made no promises. In fact the most romantic thing he'd said when they'd left this morning was that he'd see her later. No specifics on when "later" was. Of course then that car had swerved out of nowhere and nearly put an end to everything. When she thought of how close he came to being seriously hurt, or worse, it sent a shiver through her. She didn't like even—

Her breath jammed into her throat, and every meandering thought vanished as she pulled into her father's driveway. And saw his car sitting in his carport. His silver car.

With driver's-side damage and a missing side mirror.

Chapter 32

Quinn ended the call on his cell, stood still for a moment, then turned to look at Gavin. Gavin took one look at his expression and quickly wound up his own call with his contact at the hotel in San Diego; he'd connected with the manager during a bar association meeting there some years ago, and had more recently steered him to Foxworth for help on a personal problem. The man had been more than willing to help, and Gavin now had confirmation that the room allotted to Ross Carr had been paid for, for the week, but according to hotel staff it had shown no sign of being used after that first day.

Normally he would have immediately relayed that information, but something in the way Quinn was looking at him stopped him. Cutter, who had been inspecting the building as if to make sure nothing had changed here after a night away—and what a night, Gavin thought—stopped and came over to sit at his feet.

I'm lucky you can't talk, dog.

"That was Brett," Quinn said after a moment. "Ty sent him what he was able to get on the license plate." Gavin stiffened, apprehension shooting through him. It intensified when Cutter plopped his chin on Gavin's knee and looked up at him worriedly. "He narrowed it down to a dozen or so registered in the county."

Gavin waited. His stomach started to churn again because he knew what was coming. Quinn let out a breath, looked back at his phone, tapped a screen and waited a moment. Then he handed it over.

Gavin scanned the list of registrations that had come attached to an email from Brett Dunbar. His gaze snagged on the fifth one on the list.

Steven Moore.

The churning became nausea. He'd been keeping the fear at bay since the moment he'd seen the photo and recognized the make, together with the fact that the car that hit him was silver—the same color as Moore's. But now it erupted in his gut.

Theories exploded in his brain. He noticed the first ones were efforts to make this innocent, to make the obvious not true. He waited, staring at that name, trying to summon up the detachment that had always enabled him to analyze coolly and dispassionately. But when he did he regretted it because the pattern he saw once he got his emotion out of the way was an ugly one.

Steven Moore, or someone using his car, had intentionally sideswiped him on that rain-slick road, sending him into that ditch. Gavin could easily have ended up hurt much worse than he had been. Or dead. Had that been the goal?

Questions caromed through his mind, rapid fire. Did Katie know? She'd been the one to suggest the route they both took; had it been for this reason? Had she set him up for her father to take out? But why would she do that when she'd asked for Foxworth's help, or at least not said no? Why would she bring him into the case, only to try and kill him when he got close to finding an answer?

Or maybe she really had thought her father innocent, but found out he was not and then quickly and easily changed course. He thought of the women he'd met over the years who would be quite capable of doing that. He would have sworn Katie wasn't like that, but who knew better than he how wrong he could be if he cared about someone.

And he cared about Katie. In fact, ten minutes ago he'd been close to facing the possibility that he was falling in love with her. Why the hell else would he be thinking about staying here longer, perhaps long term?

Fool.

The chill that crept over him now froze out the heat Katie had fired in him. Because the final possibility, the one he'd been mentally fighting off, was hammering at him now.

"You'll have to tell her," Quinn said quietly.

Gavin let out a short, harsh laugh. "What makes you think she doesn't already know?"

Bitterness flooded him. The dominoes fell in his mind. Katie had known, known all along her father was guilty, had lied and used Gavin—and his reputation—to save him. She'd lied to him about her father, the murder…and herself. It hadn't been a simple mistake that she hadn't mentioned her father's prior career as a locksmith. She probably hadn't realized how deep Foxworth would dig, had hoped they wouldn't find it. She'd lied to them from the beginning, and to him up to the end.

The finality of those last two words hit him hard.

The end. He hadn't even been sure what it was, what had sparked to life between them. And now it didn't matter.

Because this was indeed the end.

Katie stared at her father.

"That's it? That's your story?"

"It's what happened," Steven Moore said, giving her a puzzled look. "Why are you so—"

"Somebody stole your car, and you didn't know it until you came out and found it—" she gestured toward the carport "—like that?"

"I didn't hear a thing. They must have rolled it out of the driveway before starting it."

"With your keys," she said.

He grimaced at that. "That's worse than the car. That's always been a possibility with just a carport here, but I never thought anyone would actually go into the house to get my keys."

"Through the door you just happened to leave unlocked?"

"I told you I was working in the shop all day." His brow furrowed. "Why are you talking like this? Like it's my fault my car got stolen?"

"And conveniently returned."

"Obviously someone took it for a joyride this morning and brought it back after they crashed it."

"And you never heard a thing."

"I had earphones on," he said. "The ones you gave me, the wireless ones."

Katie took a deep breath to steady herself. She was trembling, she could feel it, but kept on. Because she had to. She hadn't thought through all the aspects of this, hadn't had time to, but some part of her knew the entire rest of her life would turn on this. She looked at the side of the car for a moment, and the telltale streak of paint transfer that was the exact color of Gavin's rental.

She shifted her gaze back to her father's face, where it would stay until she was sure, one way or another. "Is that what the police say?"

He looked discomfited. "I haven't actually called them yet."

Her heart, which had kept hoping for a way out of this, sank. But even knowing there was no answer she would like, she asked, "Why?"

"Well, I only just discovered it a little while before you arrived. And…I did leave the door unlocked, as you said."

Was that hesitation, him deciding to use the out she'd already provided?

"But you will call them now?"

He didn't look happy. "Maybe I'll just have it repaired."

He didn't want to call the police. And there was only one reason she could think of for that. She was shaking now.

"And if your insurance wants a police report?"

"Don't you see?" he asked, sounding oddly eager as he rapidly spoke. "That's just it. I make a report, and both my car and home insurance is likely to go up."

It did make sense. But she couldn't judge his tone. Did he sound that way because it was true, or because she'd again given him an out, a logical explanation? And how on earth had her life degenerated to where she was questioning her own father? Suspecting him of lying to her face?

Lying. The very idea made her think of Gavin. What would he think? What would he do? What would those vaunted instincts tell him?

She tried to think as she imagined he would. She knew he was an expert at reading people. She wasn't, but she knew—or thought she knew—her father better than anyone. So she set out on an exchange that she was inwardly hoping against hope would prove the awful things she was thinking wrong.

"You're missing a mirror."

"Yes. Lucky there are a ton of these cars on the road. Shouldn't be hard to find a replacement."

Another effort at covering, pointing out his car was far from unique? God, she hated this.

She stared at him as she said, "I can tell you where to find the original."

She would swear his blink was one of genuine bafflement. "What?"

"The original mirror. The one that came off when your car sideswiped Gavin de Marco's."

"How— What are you talking about?"

Her throat tightened. Had he been going to ask her how she knew about what had happened? Of course, that could be interpreted innocently, too. And he hadn't really said it. So why was she even questioning it? This was her *father*.

"The mirror I almost ran over when it was bouncing down the road in front of me."

His eyes widened. "Katie, you were in an accident? Why didn't you—"

She cut him off, her gaze fixed on his face, searching for anything that would help her believe. "Gavin was in the accident. When your car purposely drove him off the road and into a ditch."

"My God. Is he—"

"If the goal was to kill him, it failed. But he was hurt, and it could have been fatal." It was killing her, but she kept her gaze fastened on his face, that beloved face that she had loved from her earliest memories. It showed nothing but concern, and relief, that she could see.

"Thank goodness it wasn't!" If he was faking it, he was

doing a fine job. But then, if he was capable of that, then she didn't know him at all.

"Why do you suppose someone would try to kill him?"

He frowned then. "I'm sure he's made enemies…but what are the odds someone after him would steal *my* car?"

"Exactly."

"Why here, why now?" His brow was furrowed. He was rubbing at his chin in the way he always did when thinking hard. "You don't think it's connected to him helping us?"

And again, she would swear his shock was real. As was the "us."

"I think it's connected to him having a reputation for always finding the truth."

For an instant, just an instant, something flashed in the eyes she knew so well. And more telling, he looked away. She felt something inside her squirming, twisting, as if trying to get away. She made herself go on.

"Someone is worried enough to try and kill him. Or at least take him out of action." She stared at him, hating the way he now wouldn't meet her gaze. "Someone driving your car."

Finally, after more than enough time for him to get himself in hand, he looked back at her. "Katie, surely you're not saying you think it was me?"

"I don't know anymore, Dad. Something's wrong, and I—"

She stopped before she said something irrevocable. He was holding her gaze once more, and now she was doubting her doubts.

"You know I would never do such a thing."

That she would have staked her life on.

And instead you staked your love, although you didn't know it then.

"I'm a little rattled," she said after a moment. Again kept

her eyes on his face, trying to read it as she added, "If I hadn't had to work, I would have been in the car with him."

Her father's eyes widened. "What?"

"I could have been hurt, or worse, too."

He went pale. And when he reached out to hug her, he was the same beloved father who had always been there for her, who had gone through hell with her.

And yet, for the first time in her entire life, she didn't quite believe him. Not all the way. She couldn't quash the feeling that he was hiding something. She thought about the difference between lies and lies of omission. And how Gavin felt about both.

"I'll call the police right now," he promised.

"You do that. I have to go."

"Katie, wait."

She ignored him and walked back to her car. She drove home in such a numbed state she was lucky she didn't have an accident herself. Not that Gavin's crash had been an accident.

Once home she huddled in her favorite chair, in the dark, alone.

She couldn't doubt her father's concern had been genuine when he'd heard how close she'd come to being in that car. She wondered vaguely how he'd feel when he put together why she'd had reason to be with Gavin at that hour of the morning. That seemed minor compared to the fact that she was certain, on some deep level, that her father was lying to her. Or at the least keeping something from her.

Her entire lifetime perception of him had shifted in just those few minutes. Until just now, she would have sworn—in fact had sworn—that would never happen.

She had sworn to Gavin.

Who didn't tolerate liars.

Who would probably now think her one. Again.

She shivered, not even the plush throw enough to reach the chill that went bone deep. She was caught between her suspicions of her father and the knowledge that if she told Gavin, he would walk away from the case, which was practically a conviction even if he never really was his legal representative.

But if she didn't tell him and he found out, she would certainly lose him. She knew he meant what he said about people who lied to him.

She shivered again, wondering how her life had turned once more into heart-crushing chaos.

Chapter 33

Gavin realized now what he missed about the city. The thousands of people, each with their own set of problems. Each one trying to get through their lives with the minimum of upset and discomfort, sometimes succeeding, sometimes not. Somehow all that shared, communal worry seemed to make your own seem less, because you could turn any direction and find someone in worse straits than you were.

Out here, he thought as he stared out the patio door across the meadow, you were pretty much alone with your thoughts unless you made an effort. While most of the time he found that soothing after the chaos of the city, right now it was leaving him far too much time to wallow in the mire he found himself in. It had been a hellish night, and the morning, despite being sunny for a change, had brought him no relief. Because the bottom line hadn't changed.

He'd fallen like some high school kid with his first crush.

For a liar.

He'd been lied to and used in a way he'd sworn would never, ever happen again. Damn, she'd even slept with him—

He spun on his heel away from the window as his mind recoiled from the memory…the way she'd touched him and let him touch her, the sheer consuming joy of holding her, joining with her, the way it had burned through to his very soul. It had been the most amazing night of his life. If he had to believe that was all faked, that was all a lie, then he should just drive off the bridge on his way to the airport because he was obviously too stupid to live.

But if it had been real… No, it couldn't be, because she'd lied. But maybe she hadn't lied about that.

Believing in selective lying now, are we, de Marco?

He sat down on the couch before the fire; although sunny it was still November, and cold without the cloud cover to hold in what warmth there was. He was lucky he'd found out now, he kept telling himself. It didn't improve his mood any. He'd warned Quinn when they'd arrived this morning that he was in no state to either talk or be sociable, but Quinn had only raised an eyebrow and said, "Somebody ask you to do either?"

Neither Quinn nor Hayley had bothered him beyond offering coffee and ibuprofen. He took the pills; the meds they'd given him after the crash had worn off.

When he'd declined the use of one of their vehicles, Hayley, with her usual brisk efficiency, had taken on the task of dealing with his rental car company. The accident report clearly showed the other driver completely at fault, and that he'd left the scene without stopping put the seal on it. Even on Sunday she now had delivery of a replacement car promised by midday.

He turned to her as she hung up the phone.

"Maybe he'd be better off with you," he suggested, gesturing at Cutter, who was sprawled on the couch beside him, his chin now parked on Gavin's leg. He'd been watching the dog carefully—the only distraction he'd found from his thoughts—for any sign of injury that was late showing up, but the emergency vet's assessment appeared accurate and the animal seemed fine.

"I think we'd have a fight on our hands," Hayley said as she looked at the dog. "Nope, you're his chosen task, and interfering with that does no good."

"Mmm." Gavin shook his head at her words, even though he'd caught himself more than once attributing humanlike motives and intelligence to the clever canine.

Hayley shifted her gaze to Gavin. "You know, Gavin, there could well be an innocent explanation for all this," she said, obviously reading his mood. "Or Katie genuinely might not have known."

"Not likely."

"She deserves a chance to explain," Quinn put in from where he sat nearby.

Gavin had his mouth open to say he was done with this when Cutter's head came up and he let out a soft woof. Then another as he got to his feet, jumped down from the couch and headed for the door. As soon as he got there he raised up on his hind legs and batted at the automatic opener. Gavin's gut knew who was there before the door swung open. Still, it knotted up the instant Katie stepped inside.

He realized, with a little shock, she looked like he felt. The usually tidy, together woman looked a bit ragged, her hair tousled, her jeans and sweatshirt just thrown on.

And her eyes were reddened. Seriously reddened. She'd been crying. A lot. And the slight sheen on her cheeks indicated she hadn't stopped crying on the way here. Even now she wiped at her eyes with the sleeve of her shirt, as if it had become habit.

It was instinctive for him to stand, but he made himself stop. And unlike her usual considerate self, Katie ignored Quinn and Hayley, her eyes focused only on him. In his peripheral vision Gavin saw the Foxworths exchange a look. He wondered if they'd felt the sudden ice in the room.

"We'll just let you work it out," Hayley said then.

"You've got the number if you need reinforcements," Quinn added, and Gavin noticed he didn't specify which of them that was aimed at.

They murmured something he couldn't hear to Katie as they passed. But their stubborn dog stayed, escorting—hell, herding—Katie toward him. In fact, the dog shouldered and nudged and even pushed until she had little choice but to sit in the spot the dog himself had just vacated. Next to him.

Gavin stared at her but said nothing. What she said first would determine what he would do. Silence spun out. She picked at a thread on her jeans. Again she wiped at her eyes. He felt uncomfortable ignoring her obvious distress, but he made himself do it. Even if going from the incredible intimacy of the other night—God, had it just been one night ago?—to this was stomach churning. Especially when she wouldn't look at him.

"Are you all right?" she asked first.

"Obviously," he said, his voice cool.

She winced. He felt a twinge and wondered at it. When had he started feeling anything but abhorrence for liars?

"I'm sorry," she finally said.

For lying? he wondered. But still he said nothing.

"I love my father. I never would have agreed to this if I hadn't been utterly certain of him."

Gavin went very still. He hadn't missed the past tense. She lifted her head, finally met his eyes. She drew in a long, deep, audible breath. "I went to see him last night, when you—"

She stopped. He guessed she'd been about to say something about him dropping off the radar, after the night they'd had. Under normal circumstances, it would have been a piggish thing to do. But these were hardly normal circumstances.

She took another deep breath. She clasped her hands together, as if she needed the pressure, needed to do it to hold herself together. She lowered her gaze to her fingers, and he saw a shiver go through her. Again his stomach knotted; he wanted nothing more than to reach out for her, pull her into his arms, comfort her. Only a single word stopped him.

Liar.

Once more she lifted her head and met his gaze. And this time she held it. When she spoke again, her voice was steadier, businesslike, and the words unrolled rapidly.

"It was his car that hit you. I saw the damage, the dark paint, the missing mirror. His explanation is that it was stolen while he was working in his shop, and brought back after the damage was done. That someone got into the house and took the keys. That he had earphones on so he didn't hear anything. That he'd only discovered it right before I got there."

Gavin stared at her. He hadn't expected that. Hadn't expected that she'd come here to tell him what she'd learned, not when it was evidence against her father.

For a moment she just looked at him. Then her breath caught audibly. "You already knew."

"Thanks to Ty and Brett Dunbar."

She figured it out quickly. "The traffic camera on the highway. You got a license number."

"A partial. And your father was fifth on the list of matches. I don't believe in that much coincidence."

"Neither do I."

His certainty that she'd been lying all along was shaken. Why would she come here like this, tell him about the car if she was? And her reaction when she realized he already knew had been genuine surprise, he was sure of that.

"You believe his story?" He kept all trace of accusation out of his voice.

"I want to. He's never lied to me before."

Want to wasn't the same as *yes*. "But now?"

She steadied herself again, and Gavin saw in the tenseness of her posture, the tightness around her eyes, the way she clenched her hands, just how much this was costing her. And yet she was doing it. Admiration spiked through him.

"Now I'm not sure. I still can't believe he would hurt Laurel. And he seemed totally honest about the car. And why would he want to hurt the person trying to help him? But the car being stolen out from under his nose, and just happening to hit you? That's so…implausible. He's keeping something from me. I can feel it."

He couldn't put a single name to how she sounded. Bewildered. Hurt. Confused. Yet she also sounded determined, and maybe the tiniest bit angry. He analyzed his options for a moment before he quietly repeated her own question.

"Why would he want to hurt the person trying to help him?"

"There's only one reason I can think of," she said, her voice going dark, wounded. "He doesn't want the truth found."

She was no coward, Katie Moore. When it was staring her in the face, she didn't run away, no matter the pain it had to be causing her. *Admiration* wasn't a strong enough word for what he felt for her.

But the other words that fit scared him.

"And what do you want, Katie?" he asked softly.

She steadied herself once more, and her voice was level when she answered, "I want what I said I wanted in the beginning. I want the truth."

"Do you?"

She frowned. "Why else would I have wanted you to get involved in the first place?"

There was that. He leaned back on the couch, keeping his gaze fastened on her. She met his eyes unflinchingly. So unflinchingly he found himself rethinking his assumptions. All of them.

This time it was he who found he couldn't look at her. He shifted his gaze, realized Cutter was sitting at her feet and staring up at him intently. The dog held his gaze with the intensity Gavin imagined his breed used on the animals it herded. And then he put his chin on Katie's knee. What was Cutter trying to indicate? Trust? Belief? Faith? All three?

Gavin gave a shake of his head, as much at falling into the pattern of Foxworth crediting the animal with such uncanny abilities as anything.

Were she anyone else, he'd be certain he'd been played and she'd been lying all along. Yet a dog's simple gesture made him want to believe.

"So that's it," Katie said, startling him. His gaze shot back to her face. She was watching him and frowning. "You think he did it. All of it, Laurel, too. And you think I knew all along."

She'd obviously thought his shake of the head was aimed at her, not the dog. He found himself considering denying her words. Once more thinking about lying. When had he become such a hypocrite? He steeled himself; he couldn't be less strong than she was being right now.

I don't lie.

His own words to her rang in his head. He had no idea

how she would react, and a lie would be kinder, especially after— He stopped himself before a heated string of erotic images could derail him entirely.

She wanted truth. He would give her that. Even knowing what it would do, to her and to what they had found together.

One night, that's about all you're good for, de Marco. Then you blow it to bits.

"I did think that, when it first came together," he admitted.

"You thought I was lying from the beginning?"

"I don't now," he said. But that didn't change the fact that he had.

For a moment she just stared at him. He waited for some kind of eruption, a flash of anger. After all, he'd just admitted he'd suspected her of some very devious machinations. What he saw in her face was plainly readable, but it wasn't anger. It was pain, and it echoed in her voice when she spoke.

"And you thought I was the kind of person who would do something like that? Use you like that?"

Only then did he realize he'd done worse than make her angry. Even Cutter sensed the change and straightened up.

He saw it in her eyes. It was impossible to miss. He'd shattered her. He'd taken the closeness of that night and made it a travesty, a sham, at least in her eyes.

"Katie—"

She waved him off and stood up abruptly. Cutter whined, clearly displeased by what was happening. She folded her arms in front of her, and Gavin had the distinct feeling that if she'd been alone she'd have wrapped them around herself for some small amount of comfort. Something he should be doing for her.

Except now he didn't have the right.

She walked over to the patio doors, stood for a long, silent moment staring out across the meadow. He wanted to go to her, wanted to ease her pain, but since he was the one who had caused it with his lack of trust, he would likely do more damage than good.

She turned and came back. He rose slowly as she came to a halt in front of him. When she spoke, it was so controlled it made his own muscles tense up. "Are you quitting?"

"Katie—"

"Have you decided my father is guilty, Mr. de Marco?"

The formality stung, as he knew it was supposed to. What surprised him was just how much it hurt. It took him a moment to get past the unexpected, wrenching pain. He tried to match her flat tone, and it took an effort that amazed him.

"I haven't decided anything. And I won't until I speak to your father again."

"Fine." He had the feeling that single word would have sounded the same no matter what his answer had been. "Now would be a good time. He'll be home."

She turned and walked out without another word.

Cutter growled. Gavin looked down at him.

He had never realized an animal could express disgust.

Chapter 34

She was going to see this through.

Katie repeated the words in her head like a mantra, as she had all morning while waiting for the rental, because she didn't want to be suspected of sneaking ahead to warn her father. She repeated the words as if they were the only thing that could keep her together. She'd vowed to see this through and that's what she would do. Her feelings didn't matter now. Nor did the fact that her belief in her father was on the edge of obliteration. Or her belief that what she'd found with Gavin was real, and wonderful. Because she couldn't love a man who could think her capable of what Gavin had thought.

It didn't matter, she repeated to herself. Nothing mattered but the truth.

She drove rather dangerously, since she refused to look in the rearview mirror to see if Gavin's new rental was behind her. When she got to her father's house, she saw his damaged car in the same place it had been. But there were new tire tracks in the soft dirt next to the driveway, indicating someone had turned around. The sheriff?

She felt a surge of hope. Her father had called her last night, but she hadn't answered, hadn't wanted to talk to him. But the message he left said he'd reported the theft and damage. Surely if her father had actually tried to take Gavin out of the picture, he wouldn't have actually done that. He wouldn't want law enforcement involved at all, would he?

But her certainty meant nothing to Gavin. Clearly any emotion of hers meant less than nothing to him. On the bitter thought, she heard another car pull into the driveway. It came to a stop beside her. She got out, started to head for the house, then stopped. She waited for Gavin to get out, followed by Cutter. He walked toward the car, but paused to look at her questioningly.

"Wouldn't want to give him any warning," she said, her tone as chilly as the air.

He didn't respond, only nodded and walked on to look at the car. He studied it for a moment, and she was sure he was taking in the missing mirror and the long scrape that showed a streak of color that exactly matched the car he'd been driving.

"He reported it," she said, leaving out the hopes attached to that thought. He looked at her, lifting an eyebrow. "He left a message late last night that he'd done it. And," she said, gesturing toward the tire prints in the ground, "those weren't here last night."

Again he only nodded. Plainly he didn't want to talk to her. And why would he, when he thought her capable of such deviousness? A belated thought suddenly struck, with such power it took her breath away. Did he think Friday night had been a lie, too? Did he think that part of some great manipulation on her part?

She didn't think she'd made a sound, thought she'd stifled the moan of pain, but he looked at her as if he'd heard it. Something flickered in those dark eyes but she couldn't tell what it was, and allowed herself no foolish imagining that it might be caring.

When Cutter came to her and nuzzled her hand, she automatically stroked his head. She felt a slight easing of the turmoil inside her, as if the dog had somehow taken some of the ache away.

The house was locked front and back, and her father didn't answer the door. She led the way around the back, saw a distant light on in the shop.

"At least he locked the back door this time," she said, almost to herself as they started that way. It was a bit of a trek over the soft, uneven ground, past the vegetable garden and through the trees to the small building at the very back of the property. The trees and shrubbery back there were a bit overgrown, but her father liked it that way, said it gave him a sense of peace and solitude when he was there.

"This is why he didn't see or hear the thief," she said when they had passed the first stand of greenery and the house—and carport—were barely visible. Gavin looked back, but he again said nothing. She resolved to say nothing more; obviously he didn't care to hear anything from her.

Especially that you fell in love with him.

Even in her thoughts the past tense hurt, and she kept her face steadfastly forward until they reached the shop.

Her father was busy tweaking his latest project, welding something on an intentionally crooked weathervane he was making for Mrs. Collier down the street. A few more of his pieces, in various stages of completion, adorned the workbench and shelves. She didn't look at them, she'd seen them all, but she watched Gavin look at them and saw the fleeting expression of surprise on his face as he took in the room.

Good. I'm glad you're surprised. Maybe you'll see that he's not who you think he is.

With a rueful inward laugh at herself about people not being who you thought they were, she watched as her father whipped off his helmet. His face lit up as he looked at her, clearly delighted to see her. Especially after the way they'd parted.

"Katie, honey," he said and strode quickly over to envelop her in a hug. She accepted it, although with some lingering hesitation.

When he released her she nodded toward Gavin. "He needs to talk to you," she said, not even using his name.

She saw her father's expression change, take on a look that could be fear, or simply wariness at facing the fierce Gavin de Marco.

"Let's go up to the house," her father said, and such was her state of mind that she wondered if he suggested that to give himself time to think, time to decide what he was going to say. And not say.

But Gavin didn't press, merely agreed. Once inside, she went into the kitchen she knew as well as her own and put on a pot of coffee. She'd pass on it herself. The last thing she needed was a caffeine hit when her mind was already running in circles, but she was sure her father at least would welcome it. And at a second thought, she checked the vegetable bin and found a bag of carrots, broke a chunk off of one and offered it to Cutter. The dog took the treat with a wag of his tail as a thank-you.

When the coffee was done, she poured one for her father and added his usual large dollop of milk, and pondered for a moment over pouring a cup for Gavin, as well. She hadn't asked if he wanted any. In fact she hadn't spoken to him since her explanation about the shop's location had been met with no response. In the end she poured it anyway and carried the two cups out into the living room.

Oddly, they were talking about his shop projects, her father explaining how he'd gotten into the whimsical sideline when someone had stopped to ask about the Christmas decoration he'd built one year, a row of wire structures of different sizes and shapes that, when strung with lights, looked like a little village lit up for the holiday.

She handed her father his mug first, and then held the other out to Gavin.

"It's black," she assured him as he hesitated; she knew he drank it that way or not at all. No multinamed concoctions for him; he drank it for the hit, he'd told her, not the taste.

Her father was watching them, a considering expression on his face. And then he focused on Gavin. "If you hurt my little girl," he said conversationally, "I have a welding torch."

"Dad!" she exclaimed, her cheeks flushing. Between the coffee and her telling him she would have been with Gavin yesterday morning had she not needed her car, he'd obviously put it together.

"I think," Gavin said quietly, "that warning's a little late. To my anguish."

Her head snapped around. Gavin was looking at her, not her father.

"Well, you'd damned well better make it up to her, then," her father said sternly.

"I never intended to hurt her."

Katie felt as if she should say something, but she had no words. It wasn't exactly an apology, but it was close.

"That said," Gavin went on, "why are you hurting her?"

Her father drew back, clearly startled. "What?"

"You're lying to her. Or hiding something. And she knows it. Why?"

Katie's breath caught. Her mind careened between two things, that the near-apology had not been sincere but a lead-up to this, and that it seemed strange that Gavin had asked why he was lying rather than what about.

"Mr. de Marco," her father began.

"Gavin, please," he said, and his tone was as it had been, conversational, lacking even a hint of accusation. "You had the sheriff out, for the car?"

"I did," her father said, sounding relieved at the sudden switch. "They took a report. I even told them about what happened to you. I have nothing to hide. I'm sorry about your accident, by the way."

"It wasn't an accident."

"Well, yes, but you know what I mean."

"I know several things. I'll list them for you later, if you like. But right now I'd like to know why you feel the need to hide something from your daughter."

It went on and on, Gavin letting her father veer away from the subject, get to thinking he'd successfully diverted the conversation. Then, in the moment she sensed her father relaxing, he was back to it, again catching her father off guard. First from his artwork back to the question, then from the car incident back to it again, then from what he'd been working on at the time back to why he was hiding something. And again, not what he was hiding, but why. As if he thought he would get an answer to the one but not the other. Or that only this answer really mattered.

She stayed silent, watching and listening intently, trying to shore up her faith in the father she loved. She wondered if that was why Gavin had said nothing about her staying in the room, because he wanted her to see this, to learn what he learned. But that would mean he believed she hadn't known all along, wouldn't it? If her father was lying, that is.

She cut off the circuitous thoughts that got her nowhere and continued to watch and listen. She wondered if this was what he'd been like in a courtroom, pressing, luring, ensnaring until he finally got to the truth. Quietly, determinedly relentless, knowing what he wanted and digging from whatever angle would get him there. Reluctantly, since he was grilling her father, the admiration she'd felt when she'd first watched a trial video of him sparked anew.

"Why put your shop so far from the house?" Gavin asked, seemingly apropos of nothing. Unless he was insinuating her father had buried bodies back there. The thought came with the bitter memory of Gavin admitting he'd believed she'd been lying all along.

Her father's brow furrowed, but he was apparently getting more used to the rapid switching of subjects. "I do some grinding, and other work that makes some noise. I didn't want to disturb the neighbors, so I put it as far back as I could from the other houses."

"Not hiding anything back there?"

Her father looked offended. "Nothing but Katie's Christmas present, and thanks for making me give that away."

For the first time since this had begun, Katie smiled. "I promise not to snoop."

He managed a smile back. "Then it's safe. Your promise is golden."

"Is yours?" Gavin asked her father quietly. "Will you promise her you're not hiding anything from her?"

Katie nearly gaped at him. Was there nothing he couldn't turn to his goal?

"We all have secrets," her father said, looking uneasy once more.

"But why do you feel the need to hide this one from her?"

"I love my daughter," he answered, as if that explained it.

"And she loves you," Gavin said, still quietly. "Is that it? You're afraid your secret will change her love for you?"

Katie nearly gasped aloud as her father's expression changed again. And this time there was no denying what was right before her. Gavin had hit upon the truth. Or *a* truth, at the least. Her father truly was hiding something, and it was something he was not just reluctant but afraid to tell her.

"Dad," she whispered, staring at him.

Her father wouldn't meet her eyes. Gavin's voice was barely above a whisper now. "I've gotten to know your daughter a little. And once she gives her love, only something unforgivable could change it. Something indefensible. So indefensible even her great love can't get past it."

Katie's breath caught once more. *Is this aimed at me, too? Is he talking not just about Dad, but us?* She answered her own inward questions. *This is not about you, and there is no us. Didn't he make that clear enough for you?*

"I believe you about the car," Gavin said. "Have you done something else, Steven? Something so bad that even Katie's love can't withstand it? Did you kill her best friend?"

Her father drew in an audible breath. "No."

It was flat, solid, and to Katie utterly believable. He hadn't done it. And she realized she'd never really believed he had. He was hiding something, but not that.

"Then what?" Gavin persisted, still gently.

Her father glanced at Katie, and she read an apology there for what he was about to say. She wanted to encourage him, assure him nothing could change her love for him, but she was afraid to interrupt the flow Gavin had finally established.

"Get it out," Gavin said. "It's eating you up."

Her father looked at his feet. And then, in a voice she'd never heard from him before, he answered.

"Laurel and I had an affair."

Chapter 35

Gavin heard Katie's gasp, but didn't look at her. He kept his gaze fastened on the man before him. But inside he was relieved. Katie would be hurt but not destroyed. Another warning bell went off in his head, that his first thought wasn't about Moore's guilt or innocence, but Katie. And she was apparently Cutter's first thought as well, for the dog was quickly at her feet, leaning in, offering comfort in that way he had.

"I know it sounds silly," Moore said, "me more than twenty years older, but she didn't care. Her only worry was that Katie might not like it."

He gave Katie a quick, sideways glance. She was staring at her father, clearly stunned.

"It started when we were planning Katie's birthday. The breakup with Ross was already starting. So she cried on my shoulder and then one day…she kissed me. It startled both of us, I think."

"Dad," Katie began, then stopped as if she couldn't find any words.

He didn't look at her, kept his eyes on Gavin. He was clearly uncomfortable, but now that he'd started he was going to finish. Gavin stayed silent, knowing that right now, this was nothing to do with the case and everything to do with what kind of relationship Katie and her father would have from here on.

"We laughed it off, but…it wouldn't go away. It kind of…morphed from there into something else. Something special."

"So special you kept it secret?" Katie asked. Gavin tried to assess her tone, but there was so much shock there he couldn't separate out much more.

"In the beginning, we didn't even know what it was. At first we met to make plans for the party. Then we ended up talking about other things. For hours. She'd ask for advice. I thought she looked at me as a sort of surrogate father."

Katie absently stroked Cutter's fur. "She always thought you were hot," she said slowly. "When we were in elementary school she used to joke that she couldn't wait until she grew up so she could marry you."

Gavin saw Moore's eyes widen, then saw him blink rapidly as moisture pooled there. Whatever the man had felt for Laurel, it had been real.

"I was the one who wanted to keep it quiet," Moore said. "I wanted to be the one to tell you, but I was afraid to."

She was still stroking Cutter's dark head as if it helped her think. She was processing it now, Gavin thought. Getting past the shock. "I told you I would love for you to find someone. You've been alone so long. But…"

"Not your best friend."

"It would have taken time for me to get used to it." Gavin could tell by her expression she was turning it over in her mind, looking at it from all angles. "But," she added softly, her gaze seeming to turn inward, making Gavin guess she was remembering things, "maybe I should have known. Not just because she'd always had a crush on you, but looking back...she did drop some hints here and there. I just never realized it at the time."

"You two were so close, she hated not telling you. I was the coward."

Gavin could almost feel Katie leveling out. She was dealing with it now.

"Back in high school she used to joke that if she married you, she'd be my stepmother. We both laughed hysterically at that idea, so... I guess I never took it seriously."

Moore was looking at Gavin now. "So do you believe me now? I would never have hurt Laurel."

In that moment Cutter got up, crossed over to Moore, turned and sat. He looked at Gavin, in fact stared at him with that same intensity he'd seen before. Something flashed through Gavin's mind, a memory of the first day Cutter had met the man, and the odd look that Gavin had categorized as a maybe. There was no reservation in the look the dog was giving him now. He might as well have been able to talk. It was almost as if he'd had the same instinct Gavin had, that he knew the man had been lying about something, but now that it was out, the animal sensed what was left was the truth.

In fact Gavin did believe Moore, now that he knew what the man had been hiding. But he also knew now what Detective Davidson had been talking about when he'd said they had something on Moore. "Some would say there's more motive than ever. Who ended it?"

"I did. I thought it was best. She needed to find someone her own age."

It sounded like the truth, Gavin thought. But if Davidson had found out, it would explain the police looking in Moore's direction.

Katie was shaking her head, clearly still trying to wrap her mind around this. "I felt like Laurel was hiding something, but… So when I thought I was helping her get over Ross, it was really you? And when she said there had been cheating involved, it was her, not Ross? With you? That's why you were so broken up about it, because—"

"When did you last see her?" Gavin asked, cutting off the flow of clearly distressed questions. He needed more answers before leaving Katie to deal with the personal fallout.

"About a week before she…died. She wasn't happy about my decision." His expression was bleak. "She wasn't happy about anything at that point."

Katie spoke again. "But Ross was—"

"One of the things she was unhappy about," her father finished for her. "He wanted back in her life, but she was afraid he hadn't changed. She wanted to meet, to ask one last time if I was sure."

Gavin's gaze narrowed. "One last time?"

"She was considering going back to him. I told her I didn't think she should, that I—"

He stopped as Gavin's phone beeped with an incoming text. He pulled it out, swiped the screen and glanced at the message. Timing, he thought, considering where his mind had just turned, what had clicked into place with Moore's confession.

He looked at the man, who seemed relieved to have the truth out at last. At Cutter, who was still giving him that signal that Moore was now to be trusted. And finally he looked at Katie, who was looking back at him with only mild curiosity. As she might look at anyone, not someone who just one night ago had been naked in her arms, her name ripping from his throat as he drove into her body in a heat he'd never known before.

A flame of that heat singed him, and he had to steady himself to speak with a semblance of casualness. "I need to talk to someone, so I'll leave you two to work this out."

He rose, and so did Katie. "Who?" she asked.

"Someone I've been waiting to interview."

She studied him for a moment as he got up. Cutter got to his feet as well, and before Gavin had even taken a step was headed for the door. Katie was right behind them.

"I'm going with you."

"Don't you think you need to stay with your father and talk?"

"No. Right now I need to see this through. To the end."

Something in the way she said the words sent a chill through him. The end of what? The case? Or them? Had his lack of faith in her put the finish to both? He couldn't blame her. He saw so clearly now that he should have trusted her, but hindsight wasn't going to fix what he'd done. And he was shaken to the core by how the idea of losing her, what he'd found with her, nearly shoved everything else out of his mind.

She followed him outside and toward the cars.

"Katie, just—"

"No."

The finality in her tone told him he would get nowhere arguing with her, and at the moment he didn't have time to waste. If his hunch was right, he needed to get moving now. He'd just have to keep her out of it, somehow.

"I should drive," she said as he reached for the keys to the rental.

His brow furrowed. "Why?"

She pulled out her own keys. "Because I know where we're going."

That stopped him in his tracks. He turned to stare at her. "What?"

"Tacoma, right? Ross?" She hadn't seen the text. He knew she hadn't. "Please," she said scornfully at his expression. "He's the only one you haven't talked to yet, isn't he?"

His appreciation for her quick deduction warred with the sting from the tone of her voice. For one of the few times in his life he was unable to think of a word to say. Instead he gave a half shrug and walked to the passenger side of her car. Without comment, Katie unlocked the car, and even opened the back door for Cutter to jump in. The dog did so without hesitation.

She drove, as he would have expected, with calm efficiency.

And in total silence. Which he probably should have expected, given what she thought of him at the moment.

In his mind he turned over a hundred ways to try to talk to her, but none of them seemed likely to earn him anything but more scorn. He knew now—too late—that Katie Moore was exactly what she seemed to be. Smart, kind and completely honest.

Cutter gave a low sigh from the back seat. Gavin glanced back at him, and saw that look of disgust again. He was beginning to give up on trying to rationalize the dog's traits in any ordinary canine way.

Her silence began to wear on him, and since he couldn't think of a damned thing to say, he took out his phone and called up the images of the notes he'd made on Ross Carr; he might prefer to make his notes by hand, but carting around reams of paper was another matter. He read through them, this time with a fresh eye, refocused thanks to what he'd just learned.

For the sake of completeness he added Quinn's text to the file. Brett Dunbar was true to his word, as usual, and the moment he'd heard from his friend in Tacoma that a unit had reported Carr had returned home, he had sent the information on. Quinn in turn had sent word to Gavin, and added that he and Rafe would be heading that way, just in case. Gavin knew Quinn hadn't liked Carr's disappearing act, any more than he had.

As they drove, the inkling of a suspicion that had come to him during Moore's revelations grew. He turned it over and over in his mind to inspect all sides. By the time they were nearly there, he wasn't much liking the conclusions he was drawing.

When they finally got off the highway, Katie drove so confidently he belatedly realized she knew where she was going because Ross Carr's house had once been Laurel's, as well.

"I need you to stay in the car when we get there," he said. They were the first words he'd spoken in nearly an hour.

"I'm not—"

"You've seen how I work. I need to talk to him cold."

She hesitated, and he saw her forefinger tap on the steering wheel. "All right," she said after three taps.

"Thank you." God, the formality was clawing at him, but he didn't know what else to do. And for a man used to always knowing what to do, it was an unsettling feeling.

She continued on through three more turns, then slowed after the last one. "Up here on the right, by that car with the trunk open," she said.

He nodded, glanced at the house the vehicle was parked in front of. He saw someone coming down the walkway, a large box in his arms, apparently heading for that vehicle.

Cutter was suddenly on his feet in the back seat, a low growl issuing from his throat.

"Wait, that's Ross," Katie said. "Is he packing? Moving?"

Gavin glanced at Cutter, who was pawing the door madly, wanting out. He looked back as the man set the box he'd been carrying in the trunk, then turned.

His size. Build. Way of moving. The knit hat, cuff now rolled up on his head, but still black with bright red trim on the edge. Cutter's reaction.

All that made him certain.

Ross Carr was the man with the knife.

Chapter 36

Ross spotted Cutter first. Even from here Katie could see his eyes widen. Gavin had let the dog out first, snapped an order for Katie to stay and headed after the dog at a run.

Ross darted back toward the house, vanishing behind the section that jutted out toward the road, where Katie knew the living room was. Cutter raced across the yard, disappearing in turn around the building. Gavin wasn't far behind. And then...

Nothing.

She rolled down her window. Silence.

Her mind was racing. Of course Ross would run from an oncoming, growling dog. Anyone would. The question was, why was the brilliantly clever, normally very sweet Cutter bent on mayhem against Ross? He'd never met him, why would he—

It hit her then.

Maybe Cutter had met Ross. That night outside the library.

Her breath caught. And now her thoughts were tumbling. Had it been Ross who'd attacked Gavin? Had he been here all along, not in San Diego? Had he even perhaps been the one to steal her father's car and try for Gavin again after his knife attack had failed? But why? Why would—

Again it clicked into place, the reason for the way Gavin had reacted to the news that Ross was home.

What if Ross had found out about Laurel and her father? He'd always been able to lure Laurel back from her efforts to leave him, but there had never been a third party involved before.

She couldn't bear it any longer. Her thought process had taken only seconds, but it felt like she'd been sitting there, doing nothing, for an eternity. She grabbed her phone, keyed in 9-1-1 but didn't send it. Then she got out of the car and headed for the house.

When she rounded the corner, she heard a shout. In a corner near the door, she saw the two men on the ground. Gavin nearly had Ross pinned. Ross threw a wild punch that Gavin easily dodged. And then Cutter darted forward, fangs bared and growling fiercely. He went for Ross's leg, catching his ankle. Ross screamed, kicked. Cutter held on. His growl scared even her.

And then Gavin had him, his forearm locked around Ross's neck. She ran forward.

"Get him off me!" Ross screamed again.

"You're lucky it's not your throat," Gavin snapped out. He gave Katie a warning glance, and she stayed carefully out of Ross's reach.

"Just get him off!" Ross begged. She saw now why police K-9s were so effective. A determined, fierce dog could clearly be terrifying.

Gavin ignored Ross's plea. "I know you faked being in

San Diego and came back here. I know it was you with the knife. And then the car. You clearly wanted me off this."

Ross paled at each statement. He twisted harder, trying to escape both Gavin's hold and Cutter's teeth. He failed at both.

"There's only one reason I can think of to make you go through all that."

"You did it," Katie said, barely managing to speak past the tightness in her throat. "You killed her, didn't you?"

"Stop, Katie." Gavin's order was remarkably calm, considering.

"But—"

"Don't ask him anything. That's for the police. After he's been read his rights. We don't want him to wiggle out of this, do we?"

She let out her breath. She realized then that Gavin never had actually asked anything; he'd only stated what he knew. But he hadn't needed verbal answers. Ross's face said it all.

"Cutter, release," Gavin said. The dog let go, but didn't look happy about it. But Gavin's sharp command of "Guard" seemed to cheer him up. Gavin backed off Ross, but remained crouched beside him. "If you move, he will go for the throat this time."

As warnings went, it was immensely effective; Ross was staring at the dog in near terror. Gavin looked up at her then.

"Why don't you make that call?" he suggested. "And then call Quinn. Never mind. They're here."

Katie spun around and indeed saw Quinn coming around the back corner of the house. He took in the situation quickly, then called out, "Clear!" Then Hayley came out from around the other side of the house, while a second man unexpectedly appeared above her on the roof. She recognized the other Foxworth operative she'd met, Rafe

Crawford, as he slid a weapon into a holster, then tugged his jacket over it before he dropped down to the ground. Quinn was armed as well, Katie realized. And even Hayley? She saw the other woman slide something into her belt and had her answer; Foxworth had come prepared for anything. Unnecessarily, but still comforting.

Gavin stood up then. Cutter greeted his teammates with a brisk bark, but his eyes never left his assignment.

Katie felt a sudden wave of reaction, as if the ground had rippled under her feet. If not for Gavin jumping to her side, throwing an arm around her to steady her, she very probably would have ended up on the ground beside Ross.

It was over.

"So that's it?" Katie asked. "He found out about Laurel and my father and killed her for it?"

"That's his story," Quinn said. "In his mind, they hadn't split yet, so she was cheating on him."

They were gathered at Foxworth once more, the five of them plus Cutter, who, after obtaining another carrot snack for a job well-done, settled before the fire to happily crunch. Katie herself had been unable to settle; there was too much turmoil in her head and heart. So she'd been pacing the floor since they'd arrived after turning Ross and their information over to the police, who went into action quickly and efficiently. The Foxworth name garnered respect in all corners, it seemed.

"But his alibi," Katie began.

"He drugged the woman," Hayley said in disgust. "But a small dose, so she would only be out for a while. Just long enough for him to sneak out, borrow another partier's motorcycle, leaving his car unmoved, get to Laurel and get back with no one the wiser."

"So they all assumed he was with the woman the whole time?"

Quinn nodded. "And she thought she'd just gotten drunk. When she passed out he was with her, when she woke up he was with her."

"And keeping her around was insurance," Rafe said sourly from where he stood by the fireplace.

"He manufactures this alibi, and it holds," Hayley said. "So he thinks he's going to get away with it."

"Until," Quinn said with a grin, "the famous Gavin de Marco shows up and starts poking into things."

Katie stopped her pacing on those words, saw Gavin grimace, but he didn't speak. In fact, he hadn't said anything since they'd begun to lay it all out.

She looked at Quinn. "And then he decided to try and pin it on my father?"

Quinn nodded. "One final bit of revenge."

She shook her head slowly. "It could have worked." She looked back at Gavin. "If you hadn't been here, hadn't taken this on, it could have worked."

Gavin wouldn't look at her. "Thank Cutter. He brought it—and you—to Foxworth."

"Oh, I will," she said with a glance at the dog. "Carrots for life, m'boy."

The dog gave a happy bark, so far removed from the ferocious, intense working dog she'd seen, it was hard to believe it was the same animal.

The Foxworths exchanged glances, and then Hayley said brightly, "We're going to go up and finish off our reports. There's more coffee on if you need it."

Cutter did not head up with them, but stayed where he was. He was still Gavin's self-appointed guardian, it seemed. And Rafe lingered for a moment, looking at them both. She saw Gavin lift an eyebrow at him.

The dark, intimidating man shrugged. "Just thinking. You hate liars, now she hates the results of lying. So you'll probably never lie to each other."

Katie's breath caught. He'd said that like he expected she and Gavin to...what? Be together? The unlikeliness of that jabbed at her. She watched as he went out the patio door and headed toward the warehouse building.

Cutter did not follow him, either.

She was unable to keep still. She was relieved that her father had been exonerated, but a sour taste remained when she thought of how he had lied to her all this time. Her own father, the man she'd relied on her entire life and would have sworn she knew inside out.

Not to mention Laurel. Her best friend of nearly twenty years, and she had not only had an affair with her father, but had also lied about something as major as that. She found the latter much more upsetting, and that it was a lie of omission didn't ameliorate it at all. Gavin was right about that. And yes, she hated the results of lying. Rafe Crawford had been right about that.

Now it was over. And it was time to extract herself and try to put her life back together. What there was left of it.

She stopped pacing and turned to face Gavin. Slowly, he stood up. "Katie," he began, but she shook her head.

"Thank you, Gavin," she said formally. "For...everything." She saw something flicker in his eyes and kept going. "I mean not just clearing my father, but everything. You taught me about things I never knew existed."

"Katie, stop. I—"

"I understand. You were never going to stay. I don't regret it, any of it."

"What are you—"

She put up a hand to stop him. "I get it now," she said. It came out tight, with a quaver. "I understand completely why you want nothing to do with liars. And I... I seem to attract them." She didn't care that a note of bitterness had entered her voice. But this was for his sake, so she said it. "Goodbye, Gavin."

She headed for the door. She'd meant to just walk, but halfway there she broke into a run, afraid if she was in the same room with him one more second she would break down.

He didn't say a thing, and the door swung closed behind her.

Chapter 37

Gavin stared after her, feeling unable to either speak or move. He who had the reputation for always knowing what to do next, couldn't think of a thing to say or do now. All he knew was that this felt wrong, completely wrong, more wrong than anything in his life.

He'd barely acknowledged that when Cutter exploded into action. Letting out a howl the dog raced for the door, hitting the open button with a furious swipe of his paw. The moment he could squeeze through he was gone, still howling, in a way that spoke of lonely wolves in the distance. Gavin had never heard anything like it, and it raised the hair on the back of his neck.

Galvanized by the sound, he ran to the door, just in time to see Katie pause at her car, keys in hand, and look back at Cutter. Something slammed into his chest when he saw the tears streaming down her face. Not Katie, who was so strong, so tough, who had handled all this with a strength that had amazed him. She wouldn't break. Not his Katie...

And then Cutter was back, nudging at him, then flat-out pushing him toward her. When he looked at Katie again, she was looking at him. And there was no mistaking what he saw in her face. Not just sadness, not just longing, but…love. It was there, written large, and in that instant he knew.

If he let this woman go, it would be the biggest mistake of his life.

"Katie," he whispered, even knowing she couldn't possibly hear him.

He didn't need Cutter's urging. He simply ran, caught her up in his arms, the words that wouldn't come before coming in a rush now. He doubted if they made any sense at all, yet somehow she understood.

"You can't go. Don't. Please. Stay. He doesn't matter. Their lies don't matter."

"Gavin," she began to protest, but he shook his head. He felt like he was about to cry himself, and tried to put some sensible words together.

"You've given me back everything, Katie. I went too far down that path. Lost my trust, my faith in people, my willingness to believe anyone who hadn't already proven themselves to me. But you've changed that. No more guilty until proven innocent."

"But you were right. Because I'm obviously surrounded by liars. And you don't want that around you, so this is for your sake."

He drew back, stared at her. His sake? "But what I did… suspecting your father…"

She gave a sad smile. "It's what lawyers do, isn't it? You cover anything that could go wrong by thinking everything could go wrong?"

"So it wasn't…unforgivable?"

Her expression changed, and he knew somehow she was

thinking of what he'd said to her father. Only something unforgivable could ever change her love. With a sigh she said, "That's probably the most forgivable thing that's happened."

He hated that she sounded so beaten. "No. Don't let my mistrust infect you. They made mistakes, big ones, but... Please, Katie, don't lose that thing that makes you you, that sweetness, the kindness, the honesty. It's what makes you so strong."

She was staring at him, and he had the feeling she was holding her breath. Waiting. If she'd been willing to leave for his sake, he had to say this for hers.

"It's what I love," he said hoarsely.

Her eyes widened.

"I love you, Katie. I know it's too fast and too crazy, but—"

He stopped when she lifted a finger to his lips. Just the touch sent fire racing along every nerve.

"I love you, too," she whispered, and his heart jammed up into his throat. "No matter how fast or crazy. But what I said is still true. I have liars all around me."

He swallowed tightly. "But you're not one of them. And that's all that really matters. And I wouldn't blame you if you walked away, after what I thought, but don't. Please don't."

"You're sure of that?"

"Yes. Are you sure you want to take on that lifelong challenge?"

He saw her remember her own words, and a slow smile curved her lips. Those lips that drove him mad. "I think I'm up to it," she whispered. "In fact, I think I'll start right now."

It was much later, long after Quinn and Hayley had discreetly departed—Cutter with them, after a last, happy

woof that seemed to indicate he knew his job was done—
that Gavin broke a long, slow kiss and broached the subject he'd been pondering.

"You've had a rough time here the last few months."

Katie nodded, then smiled up at him from where she
lay beneath him on the couch. "But things are definitely
looking up."

He smiled back. "But maybe a change of scenery for a
while might be good."

"I kind of like the scenery here."

She ran a finger down his chest. He put a hand over
hers, knowing if she continued he was going to forget everything he wanted to say.

"I need to go back to St. Louis, for a while at least. There
are logistics I have to figure out."

She went still. "What are you saying?"

"Come with me," he said. "Away from all the reminders,
where you can think more clearly. Just for a while. While
we decide what happens next."

"Next?"

"You love your work here," he said, "and you're damned
good at it. And I can work anywhere. It's easier from St.
Louis because it's in the middle of everywhere, but I don't
have to be there."

"You'd move? Here?"

"I like it here." He wasn't sure if it was the place, or just
her, and in the end it didn't matter. "I would, if that's what
works best. For us."

She kissed him, hot and fierce. "I love you, Gavin de
Marco."

He kissed her back. This time they ended up on the
floor before the fire, and it was more explosive than ever.
He thought he might have shouted her name when they hit

the peak. And it took him a long time to work up the energy to speak again.

"Fair warning. If you come with me, you'll have to meet Charlie."

"That sounds like you're going to introduce me to royalty."

He laughed. "That's more fitting than you know."

"I'll practice my curtsy."

He laughed again, thinking he was almost getting used to doing it. "Does that mean yes?"

"I'd go anywhere with you."

He raised up on one elbow and looked down at her, smiling.

"Welcome to Foxworth," he said.

* * * * *

*And don't miss Justine Davis's next thrilling romance,
coming in October 2018 as a part of*
THE COLTONS OF RED RIDGE *continuity!*

*And catch up with everyone at the Foxworth
Foundation with previous books in the*

CUTTER'S CODE *miniseries:*

*OPERATION ALPHA
OPERATION SOLDIER NEXT DOOR
OPERATION HOMECOMING
OPERATION POWER PLAY*

Available now from Harlequin Romantic Suspense!

#1975 COLTON BABY RESCUE
The Coltons of Red Ridge • by Marie Ferrarella

A murder, a family feud, a missing suspect—and a couple who can't deny their attraction. Despite having exact opposite life goals, Carson Gage and Serena Colton can't resist each other. And when a murderer comes after Serena and her baby, Carson is the only one who can save them!

#1976 IN THE BODYGUARD'S ARMS
Bachelor Bodyguards • Lisa Childs

Jordan "Manny" Mannes would rather risk his life than his heart. So finding out that his new assignment—Teddie Plummer— is a supermodel puts quite a wrench in his plans to avoid relationships. But as the danger to Teddie ratchets up, so does the desire, and they might not have a chance to prove their love before a stalker takes them both out—forever!

#1977 POWER PLAY
Wingman Security • by Beverly Long

When Trey Riker's old college roommate asks him to check on his little sister, Trey agrees, thinking it's the least he can do for the man who once saved his life. Kelly McGarry says everything is fine and promises to call her brother. When she suddenly goes missing and her apartment has been trashed, Trey has to earn her trust before he can save her life.

#1978 SECRET BABY, SECOND CHANCE
Sons of Stillwater • by Jane Godman

Beth Wade walked out on Vincente Delaney sixteen months ago. Now he discovers she has been hiding his baby daughter from him. When Beth is in danger after witnessing a murder, Vincente must save the woman he has always loved to claim the family he never knew he wanted.

ROMANTIC suspense

A murder, a family feud, a missing suspect—and a couple who can't deny their attraction. Despite having exact opposite life goals, Carson Gage and Serena Colton can't resist each other. And when a murderer comes after Serena and her baby, Carson is the only one who can save them!

Read on for a sneak preview of
COLTON BABY RESCUE
by USA TODAY *bestselling author*
Marie Ferrarella, *the first story in*
THE COLTONS OF RED RIDGE *continuity.*

"Just what is it that you want me to do?"

Serena threw her hands up, angry and exasperated. "I don't know," she cried, walking back around to the front of the building. *"Something!"*

"I am doing something," Carson shot back. "I'm trying to find the person who killed my brother," he reminded Serena.

From what she could see, all he was doing was spinning his wheels, poking around on her ranch. "Well, you're not going to find that person here—and you're not going to find Demi here, either," she told him for what felt like the umpteenth time, knowing that no matter what he said, her cousin was still the person he was looking for.

HRSEXP1217

"If you don't mind, I'd like to check that out for myself," Carson said, dismissing her protest.

"Yes, I do mind," she retorted angrily. "I mind this constant invasion of our privacy that you've taken upon yourself to commit by repeatedly coming here and—"

As she was railing at him, out of the corner of his eye he saw Justice suddenly becoming alert. Rather than the canine fixing his attention on Serena and the loud dressing down she was giving Carson, the German shepherd seemed to be looking toward another one of the barns that contained more of the hands' living quarters.

At this time of day, the quarters should be empty. Even so, he intended to search them on the outside chance that this was where Demi was hiding.

Something had gotten the highly trained canine's attention. Was it Demi? Had she come here in her desperation only to have one of the hands see her and subsequently put in a call to the station? Was she hiding here somewhere?

"What is it, Justice? What do you—?"

He got no further with his question.

The bone-chilling crack of a gun—a rifle by the sound of it—being discharged suddenly shattered the atmosphere. Almost simultaneously, a bullet whizzed by them, so close that he could almost feel it disturb the air.

Find out who's shooting at Carson and Serena in
COLTON BABY RESCUE by Marie Ferrarella,
available January 2018 wherever
Harlequin® Romantic Suspense books and ebooks are sold.

www.Harlequin.com

HRSEXP1217

Get 2 Free Books,
Plus 2 Free Gifts—
just for trying the
Reader Service!

LOVE
Harlequin
romance?

Join our Harlequin community to share your thoughts and connect with other romance readers!

Be the first to find out about promotions, news, and exclusive content!

Sign up for the Harlequin e-newsletter and download a free book from any series at

www.TryHarlequin.com

CONNECT WITH US AT:

Harlequin.com/Community

 Facebook.com/HarlequinBooks

 Twitter.com/HarlequinBooks

 Instagram.com/HarlequinBooks

 Pinterest.com/HarlequinBooks

ReaderService.com

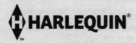 **HARLEQUIN**®

**ROMANCE WHEN
YOU NEED IT**

HSOCIAL2017